THE
FIRST BOOK
OF
LOST SWORDS

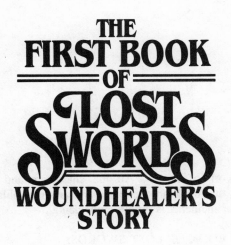

THE
FIRST BOOK
OF
LOST SWORDS

WOUNDHEALER'S STORY

FRED SABERHAGEN

TOR

A TOM DOHERTY ASSOCIATES BOOK

THE FIRST BOOK OF LOST SWORDS:
WOUNDHEALER'S STORY

Copyright © 1986 by Fred Saberhagen

First printing: October 1986

A TOR Book

Published by Tom Doherty Associates, Inc.
49 West 24 Street
New York, N.Y. 10010

ISBN: 0-312-93243-X

Library of Congress Catalog Card Number: 86-50319

Printed in the United States

0   9   8   7   6   5   4   3   2   1

For Joan
As are all the others, whether labeled so or not.

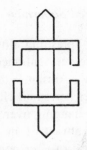

CHAPTER 1

HERE in the green half-darkness an endless melody of water ran, a soft flow that played lightly and moodily over rock. The surrounding walls of dark rock oozed water like the Earth's blood, three clear rivulets that worked to fill a black pool no bigger than a royal bath.

At the single outlet of the pool a stream was born, to gurgle from the vessel of its birth across a rocky floor toward the distant sunlight. What little light inhabited the cave, a dim, funneled, gray-green, water-dappled illumination, came in through the small air space above the tumbling surface of the small outflowing stream.

Now multiple moving shadows were entering from the sunlight, distorting the gray-green light within the cave. Bold, purposeful splashings altered the endless murmur of the water. Rocks in the streambed were kicked and tossed aside, with hollow echoing sounds. The voices of children, pitched to quiet excitement, entered the cave too.

There were three of the visitors. Two of them, a girl and boy in their middle teens, were sturdy waders who supported and guided between them a smaller and much more fragile-looking figure. All three had rolled their trousers above their knees for wading; a useless precaution, for all three were dripping wet from feet to hair. It had been necessary to

1

crawl, half in the cold splashing flow of water, to get in under the low rock at the very entrance.

"We're in a cave now, Adrian," the girl announced with enthusiasm, bending over her small charge. She was perhaps fourteen, her brown hair hanging over her face in long, damp ringlets. Her face was attractive in its youth and health, though it gave no promise of ever being known for its great beauty.

The little boy to whom she spoke said nothing. He was no more than seven years old, with long, fair hair falling damply around a thin, sharp-featured face. His mouth was open just now, and working slightly, the lips rounded by some inner tension into a silent cry. His eyes, remarkably wide and blue, were sightless but active, sending their blind gaze wavering across the rough and shadowed ceiling of the cave.

Now he pulled free his right hand, which the older boy had been holding, and used it to grope in the empty air in front of him.

"A cave, Adrian." The sturdy youth, in a voice that was just starting to deepen, repeated what the girl had said. Then, when the child did not respond, he shrugged his shoulders slightly. He was somewhat bigger than the girl and looked a little older. His hair was of the same medium brown as hers and showed something of the same tendency to curl; and his face resembled hers enough that no one had trouble in taking them for brother and sister.

The girl was carrying three pairs of shoes tied at her belt. All three of the children were plainly dressed in rough shirts and trousers. Here and there, at throat or wrist, an ornament of gold or amber indicated that the choice of plain clothing had not been dictated by poverty.

The explorers had all waded out of the ankle-deep stream now and were standing on the flat sandy floor of the cave. The girl halted after a couple of steps on dry sand, studying the surprisingly large room around her. She frowned into the dark shadows ahead, from whence the sounds of running water had their deepest origin.

She asked: "Zoltan, is this place safe?"

Her brother frowned into the deeper shadows too. Self-consciously he felt for the dagger sheathed at his belt. Then he dropped into a crouch, the better to scan the cave floor in the half light.

"No droppings," he muttered. "No gnawed bones. I don't even see any tracks." He brushed his strong, square fingers at sand and rock. "Ought to be safe. I don't think that anything large can be living in here. Besides, the wizards checked out this whole area this morning."

"Then we can hide in here." The girl's voice returned to the conspiratorial tones of gaming, and she stroked the small child's hair protectively, encouragingly. "We'll hide in here, Adrian; and Stephen and Beth will never find us."

Adrian displayed no interest in the question of whether they would ever be found or not. "Elinor," he said, in a high, clear voice. The name sounded as if he were pronouncing it very thoughtfully and carefully. At the same time he reached his groping hand toward the girl and touched her clothing.

"Yes, it's me. I've been with you all the morning, remember? So has Zoltan." She spoke patiently and encouragingly, as if to a child much younger than seven.

Now Adrian seemed to be giving her last statement his deepest thought. He had turned his head a little on one side. His round mouth worked, his blind eyes flickered.

Zoltan, standing by with folded arms and watching, shook his head. "I don't think he even understands we're playing hide-and-seek," he remarked sadly. In relation to his young cousin, the Prince Zoltan stood more in the role of companion and bodyguard than that of playmate, though at fifteen he was not too old to slide from one character to the other as conditions seemed to require.

"I think he does," Elinor said reproachfully. "Something's bothering him, though."

"Something's always bothering him—poor little bugger."

"Hush. He can understand what you're saying." Kneeling in dry sand, she patted the cheek of their young charge soothingly. The Princeling slowly patted her hand in return.

Elinor persisted with her cheerful encouragement. "Beth and Stephen are 'it' this turn, Adrian, remember? But we've got a great place to hide now. They're never going to be able to find us, here in a cave. Can you tell we're in a cave, by the way things sound? I bet there are a lot of blind people who could do that. Isn't it fun, playing hide-and-seek?"

The small boy turned his head this way and that. Now it was as if he were tired of listening to Elinor, thought her brother, who couldn't blame him if he were.

"Water," Adrian whispered thoughtfully. It did not sound like a request, but a musing comment.

The girl was pleased. "That's right, we had to wade through the water to get in here. I was afraid the rocks would bother your feet, but I guess they didn't. Now you're out of the water, you're sitting on a dry rock." She raised her head. "Zolty, will we be able to hear Beth calling if they decide they want to give up?"

"Dunno," her brother answered abstractedly. He had turned his back on the others and was facing the cave's single entrance, his eyes and ears intently focused in that direction. "I thought I heard something," he added.

"Beth and Stephen?"

"No. Not a voice. More like a riding-beast. Something with hooves, anyway, clopping around out there in the stream."

"Probably some of the soldiers," Elinor offered. There had been a small patrol sent out from High Manor, in advance of the children's outing. Not that the adults of the royal family, as far as she knew, were particularly worried about anything. It had been purely a routine precaution.

"No." Her brother shook his head. "They're supposed to be patrolling a kind of perimeter. They wouldn't be riding through here now. Unless . . ."

"What?"

Zoltan, without taking his eyes off the entrance, made an abrupt silencing motion with his hand.

His sister was not going to let him get away with becoming dramatic. She began to speak, then broke the words off with a hushed cry: "Adrian!"

The child's eyes were only half open, and only the whites of them were showing. A faint gasping noise came from his throat. He had been sitting bolt upright where Elinor had placed him, but now his thin body was starting to topple slowly from the rock.

Zoltan turned to see his sister catch the child and lower him into the soft sand. But then just as quickly he turned back the other way. Something was now outside the cave that could shadow the whole entrance. The darkness within had deepened suddenly and evenly.

Elinor was curled on the sand, lying there beside the child, and when Zoltan took another quick glance at her he could see that she was frightened. Adrian was starting to have a real seizure, what looked to Zoltan like a bad one. The Princeling's little body was stiffening, then bending, then straightening out again. Elinor had stuffed a handkerchief into his mouth to keep him from biting his tongue—her eyes looking back at her brother were full of fear. Not of the fit; she had seen and dealt with those before. The nameless presence outside the cave was something else again.

Then suddenly the shadow outside was gone.

Only a cloud shadow? As far as Zoltan's eyes alone could tell, it might have been nothing more than that.

But he didn't think so.

He waited. Something . . .

And now, from out there in the renewed sunlight, in anticlimax, came childish voices calling; shouting imperiously, and not in fear. Calling the names, one after another, of the three who waited in the cave.

Then silence, stretching on, one heartbeat after another.

Zoltan had a strong impulse to return the call. But somehow his throat was misbehaving, clogged with relief and lingering fear, and at first no sound would come out.

But no answer was necessary. Their trail must have been plainer than he had thought. Again the entrance of the cave dimmed slightly, with small, wavering shadows. Two more children entered, splashing.

"We found you!" It was a cry of triumph. Beth, as usual, had no trouble finding her voice or using it, and there was no indication that she had encountered anything in the least unusual on her way to the finding. She was a stout ten-year-old, inclined to try to be the boss of everyone in sight, whether or not they might be older than she, or related by blood to the rulers of the land while she was not.

Clamped firmly in the grip of one of her stout fists was the small arm of Stephen, Adrian's younger brother.

Adrian and Stephen shared a certain similiarity in face and coloring. But with that, even the physical resemblance ended. Already Stephen, no more than five, was pulling his arm fiercely out of Beth's grip and beginning to complain that their three rivals in the game had cheated by coming into the cave to hide.

Zoltan grabbed small Stephen suddenly and clamped a hand across his chattering little mouth, enforcing silence.

Whatever had shaded the cave mouth before was coming back, just as silently as before, and more intensely. The shadow that now lay across the sunlight seemed deeper and darker than any natural shadow had the right to be.

Now even Zoltan's eyesight assured him that this must be more than just a cloud.

Stephen, awed by the strange darkness and by the seriousness of the grip that held him, fell silent and stood still.

Presently Zoltan let him go, and drew his dagger from its sheath.

Now Adrian, with a grunt and a spasmodic movement, reared himself almost to his feet, then fell back on the sand. Elinor lunged after him, but one loud shrill cry had escaped the boy before she could cover his mouth with her hand.

An echo of that cry, in a different voice, deep and alien and perhaps inhuman, hideously frightening, came from outside.

And with that echo came a noise that sounded like a large number of riding-beasts splashing in the stream outside. Stones were being kicked carelessly about out there, and there were men's voices, rough and urgent, speaking to each other in unfamiliar accents, not those of the Tasavaltan Palace Guard. Zoltan could not make out words, but he was sure that the men were confused, upset, arguing about something.

Now waves of sickness, almost palpable, came and went through the atmosphere inside the cave. The children stared at each other with ghastly faces, pale in the deep gloom. Zoltan had the feeling that the floor was tilting crazily under his feet, though his eyes assured him that the stream was undisturbed in its burbling course. The child in Elinor's arms emitted another pitiful cry; she clamped her hand over his mouth more fiercely than ever.

Beth was standing stock still. Her eyes met Zoltan's, and

hers were wide as they could be. But she was biting her lip and he thought there was no sign that she was going to yell.

There was now almost no light left in the cave, and it was difficult to see anything at all, though by now his eyes had had time to adapt. Shadow, imitating rock, bulged and curled where once the entering sunlight had been strongest.

Something, thought Zoltan, is trying to force its way in here. Into the cave. To us.

And he had the inescapable feeling that *something else* was keeping the shadow, whatever the shadow represented, from forcing its way in.

How long the indescribable ordeal lasted he could never afterward be sure, nor could Elinor. Nor were any of the younger children able to give consistent estimates. But eventually, with renewed kicking of rocks and splashing by their mounts, the riders outside withdrew. The shadow moderated. But no component of the threat retreated very far. From time to time Zoltan could still hear a word or two of the riders' talk or the sharp sound of a shod hoof above the constant murmur of the stream.

Beth moved. Almost calmly, though timidly, one quiet step after another, she went to Elinor's side, where she sat down in the sand. Stephen continued to stand rigid, his eyes moving from Zoltan's face down to the useless dagger in Zoltan's hand, and back again.

And once more the sickness came, like an evil smell. It seemed to burrow in and grip, somewhere even deeper than the belly and the bones. A sudden realization crossed Zoltan's mind: *This must be the sensation that people describe, that they have when a demon comes too near them. Quite likely we are all going to die.*

But once more the sickness in the air abated.

Adrian's seizure was growing more intense, but so far Elinor was coping with it somehow. She and Zoltan had both seen some of his fits before that were as bad as this, or almost as bad.

Now a new feeling, curiosity, grew in Zoltan, until it was almost as strong as the fear he felt. Dagger still in hand, he got down slowly on all fours in the sand until he could peer out all the way into the restored sunshine outside the cave.

In the distance, slightly downhill from Zoltan and far enough away so that he could see only her head and pale, bare shoulders above a rock, there was a girl. Black-haired and comely, perhaps his own age or a little older, she appeared to be sitting or kneeling or crouching right beside the stream.

What caught Zoltan's attention most powerfully was that the girl was looking straight at him. He was sure of it. Despite the distance, some thirty or forty meters, he thought that he could see her gray eyes clearly, and he was certain about the finger she had lifted to her smiling lips. It was as if she were trying to convey a message: *Say nothing now. In good time. You and I will share great secrets, in good time.*

The way her black hair fell round her ivory shoulders reminded him at once, and irresistibly, of a little girl he had known, years previously, when he had been but a small child himself. Zoltan had loved her, in the way of one child for another, though until this moment he had not thought of her for years. Somehow his first look at this older girl in the sunlight brought back the vision of the child. And the suspicion, the hope, began to grow in him that this was she.

With a start Zoltan became aware of the fact that Elinor was calling his name in a frantic whisper, that she must have been calling it for some time. He turned his head to look helplessly at his sister.

"He's getting worse!" The words were uttered under her breath, but fiercely.

And indeed, the child's fit was now certainly the worst that

Zoltan had ever seen him undergo. Zoltan got to his feet, the girl outside temporarily forgotten.

There was a lull outside, a certain lightening of the shadow.

And then, suddenly, a confused uproar. Whatever was happening out there, the noise it made was for the moment impossible to interpret.

Then Zoltan understood. With a rush, new hoofbeats and new voices made themselves heard in the distance. As if blown off by a sharp breeze, the sickness faded from the air, the darkness lifted totally. Abruptly there began the sounds of a sharp fight immediately outside the cave, the honest sound of blades that clashed on other blades and shields. To Zoltan's ears it sounded like the soldiers' practice field, but in his mind and in his stomach he knew that this was more than practice.

Now one man's voice in particular, shouting powerfully outside the cave, was recognizable to them all. Zoltan's knees, which until now had stayed reliable, went suddenly shaky with relief. "Uncle Mark," he gasped.

Elinor looked back at him. "Uncle Mark," she echoed, prayerfully.

Adrian, twisting his body and pulling with both hands, somehow tore his face free of her grip. "Father!" he cried out loudly, once, and fell into a faint.

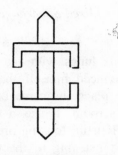

CHAPTER 2

ON the night following their temporary entrapment in the cave, Zoltan and Elinor slept soundly at High Manor, in their own beds. In contrast, it was well after midnight before the Princes Adrian and Stephen, and their playmate Beth, were returned to their homes in Sarykam, the capital city of Tasavalta. When Prince Adrian was put to bed in his own room in the Palace, the fit was still on him, though the fierceness of it had diminished.

Prince Mark, Adrian's father, had brought his family home himself because there had seemed to be little or nothing more that he could accomplish personally at High Manor in the aftermath of the attack. Next morning's sun was well up before he roused from his own uneasy and sporadic slumber.

He was alone on waking, but felt no surprise at the fact. He assumed that his wife had remained all night at the child's bedside, getting such sleep as she was able in a chair. She had done the same thing often enough before; and Mark himself was no stranger to such vigils either.

Presently Prince Mark walked out onto the balcony that opened from his and the Princess's bedroom. Squinting into sunlight, he looked about him over the city and the sea. The far horizon, which had once seemed to promise infinite possibilities, was beginning to look and feel to him like the high wall of a prison.

*   *   *

Having filled his lungs with sea air and his eyes with sunlight, and convinced himself that at least most of the world was still in place, he came back indoors to join his wife in the child's room. It was a small chamber that adjoined their own. Kristin, looking tired, was standing beside the small bed and listening to the Chief Physician of the Royal Household. There was visible in her bearing a certain aristocratic poise that her husband permanently lacked. Her hair was blond, her face as fine-featured as that of her older son, and her eyes blue-green, with something in them of the sea, whose sharp horizon came in at every eastern window of these high Palace rooms.

The current Chief Physician—there had been several holders of the office during the seven years since Adrian was born—was a gray-haired, white-robed woman named Ramgarh. She had been in attendance on the Princess and her elder son since their return to the Palace in the middle of the night.

As Mark entered, the doctor was saying, in her calm, soothing voice: "The child is breathing steadily now, and his pulse is within the range where there is no cause for concern. If the history of recovery from past seizures holds for this one, he will probably sleep through most of the day."

It was only what the father had expected to hear. In the past seven years he had endured more of his firstborn's fits and seizures than he could begin to count. But still he put back the curtain from the bed to see for himself. There was Adrian, asleep, looking as if nothing in the world were wrong with him.

Mark, Prince Consort of Tasavalta, was a tall man of thirty. His hair had once been as fair as that of his sons'; but age had darkened Mark's hair into a medium brown, though hair and beard still tended to bleach light in the sun. This morning Mark's face wore a tired, drawn look, and the lines at the corners of his mouth were a shade deeper than they had been the night before.

Princess Kristin had come silently to stand beside her husband, and he put an arm around her. Their pose held more than a suggestion that they were leaning together for mutual support.

The physician, after dispensing a few more soothing words for both the parents, departed to get some rest. Mark scarcely heard the doctor's parting words. They were almost always essentially the same: an exhortation to hope, a reminder that things could be worse. For about two years now there had been no more promises that new kinds of treatment would be tried. The catalogue of treatments that the doctors were ready and willing to attempt had been exhausted.

When the door had closed behind the physician, the Prince and Princess looked at each other, and then both turned their eyes back to the small form in the bed.

She said: "He will be all right now, I think."

Mark's voice was flat and heavy. "You mean he will be no worse off than before."

Before the Princess could answer there was an interruption. A nursemaid had just entered the room, leading their second child, who had just awakened, his usual healthy self. Stephen was carrying, rolled up in one hand, the hand-lettered storybook that had been with him all during the long ride from High Manor.

Stephen was obviously still somewhat fogged with sleep, but he brought with him an image of hearty normality. Though almost two years younger than his brother, he was the sturdier. And now, in the way that Stephen looked at his sleeping brother, there was a suggestion of his resentment, that Adrian should be getting so much attention just because he had had another fit.

But Stephen, aware that parental eyes were on him, tucked the colored scroll of the book in at the edge of Adrian's bed, a voluntary and more-or-less willing sharing. Then he tugged at his father's trouser leg. "Can we go back to High Manor again today? I want to watch the soldiers."

His father smiled down at him wanly. "Didn't you have enough excitement there yesterday?"

"I want to go back."

"You'll be a warrior." Mark's big hand brushed the small blond head.

The mother stood by, saying nothing, not smiling.

The nursemaid returned to take the energetic child away for breakfast.

Driven by the need to do something, Mark strode out upon a balcony, where he drew a deep breath and looked out over the tile rooftops of the city well below him. From the outer wall of the Palace, Sarykam spread downhill to the sea, which here made first a neatly sheltered bay, then endless blue beyond a thin, curving peninsula of docks and light-houses and fortifications.

A favorable combination of warm latitude and cool ocean currents made Sarykam a place of near-perpetual spring. Behind the Palace and the western fringe of the city, the mountains rose up, rank on rank, and topped with wild forests of pine. The trees upon the eastern side of the crest, toward the city and the sea, were warped by almost everlast-ing winds, fierce at that altitude but usually much milder down here near sea level. Six hours' ride inland, beyond those mountains, lay High Manor, which, among its other functions, served sometimes as a summer home for royalty. And only a couple of kilometers from the Manor was the cave where yesterday's mysterious kidnapping attempt—Mark had to interpret the violent incident as such—had been thwarted.

There was much about that attempt that the Prince still found mysterious. Naturally investigations on both the mili-tary and the magical level had been set in motion last night—as soon as the fighting stopped—and were going forward.

Even now Mark could see a winged messenger coming from inland, perhaps bearing news of some results. There, halfway between the highest tower of the Palace and the crest of the mountains, were a pair of small, fine wings beating swiftly. He could hope that the courier was bringing word of some success by the searching cavalry.

Had the attempt been only the impulsive gamble of some bandit chief, reckless enough to accept the risks in return for the chance of a fat ransom? The Prince thought not, for several reasons.

The enemy had come with powerful magical assistance. The small detachment of the Palace Guard that had been stationed, as a matter of routine protection, in the area where the children were playing had been surprised and wiped out ruthlessly. The children had been tracked to the cave where they were hiding.

And then, just when the greatest tragedy should have been inevitable, came inexplicable good fortune. The enemy, for all the competence and determination they had displayed up to that point, had been unable to determine that the children were actually in the cave. Or—and this alternative seemed even more unlikely—the enemy had known they were there, but had simply been unable to get at them. Either explanation seemed quite incredible under the circumstances. It was true that Elinor and Zoltan had both reported the subjective feeling of some protective power at hand, but in Mark's experience such feelings had little to do with the real world.

Of course in this case the feelings could have had some basis in fact. Karel, who was Princess Kristin's uncle as well as her chief wizard, had divined from his workroom in Sarykam that something was wrong out near High Manor and had done what he could do at a distance. Meanwhile one of the winged messengers employed by the military had fortunately witnessed the wiping-out of the Guard detachment and had darted back to its roost at High Manor to report the attack. Mark, who was at the Manor, had hastily gathered a force and ridden out at once. The children had been completely unprotected in the presence of the enemy for only a few minutes.

Mark and his swordsmen had surprised the attackers—who to all appearances were no more than a group of bandits—at the very mouth of the cave in which the children were sheltering. Fortunately it had been possible to drive off the demon at once. Mark had assumed at the time that the enemy had been on the point of entering the cave, and that his arrival was barely in time to save the children. But the children, when questioned later, insisted that the intruders, including their demonic cohort, had been immediately outside the cave for a long time. The adults took this estimate as an exaggeration—no doubt the time had seemed an eternity to children who were thus trapped.

The fight at the entrance to the cave had begun without any attempt to parley, without even a single word of warning on either side. And it had been conducted to the death. None of the nameless human invaders had shown the least inclination to surrender, or even to run away. Mark had shouted for his soldiers to take prisoners, but even so none of the attackers had survived long enough to be questioned. Two who were only lightly wounded when captured were nevertheless dead, apparently of magical causes, before the Prince could begin to interrogate them.

Now a new figure appeared at the doorway to the balcony. It was Karel himself, come down from his eyrie in the second-highest tower of the Palace to talk to Kristin and Mark. This wizard was not only highly skilled and experienced, but he looked the part—as so many of the really good ones did not—sporting a profusion of gray hair and beard, a generally solemn manner, and a massive and imposing frame clothed in fine garments. Karel departed from the popular image by having red plump cheeks, giving him a hearty outdoor look he did not deserve.

Yesterday, as the wizard had already explained, he had done what he could do at a distance. First in his own workshop, then mounted and driving his riding-beast with blessings and curses through the mountain pass toward High Manor. Grasping at every stage for whatever weapons of magic he could find, Karel had endeavored to raise elementals along the course of the small stream that issued from the cave. He thought now that his try with the elementals had been more successful than he had realized at the time, evidently good enough to confuse and delay the enemy until Mark and his force were able to reach them.

Karel's voice rumbled forth with his habitual—and generally justified—pride. "Might have tried to produce a hill-elemental right on the spot, but that could be a problem to anyone in a cave, as I divined our people were. When you confront a hill-elemental it will tend to keep in front of you, so that what you're trying to reach is always behind it. It'll tumble rocks about and tilt the ground beneath your feet, or anyway make it seem to tilt, so that you go tumbling on what had been a gentle slope, or even level ground."

"Zoltan reported feeling something like that."

"I know, I know." Karel made dismissive motions with a large hand. "But that sounded more like a demon outside the cave, the way the lad described it."

"There was a demon, I am sure of that. And mere bandits do not ordinarily have demons at their disposal."

"I am sure that you are right in that, Your Highness."

"Go on. You were talking about the elementals."

"Ah, yes. Your river-elemental, now, is distance, length, and motion. But it can also be stasis. It sweeps things away, and hides them, and separates things that want to be together. I kept the river-walker on the scene, and the rock-roller in the background.''

"Whatever your methods were, they seem to have been effective. We are very grateful to you, Karel.''

The graybeard brushed the words away, though it was not hard to see that he was genuinely pleased by them. "Sheer good fortune was on our side as well. As to our investigation, I want to talk to Zoltan again. There are things about his account that still puzzle me a little.''

"Oh?''

"Yes—certain details. And he's the oldest of the young ones in the cave; maybe the most levelheaded, though there perhaps his sister may have something of an edge. Not much that one can hope to learn from children in a situation like this. Apparently none of them even made an effort to look out of the cave mouth while the enemy was there.''

"Shall I send a messenger to bring Zoltan here? He and his sister are still at High Manor.''

"No great hurry. There are other avenues of investigation I must try first. I have a strong suspicion now of who was behind yesterday's atrocity.'' Karel paused for a deep breath. "Burslem.''

Prince and Princess exchanged looks. Mark had the feeling that their tiredness had frozen them both into shells, leaving them unable to communicate freely with each other. And his own tiredness, at least, was not of the kind to be swept away by a night's sleep.

Mark said to the wizard: "Worse than we thought, then, perhaps?''

"Bad enough,'' said Karel. "Just how bad, I don't know. We can be sure that a man who once headed magical security operations for King Vilkata himself is a wizard of no mean capacity. And there's been no word of Burslem for eight years.''

"Where is he now?" the Princess asked.

Her uncle signed that he did not know. "At least he doesn't have an army lurking on any of our frontiers. Those were ragtag bandits he recruited somehow for yesterday's adventure. Having spent much of the night with their corpses I can be sure of that much at least. I think he'll wait to see if we've caught on to the fact that he was behind them."

"And then?"

"And then he'll try something else, I suppose. Something nasty."

"What can we do?"

"I don't know. I see no way as yet in which we can retaliate effectively." And Karel shortly took his leave, saying that he had much to do.

Husband and wife, alone again on the balcony, embraced once more then walked back into the room where their older son still slept. On the walls of Adrian's room were paintings, here brave warriors chasing a dragon, there on the other wall a wizard in a conical hat creating a marvelous fruit tree out of nothing. The paintings had been done by the artist of the storybook, in those happy months before Adrian was born, created for small eyes that had never seen them yet.

Princess Kristin said in a weary voice: "His mouth is bruised as well, I suppose from Elinor trying to keep him quiet in the cave. I never saw a child who bruised so easily."

Mark said nothing. He stroked her hair.

Kristin said: "It's only great good fortune that any of the children are still alive, that that cave was there for them to hide in while Karel's elemental moved the river around outside. Otherwise who knows what might have happened to them?"

"I can imagine several things," said Mark, breaking a silence that threatened to grow awkwardly. "If Burslem is really the one behind it. And in the cave Adrian kept crying out, or trying to cry out, as Elinor told us. You realize it's quite possible that he almost killed them all, betraying that they were there.''

His wife moved away from him a little and looked up at him. ''You can't mean that what happened was somehow his fault.''

''No. Not a fault. But already his blindness, his illness, begin to create problems not only for us, for you and me. Problems already for all Tasavalta.''

''It is Burslem who creates problems for us all,'' the Princess said a little sharply. ''I will confer with Karel again, of course, but I don't know what else we can do for Adrian. We have tried everything already. Are you going to make him feel guilty about being the way he is?''

''No,'' said Mark. ''But if we have tried everything, then we must find something else to try. My son—our son—must grow into a man who is able to guard others. Not one who will forever need guardians himself.''

''And if he cannot?''

''I am not convinced that he cannot.''

Word of the Prince's intentions went out through the Palace within the hour, and within another hour was spreading throughout the city of Sarykam. Prince Consort Mark, determined on an all-out effort to find a cure for the blindness and the strange seizures that had afflicted his elder son since birth, was calling a council of his most trusted advisers. The council was to meet early on the following morning, which was the earliest feasible time for all of its members to come together.

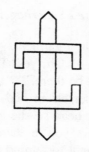

CHAPTER 3

O N the morning appointed for the council, Ben of Purkinje was up even earlier than usual.

He was an enormous man, a pale beached whale rolling out from under the silken covers of his luxurious bed. The stout, carven frame supporting the mattress creaked with relief when his enormous weight was lifted from it. Comparatively little of that weight was fat.

Once on his feet he cast a quick glance back at the slight figure of his dark-haired wife and noted with a certain relief that she was still asleep. Then he padded into the marble bath adjoining the bedroom. Presently the sounds of water, flowing and splashing in great quantities, came into the bedroom; but they were not heard by the woman in the bed, who slept on.

The subtler sounds of her husband's return awoke her, though. Her eyes opened as Ben came back into the room, cast aside a towel that might have served as a ship's sail, and started to get dressed.

"I was up late," she greeted him, "with Beth. She was babbling about strange wizards and I don't know what. What happened is catching up to her. You can't expect it not to."

"How is she now?"

"Sleeping. I was up with her most of the night, while you slept like a log."

21

He grunted, pulling on a garment.

"Why are you up so—? Oh, yes. That council meeting."

"That's right, I must be there."

Barbara rearranged herself in bed, grabbing pillows and stuffing them under her head so she could sit up and talk in greater comfort. "While you're there, I think there are a couple of things you ought to remind the Prince about."

"Ah."

"Yes. It was you who gave him the most valuable Sword of all, before he had any thought that he was to be a Prince. See if he remembers now who his friends were in the old days. See if he remembers that."

"He remembers it, I'm sure."

> *I shatter Swords and splinter spears*
> *None stands to Shieldbreaker*
> *My point's the fount of orphans' tears*
> *My edge the widowmaker*

The verse had in fact been running through Ben's head ever since he had awakened. The recent fighting had brought the Sword of Force to everyone's mind, it seemed. Now Ben whistled a snatch of tune to which he'd once heard someone try to set the Song of Swords, or a couple of verses of it anyway. When Ben was very young he had decided that he was going to be a minstrel. The dream had stayed with him stubbornly for years. By all the gods, how long ago and far away that seemed! He'd be thirty-five this year, or maybe next; he'd never been able to find out for sure exactly when he'd been born. Anyway, there'd be gray showing up in his hair soon enough.

"Yes, Shieldbreaker." Barbara was musing aloud, energizing herself for the day by discovering extra things to fret about, as if she, like everyone else, didn't have enough of them already. "I wonder if he does remember where he got it."

Ben grunted again.

Giving the Sword of Force to his old friend Mark hadn't really been any great act of sacrifice for him, or for Barbara either—or at least he had never thought of it that way. Eight years ago, on that last day in the war-torn city of Tashigang, Shieldbreaker had come into Ben's hands unexpectedly, and his first impulse had been simply to hide it somewhere. But his own house in the city had been in danger of total destruction, the tall structure so badly damaged on its lower levels following the fight with the god Vulcan that it was ready to collapse into a heap of rubble, rooftop gardens smashing down into servants' quarters, then the family rooms, then everything into the weapons shops that had occupied most of the ground floor.

Surrounded by dangers, faced with a multitude of other problems, including their own survival and that of their baby daughter, Beth, neither Ben nor Barbara had been able to think of anything better to do with the Sword of Force than take it to Mark, as soon as they heard he had survived the day, and was in good favor, to say the least, with the victorious Princess Kristin and her generals. Ben, looking back now, thought silently that he'd do the same thing again. The Swords, any and all of them, were too much trouble for anyone to own who aspired to any kind of a peaceful life—yet there was no practical way to destroy the god-forged weapons. And no way to hide them so they'd nevermore be found—the Swords themselves seemed to take care of that.

Dressed and as ready for the day as he could be, Ben said good-bye to Barbara with a kiss, to which she responded enthusiastically for all her nagging. On his way out of the house, Ben looked in on sturdy little Beth, still their only child and twice precious to both of them for that. Beth was, as her mother had said, asleep. Her father stopped off in the kitchen and grabbed himself a fresh pastry to eat for breakfast en route. Later in the day would be time enough to get down to serious feeding.

He was not a vindictive man, and as a rule he detested violence. But if he'd been able to get one of those bandits from in front of the cave mouth into his hands . . .

To reach the Palace from his house required only a short walk through the busy morning streets of Sarykam. High official that he was, Ben made his way there on foot, amid the sometimes jostling throngs of merchants and customers, workers and passersby. In Tasavalta, most people walked unless some physical disability prevented it. Outward display of wealth or position, except by means of certain subtle modes of dress, was considered in bad taste for anyone except actual royalty. Ben and Barbara, as much outlanders here as was the Prince their patron, had adapted. The condemnation of display was another thing that bothered Barbara, her husband supposed, though she could hardly complain about it openly.

Well, Ben and his wife no longer possessed the riches that had briefly been theirs when they dwelt in that great house of their own in Tashigang. Wealth had been lost, along with the house, the business, and the treasury of elegant weapons that for a while had been their stock in trade. But certainly they had done well enough here in Tasavalta, where they stood high in the councils of the Prince and Princess. Well enough, perhaps, for anyone Ben knew except Barbara.

Ben rated a sharp salute from the two guards in blue and green who flanked the small and almost private gate through which he entered the complex of the Palace proper. The guards, who knew him well, took care to look alert while in his presence. Ben's job included a number of duties, all related in one way or another to security, and to the gathering of intelligence in foreign lands. It was a post that had been created for him at Mark's behest, and when Ben was appointed to it there had arisen something of a storm of quiet protest among influential Tasavaltans who did not yet know their new Prince well, and did not know Ben at all. It would have been hard to find anyone in the whole realm who looked the part of intelligence adviser less than Ben of Purkinje did.

The first matter to occupy Ben's attention this morning, once he was inside the Palace, was not the council meeting, but something more routine. He thought it was time that he looked in at the private section of the royal armory, to check for himself on its most valued contents.

To reach the private armory he had to pass two more sets of guards, each more determined-looking than the last. Each of these also saluted sharply when he approached them, and took care to be alert while in his presence.

Now Ben entered a cavelike, windowless room, lighted only by a rare Old-World lantern on one wall, which bathed the whole chamber in a cool, perpetual glow. This room was fenced round with powerful magic as well as with physical barriers and human guards.

Once alone inside the room, Ben approached a large shelf built out of one wall at waist level and opened the first of a series of ornate wooden cases resting on it. Each case had been made, with great craftsmanship, in the shape of an enlarged Sword, with intertwined serpents carved to form the lid at the place where it looked like a hilt. Inside this first case, the Sword Coinspinner had lain for several years following the last war. Mark had fought the last day of that war with Coinspinner in his hand, and it had sent certain of his enemies to death and had kept him alive where no ordinary sword could have. Upon its ebon hilt the Sword of Chance bore as its symbol a pair of dice outlined in stark white.

Today Ben was able to see that hilt only in his mind; for the Sword itself had taken itself away, and the blue velvet of the interior of the case was empty when he opened it. To Coinspinner, the spells of Karel that bound the armory around had mattered no more than had the human guards. Like its eleven brothers, the Sword of Chance disdained all magics lesser than its own.

Who holds Coinspinner knows good odds
Whichever move he make
But the Sword of Chance, to please the gods,
Slips from him like a snake

And quietly, sometime during an otherwise unremarkable winter night, Coinspinner had vanished from its triply guarded case. Where it might have gone, no one in the Palace could begin to guess.

The Palace authorities would have preferred to keep the disappearance of the Sword a secret. But word of it had got out, though in a somewhat garbled version. Now, years later, it was still widely whispered among the people that a gold coin bearing the likeness of the god Hermes had appeared in the place of the Sword of Chance, within its magically sealed case. Actually there had been no such coin on this occasion of the Sword's vanishing, and efforts had been made to set the story straight, though to no avail. The people knew what they knew. Even some who lived in the Palace accepted what most of the populace outside still believed as a matter of course—that the god Hermes, along with the multitude of his vanished peers, was still alive somewhere and likely someday to return.

Ben knew better than that, or thought he did, in the case of the multitude of divinities. In the case of Hermes he was certain. With his own eyes, and with Mark standing beside him, he had seen the Messenger lying dead. In the god's back had gaped a great mortal wound, a mighty stab that they thought could only have been the work of Farslayer.

With a shake of his head Ben put memories away. He closed up the carven case, which some wizards had hoped would be able to confine Coinspinner, and moved on.

Here, a little distance along the stone shelf, was a second protected case, in its construction and decoration similar to the first. And this one, when opened, showed itself occupied. Ben touched the Sword inside, but did not take it out. Stonecutter's blade, identical in size and shape to those of its eleven mates, was a full meter long, and the mottled pattern of the bright steel seemed to extend far below the smoothly polished surface.

> *The Sword of Siege struck a hammer's blow*
> *With a crash, and a smash, and a tumbled wall.*
> *Stonecutter laid a castle low*
> *With a groan, and a roar, and a tower's fall.*

Letting the case stay open, Ben rested his huge right hand affectionately for a moment upon the black hilt. His grip covered the symbol of a small white wedge splitting a white block. Ben could well remember how this Sword had saved him and Mark, upon one day of danger now long years ago. Stonecutter had not been much used since that day, but unlike Coinspinner it was still here, waiting faithfully until it should be needed by its owners.

There was, as Ben always took care to drill into the armory guards, one more advantage in having this or any other Sword of Power: As long as we have it, we can be sure that our enemies do not. So we must either keep safe the Swords we know about, or destroy them. And no human being had

yet discovered a way of destroying one, other than by bringing it into violent opposition with Shieldbreaker.

Ben closed the second case. He walked on to the third,
which for the last eight years had been the repository of the
Sword of Force.

This case, when he opened it, showed him only its blue
velvet lining, and Ben had a bad moment until he saw the
little marker, dutifully placed there by the Prince himself and
signed by him. It was meant to assure the people of the
armory that he had taken Shieldbreaker out with his own
hands.

Ben hurried on to join the council.

Its members were already assembling, in a pleasant room
high in one of the taller Palace towers. Most were in the
room when Ben arrived, but were not yet seated. Ben's first
glance on entering the room had been directed at Mark, in an
effort to make sure that the Prince did now indeed have
Shieldbreaker in his personal possession. Mark did have on a
swordbelt, an item not usually worn by anyone inside the
Palace. And there was the unmistakable hilt, its tiny white
hammer-symbol visible to Ben's eyes across the room. A
faint suspicion died; being responsible for security meant that
you became ever more imaginatively suspicious.

Standing at the middle of one side of the long table, Mark
had Karel on one side of him and on the other, Jord, the man
Mark had called father all through his childhood and youth.
Mark continued to call Jord his father even now, and to
respect him as such, even though the truth of a somewhat
more exalted parenthood for the Prince had become known
during the last war.

Ben was mildly surprised to see Jord here now. The older
man was tall, and still strong, bearing a superficial resemblance to his adopted son. Jord was intelligent enough, and

certainly trustworthy, but he was not usually called in to discuss affairs of state. Of course today's affair was a family matter also. Not that Princess Kristin had ever been noticeably eager to emphasize the humble origins of her now-royal husband. Of course, if today's discussion should turn out to be substantially about Swords, there would be another reason for Jord's presence—no one else in the world could bring to it his fund of experience. Of the half dozen men recruited by Vulcan to help forge the Swords some thirty years ago, Jord was the only one to survive the process; and he was still the only human being who had ever touched all of the Twelve.

Next Ben looked around the table for General Rostov, commander of the Tasavaltan army. But the General's burly frame and steel-gray beard were nowhere to be seen. Probably Rostov, as usual, had many other things to do, particularly in the light of recent events. And probably, too, Mark did not count this meeting as having a great deal to do with military strategy.

Also in the group around the council table were several White Temple physicians, several of whom had been in attendance upon Prince Adrian since he was born. During that period a heavy turnover had taken place among Palace physicians; but everyone knew that there were none better anywhere than those of the White Temple.

Present also was the Royal Master of the Beasts, who was in charge of winged messengers, among other things, and therefore was likely to be called in on any council where quick communications or late news were of importance. Completing the assembly were two or three minor magicians, aides to Karel.

Mark had seen Ben come in, and beckoned him over for an almost-private word before the meeting started. "How's Beth this morning?" the Prince asked.

"Sleeping like a small log when I left. And your boys?"

"As well as can be expected."

"It's great to be young, Your Highness." Ben usually favored his old friend with one "Your Highness" every day. He liked to get the formality in early, and made sure to do so always when others were listening, so everyone would know that the Prince did not carry his familiarity with his old friends too far.

"I can remember that being young was pleasant," said the man of thirty, smiling faintly. "And how is Barbara?"

"Fine," said Ben promptly. "But she won't admit it. Sometimes I think I'm married to the Blue Temple." And he made a little money-rubbing gesture with his massive thumb and forefinger.

The faint smile got a little wider. Even that much was good to see on Mark's worn face. He said: "I feel a little better myself. Some hopeful news has just come in—you'll hear it in a minute. I'd better get this thing started now." And he turned away, rapping the table with a hard knuckle.

Ben went to take his seat in the place assigned him by protocol.

As soon as the meeting was in order, Mark repeated to his assembled advisers his absolute determination to find a cure for Adrian's blindness and his seizures—or at the very least, to prove beyond doubt, once and for all, that the illness they represented was incurable.

Having done that, he threw the meeting open to comments and suggestions.

The wizard Karel stroked his gray beard and his red cheeks and wondered aloud, tentatively, if the child's condition might not be the result of some last stroke of vengeance on the part of the Dark King. King Vilkata was almost certainly dead now, but his whereabouts had never been learned with any certainty since he was seen to flee the battlefield where

he had stood in opposition to the Silver Queen. The Dark
King Vilkata had been Mark's bitter enemy. And he had also
been blind.

Karel's suggestion was not a new one to the ears of anyone
around the table. Mark had often pondered it. But no one had
ever been able to come up with any means of confirming it,
or disproving it absolutely. It was plain that Karel only raised
it again now because the possibility still tormented him that
he might have been so outmatched in magic.

There was a brief silence around the table. Then Jord spoke
up, as a grieving grandfather. "Whatever the cause of the poor
lad's suffering, Woundhealer could cure him—I know it could."
This was not a new suggestion either; the only problem with
it was that for the past eight years no one in Tasavalta had
known where the Sword Woundhealer might be found.

Mark had paused respectfully to hear both of these remarks
yet once more. Now he continued.

"As I see it, when a particular case has resisted all normal
methods of healing, magical and otherwise, there yet remain
three possible remedies to be tried."

The Chief Physician, frowning slightly, looked across the
table at the Prince. She said: "The first of those would
be—as Jord has reminded us—the Sword Woundhealer. Second, the God of Healing, Draffut—if it is possible that he has
survived what seems to have been the general destruction
visited upon the gods." The physician paused. "But I confess
that I do not know what third possibility Your Highness
has in mind."

Mark sighed wearily. "At the moment it seems to me not a
very practical possibility. I was thinking of the Emperor."

"Ah," said the physician. The syllable emerged from her
lips in a way that only a wise old counselor could have
uttered it, suggesting a profound play of wisdom without
committing her to anything at all.

Jord had frowned as soon as the name of the Emperor was mentioned. A moment later almost everyone around the table was frowning, but no one spoke. No one really wanted to talk about the Emperor. Most of these folk had accepted the Emperor's reputed high status more or less on faith, as the basis for granting Mark high birth. That assumption in turn had allowed them to accept him as their Prince. But to most of the world at large, the Emperor, if he was admitted to exist at all, was accorded no status higher than a clown's, that of a low comedian who figured in a hundred jokes and proverbs.

Mark took in the reaction of his counselors without surprise. "I have spoken to him," he told them quietly. "And you have not, any of you. But let that pass for now."

At this point Ben shuffled his feet under the table. He might have had something to say. But he went along with his old friend and let it pass.

The Prince resumed. "Regardless of how helpful the Emperor might be to us in theory, in practice I know of no way to call upon him for his help. Some think that he perished too, eight years ago, with the passing of the gods from human sight and ken. For all I know it may be so."

Mark paused for a long look around the table before going on. "From him—who was my father—I have a power that few of you have ever seen in operation. I know not why I have it; there are others, doubtless worthier than I am, who do not. But for the sake of the majority of you, who do not know about this power, or who have heard about it only through some garbled tale, I want to tell you the plain truth now.

"What I have is the ordering of demons, or rather the ability to raise a shield against their powers, and to cast them out, to a great distance. Yesterday I used this power to drive what I am sure was a demon away from the entrance to the cave."

There was a murmuring around the table.

Mark went on. "Over the last seven years I have repeatedly tried to use the same power for my son's benefit, but to no avail. Whatever ails him, I am convinced that it is not possession by a demon."

There might, Ben supposed in the silence of his own mind, there might exist a demon so terrible, and yet so subtle in its potency, that it could work without being recognized for what it was, and not even the Emperor's son had power to cast it out. The huge man, who had seen demons at close range, shuddered slightly in the warm sunny room.

Or, he thought, it might be that the Emperor, from whom Mark's power derived, was now dead, and all his dependent powers beginning to lose their force. That same thought had probably occurred to others around the table now, but no one wanted to suggest it to the Emperor's son.

Mark was speaking again.

". . . the same objection holds to seeking the help of the Healing God. Draffut is of a different order of being than most of those we called gods—Hermes and Vulcan and so on. Those who have met them both can swear to that. Still, even if Draffut has survived until this day, we know of no way to contact him and ask his help."

"It is so." Old Karel nodded.

The Prince raised his chin and swept his gaze around the table. "We come now to Woundhealer. And that may be a different matter. Here at last I see a ray of hope. Only this morning a report has reached us by messenger—it is a secondhand report and I do not know how reliable—that a certain branch of the White Temple, in the lands of Sibi, far to the southwest, now has the Sword of Mercy in its possession."

There was a stir around the table.

Mark went on: "According to the message we have received this morning, the diseased and the crippled are being healed there every day.''

Jord was now gazing at his adopted son with fierce satisfaction, as if the news meant that Mark had at last decided to listen to his advice. And the Master of the Beasts was nodding his confirmation of the message. It had been brought in shortly after dawn by one of his semi-intelligent birds.

Mark said: "I propose to take my son to that Temple, that he may be healed. The journey, even by the most optimistic calculation, will take months. It may of course be difficult, but the lands in that direction have been peaceful, and we think that Burslem is elsewhere. I foresee no very great danger in the trip.''

"How many troops?" asked Ben.

His old friend looked at him across the table. "I don't want to march with an army, which would very likely provoke our neighbors in that general direction, and would at least call great attention to our presence. To say nothing of the problems of provisioning en route. No, I think an escort of thirty or forty troops, no more. And, Rostov may not like it, but I am bringing Shieldbreaker with me, to protect my son. I did not have it with me near High Manor two days ago, when it was needed. I'll not make that mistake again.''

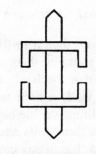

CHAPTER 4

O N two successive nights following his strange experience
in the cave, Zoltan was prey to peculiar dreams. Each
morning he awoke with the most intense and mysterious parts
of those visions still tangled in his mind—running water, soft
black hair that fell in sensuous waves, a beckoning white
arm. A certain perfume in the air.

On the second morning, as soon as he was fully awake, it
came to Zoltan that he had known this fragrance before, in
waking life. It was that of a certain kind of flower, whose
name he had never learned, that grew in summer along the
course of the newborn Sanzu. In summer and early fall there
were many flowers along the banks below the point where
the river left the hills of its birth and, already joined by its
first tributary rivulet, began to meander across a plain.

Once he had recognized that perfume the dreams no longer
seemed strange and new. Rather, they felt so familiar that
Zoltan could comfortably put them from his mind. There was
no point in telling anyone about them, as he had considered
doing. Not anymore.

Sitting up in bed on that second morning, he squinted out
through the open window of his room into the entering
sunlight. High Manor, though it sometimes served as a royal
residence, was definitely no palace. Though very large and

old, it was not much more than a fortified stone farmhouse. The view from Zoltan's room on the ground floor was appropriately homely. There was the barnyard in the foreground, then the manor's outer wall, a little taller than a man, and then green and rocky hilltops visible beyond that. Something winged was circling over those hills now. In all probability it was only a harmless bird, but in any case it was too far away to be identifiable.

Many of the hills in the area had caves in them, and the cave where the children had taken shelter, and where the river was born, was one of them. It burrowed into the foot of a hill just beyond those that Zoltan was able to see from his room.

After staring for another few moments at the hills, he jumped up and began putting on his clothes.

In the great hall downstairs, Zoltan found that the usual morning routine had not yet been reestablished. His mother and sister were not yet up, and formal breakfast for the family was not yet ready. He made his way into the kitchen, exchanging morning greetings with the cooks and servants, wheedling and pilfering to assemble a breakfast of fruit, cooked eggs, and fresh bread.

Stowing a second small loaf inside his jacket, he went outside. Summer was showing signs of waning—the leaves and fruit on the nearby trees established that—and the early air was cool. Zoltan gave good morning to the stablehands, who were busy, and saddled his own riding-beast, Swordface. The name derived from a bold forehead patch of bright white hair.

Soft black hair . . . and the scent of certain flowers. They were sharper memories than mere dreams should ever leave in waking life, and during the daytime they kept coming back to Zoltan at moments when he least expected it.

He rode out through the open front gate of the Manor. A

soldier was stationed there this morning, and Zoltan waved before heading his mount at a steady pace toward the hills. He had said nothing to anyone about his destination, but he was going back to the cave. When he got there he . . . but he didn't know yet exactly what he was going to do.

Two days ago, coming out of the cave with the other children, all of them shaken and unnerved, he had got a close look at some of the bandits, who of course by that time were already dead. Neither Zoltan nor any other Tasavaltan had been able to recognize any of them. At the time, looking at the corpses, about all Zoltan had been able to think of was that men like that would never have had a beautiful young girl traveling with them. Unless, of course, she were their prisoner. And then she'd have to be tied up, hobbled somehow, to keep her from running away. But he had the impression that the girl he had actually seen had been perfectly free.

Now, two days later, there were moments it seemed to Zoltan strange that he had not yet mentioned the girl to anyone. It was not that he had deliberately decided to make a secret of her existence. It was just that when Karel, and Uncle Mark, and others had talked to him, questioning him about what had happened while he was in the cave, she had vanished from his mind completely. Zoltan had told his questioners that he hadn't even looked out of the cave. Later on, dreaming or awake, the memory of her would pop back, and he'd think: *Oh yes. Of course.* And then he'd wonder briefly how he could ever have forgotten, and wonder whether he ought to tell someone next time he had the chance.

Maybe going back into the cave this morning and looking out again from the exact same spot would help him to fix the whole experience in his memory. Then he could tell everyone all about it. He really ought to tell someone. . . .

That girl, though. The more Zoltan thought about her, the more he realized she was a great mystery. He wasn't at all sure that she was the little dark-haired girl that he remembered from his childhood. Sure looked like her, though. It might take a wizard as good as Karel to figure out who this one really was.

Zoltan's brow furrowed as he stared forward over the neck of his riding-beast, for the moment not paying much attention to where Swordface was taking him. It was more than strange, it was really alarming that he hadn't mentioned the girl to anyone, not even to Karel when the wizard had questioned him. It was very peculiar indeed. Almost as if—

Swordface stumbled lightly over something, recovering quickly. Zoltan raised his head sharply and looked around him. He had the sensation that he'd almost fallen asleep in the saddle, that he'd just been riding, without being able to think of anything, for an uncomfortably long time. Where was he going? Yes, out to the cave. He'd had a sudden sense that there was something . . . watching? Calling him?

What had he been thinking about before he almost dozed off? Oh, yes, the girl.

Maybe she was really an enchantress of some kind, just observing, or trying to help the children, and the attacking villains hadn't been aware of her presence at all. That would explain things satisfactorily. Or maybe . . .

It seemed like one of those great questions about which it was almost impossible to think clearly, like life and death, and the meaning of the universe. Anyway, it was all a great mystery, and he, Zoltan, ought to be trying somehow to solve it. Maybe that had been the message of her eyes.

Usually it took a little less than half an hour to ride out to the cave from the Manor. This morning Swordface was ready to run, and Zoltan, his own eagerness growing, covered the distance a little more quickly than usual. It remained a fine, cool morning, with a little breeze playing about as if it could not decide which way it meant to blow over the uneven sea of grass that stretched over most of the country between the Manor and the high hills.

And Karel had tried to raise elementals here. Zoltan had never seen anyone raise an elemental, or even try, and he was curious; he had heard people say that particular kind of magic was almost a lost art. And it seemed that the effort must have helped somehow; Karel was very good. The boy wondered if there could be anything left of those powers now, two days later. If today he might feel a hillock twitch when he stepped on it, or find the stream somewhere suddenly twice as wide and deep and full of water as it was elsewhere.

Twice in the next few minutes, as he drew ever closer to his destination, he passed small squadrons of cavalry, and on both occasions the soldiers rode near enough to make very sure of who he was before they saluted and went on with their patrol. Zoltan's growing sense of adventure faded each time as the patrols approached him, then began to grow again. He felt confident that he could avoid being spotted by the soldiers if he tried.

Presently he drew in sight of the cave burrowed into the base of a high, rocky hill. From the low, dark mouth of it the Sanzu issued, and the open place in front of the cave was still torn up and stained where the clash between bodies of mounted men had trampled the rocky soil and littered it with death. There were no graves here—the bodies of friend and foe had all been removed elsewhere for examination and burial.

Now a few more mounted soldiers came in sight, and Zoltan exchanged a few words with their young officer, explaining that he had felt an urge to ride out to see what was happening.

"There's nothing much happening now, Prince." Zoltan as a royal nephew did rate that title, but ordinarily he heard it only on the most ceremonious of occasions. This soldier was one he did not know. The two talked for another minute, and then the patrol moved on.

Zoltan, alone again, sat his mount, listening to the murmur of the stream, and looking at the dark, low aperture from which it issued. There was no use going into the cave again, he decided. The black-haired girl was not here any longer. She had to be somewhere, though.

For just a moment it seemed to Zoltan that a cloud had passed over the sun. But when he looked up, the sky was clear and empty.

The scent of certain flowers . . .

The memory this time was as sharp as reality. He thought that it was the same perfume that had come to him in his dreams, and that the flowers grew downstream, not really very far from here. He turned his riding-beast in that direction, following along the bank.

Zoltan had a good idea of the lay of the land for perhaps a kilometer or two downstream from the point where he was now. Beyond that point, if he should have to go that far, everything would be strange and new.

He looked ahead eagerly, feeling ready for some undefined adventure.

There were no soldiers in sight now. The last patrol he had seen had ridden off in a different direction.

The high plain ahead of Zoltan as he rode was dotted with a thin, scrubby forest, and there were very low hills on the horizon, between which, somehow, the Sanzu must find its way.

Half an hour after Zoltan had seen the last soldier, he was still following the Sanzu downstream, without any clear idea of exactly what he expected to find in that direction besides the flowers. He was now entering the region where the land started to turn rough again after the strip of plain, and the stream started trying to get away from the high country in one little rushing descent after another. There were still signs everywhere of the recent passage of Tasavaltan patrols, but he ignored them.

Half an hour after that, and now far out of sight of home, the boy was stretched out on a flat rock beside the tiny river, reaching down to where a patch of tall white flowers grew at the water's edge. The flowers were delicate things with long stems and almost frothy petals, and there was a golden center in each blossom. The perfume was here, all right, but it was still not as strong as Zoltan had expected it would be—he would get only a tantalizing hint, and then another one, long moments later.

A few meters behind Zoltan, his riding-beast was placidly cropping grass.

Somehow, once Zoltan had found the flowers, his craving for adventure was temporarily forgotten. He lay there looking long and long into the pool.

He gazed into the murmuring water until he saw the reflection of white shoulders and black hair.

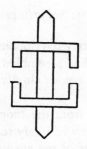

CHAPTER 5

ON that same morning, in the city of Sarykam, there were trumpets and drums at parting: a demonstration by the people of the city for the Prince they had come to love and respect over the last eight years of peace, and during the war that had gone before.

Prince Adrian, his small body clad in plain garments of rich fabric, a scaled-down version of his father's clothing, perched in the saddle of a sturdy riding-beast beside his father's mount. Jord, in the role of grandfather, held one of the Princeling's tiny hands in his huge ones and said good-bye. Mark's mother, Mala, a plain woman in her late forties, was there too, to wish the travelers well.

Adrian had ridden before, briefly, in parades and on the practice ground. Perhaps he thought that this was to be another parade. His parents had told him repeatedly what the purpose of this journey was. But there was no indication that their explanations had penetrated very far into the darkness that sealed his eyes, and more often than not closed off his mind. He held his head now in a characteristic pose, tilted on one side as if he were listening to something that only he could hear. His sightless eyes were busy. And one small hand, when Jord released it, rose and questioned the air ahead of him. His other hand continued to clutch the reins.

Now Karel, on a balcony overlooking the Palace courtyard in which the expedition had assembled, was giving the travelers such blessings as he could, chiefly by invoking the name of Ardneh.

One notable absence from the scene was that of General Rostov. There were plenty of likely reasons for his not being present—the near-success of the apparent kidnapping attempt seemed to require a thorough revamping of some of the defenses, and the General's full attention was required for that. But he had let it be known that he disapproved of Mark's taking Shieldbreaker out of the country. Rostov considered the Swords in the royal armory, like the other weapons, all public property and liable to be required at any time for the defense of the realm.

A short distance away from where Mark and Adrian sat their mounts, Ben, too, was mounted and ready. His wife had come to see him off and to offer him a few last words of advice and admonition.

When he had had what he thought enough of this, Ben excused himself to take a final count of heads. Making sure that everyone who was supposed to be in the train was actually present was really someone else's job, but an independent checkup wouldn't hurt. There were thirty mounted troops under the command of a young cavalry officer, and a handful of skilled wizards and physicians. Cages in the baggage train held half a dozen small winged messenger-beasts, and near them rode a journeyman beastmaster to manage and care for them.

Finally the order to march was given, hard to hear amid the noise and confusion that invariably took over any attempt at ceremonious departures. Tumult passed through the gates of the Palace, and then the city streets.

As Mark passed out through the great main gate of the city onto the high road that led to the southwest, he was engulfed by a last roar of good wishes that went up from people assembled on the city walls and on both sides of the road. In return he drew Shieldbreaker and saluted them all. The sun, exploding on the blade, provoked yet another outcry from the people. Mark felt a brief twinge of conscience for taking the Sword with him on what was essentially a private mission; but then he reminded himself that nothing that affected the royal family could be purely private, especially not a matter of such importance as Adrian's illness. Besides, in his heart the Prince felt that the Sword was his to do with as he wished; it had been given to him eight years ago, and not to Rostov.

Only let young Adrian come back strong and healthy from this pilgrimage; everything else was secondary to that. Apart from his feelings as a father, Mark, who had never felt he had a homeland of his own before this one, saw how important a healthy heir to the throne could be to the land and people of Tasavalta. He had read much history in the last few years, and he realized how important it was to everyone that the firstborn of the royal family should be strong and healthy, with two good eyes, and a keen mind to place at the service of his people. When the eldest child did not inherit this throne, it seemed that a time of trouble, perhaps even civil war, was practically guaranteed.

Twisting in his saddle, Mark looked back. He was far enough from the walls of the city now to be able to see above them. Kristin had evidently returned to other affairs that were demanding her attention; but high on a parapet of the Palace the fair head of little Stephen was still visible, watching intently after his father. As soon as Mark turned, his tiny, distant son waved to him yet once more; and Mark returned the wave.

Some time passed before the Prince looked back again, and when he did it was no longer possible to see who might be on the walls. The city was vanishing piecemeal now, disappearing almost magically by sections in this folded land- scape. One piece or another would drop out of sight behind one hill or another, or slide sideways behind an edge of cliff. Then sometimes the walls and towers would move into view again as the road rose up beneath the travelers or carried them through another turn.

Now Mark's gaze kept returning to the small figure that rode—so far in silence—at his side. Adrian's riding-beast had been specially selected, and specially trained, with magi- cians as well as beastmasters taking part in the instruction. The animal was an intelligent one, for its species—no riding- beast approached the mental keenness of the messenger- birds, some of which were capable of speech. It was also phlegmatic and dependable.

The boy usually sat in his saddle as he did everything, indifferently, when he could be persuaded to do things at all. Sometimes when riding he would forget to hold the reins that had been placed carefully in his right hand. Instead he would extend one arm, or both, groping into the air above the animal's neck. At the moment, one of the young physicians, alert for any sign that the child might be going to topple from his saddle, was riding on his other side.

So far all was well. Adrian's father had already observed that the child looked comparatively well this morning. The boy had spoken several connected words to his mother just before their departure and had seemed to understand at least that his father and he were going on a ride together. Now he was humming and crooning to himself in apparent content- ment, and he had not yet dropped his reins.

Mark turned again in his saddle and glanced back toward the rear of the column. Somewhere amid the baggage carried by the train of spare mounts and laden loadbeasts were the components of a litter, in which, strapped to a sturdy loadbeast or slung between two animals, Prince Adrian could ride when keeping him mounted became too difficult. Of late his seizures had increased in frequency, and it seemed inevitable that on this long journey the litter was going to see substantial use.

But only on the outward-bound leg of the journey, his father thought. Mark was consumed with hope that the litter would not be needed on the way back. *Pray Ardneh that on the way home my son will ride all the way at my side. And he'll talk to me. And he'll see me, look at me with his eyes and see me. He'll look at the world, and I'll explain the world to him. We'll talk, every day and every night, all the way as we're riding home.*

At last the walls of Sarykam and the towers of the Palace dropped permanently out of sight among the folds of the mountainous landscape. The journey still proceeded along well-kept roads, past neat villages whose inhabitants more often than not came out to wave. The border was still ahead.

But it was not very far ahead. Tasavalta was not, in terms of geographical area, a very large domain.

Now Mark looked back over his other shoulder. Three or four meters behind him, mounted on the biggest and strongest riding-beast that could be found in Sarykam, an animal of truly heroic strength and dimensions, was Ben of Purkinje.

As soon as Prince Mark caught his eye, Ben urged his mount forward and rode at the Prince's side.

Mark said, in a low voice and with feeling: "Truly, I am glad that you are coming with us."

Ben shrugged his shoulders, beside which Mark's looked thin. "And I am glad to be here, for more reasons than one." He sighed faintly. "Barbara grows a little more shrewish with each passing year."

"I suppose that she still nags you about giving me the

Sword?'' Mark tapped the hilt of Shieldbreaker at his side. He too had known Barbara for a long time.

"About that, and several other things. So I'm glad enough for the chance to ride out of the city for a time. Besides, I grow fat and immobile sitting there in my office, trying to look to the clerks as if I know what I am doing.''

"Or sometimes trying to look as if you didn't. . . . I have no doubt, my friend, that you know what you are doing, in your office or elsewhere. I don't suppose that any last bits of useful information reached your ears before we departed?''

"This morning? No.'' Ben shook his head. "Were you expecting something in particular?''

Mark gestured. "I hardly know, myself, what I am expecting. Perhaps some news of one of the other Swords.''

Ben cuffed at a fly on his mount's neck. "There's been nothing really new about any of them since we heard from that fellow Birch about two years ago.''

Mark remembered the fellow called Birch. A poor man, he had come to the rulers of Tasavalta saying he was breaking a long silence and hoping to be rewarded now for his information. Birch's report had been to the effect that once, years even before the battle of Tashigang, the god Vulcan had been seen, by Birch himself, with the Sword Farslayer in hand. Birch even claimed to have seen Vulcan kill Mars with it; in that claim both Mark and Ben were inclined to believe him. But there were no other witnesses to the Wargod's death, or at least none had come forward.

Another minute or so passed in silence, except for the sounds of moving animals, and a faint, contented crooning from Adrian. Then Mark said: "Doomgiver and Townsaver are gone.'' The statement sounded like what it was: the hundred-and-first rehearsal of the first condition of a puzzle or a riddle, which in a hundred trials still had not been solved—and to which, for all the puzzlers knew, no final answer existed.

Ben nodded. "Both destroyed by Shieldbreaker, in Vulcan's hand. No doubt about that, for either of them. And Shieldbreaker, thank Ardneh, now rides there at your side. Stonecutter's safe in our deepest vault at home. And tricky Coinspinner's vanished from the same place, gone we don't know where."

"That's five of the twelve more or less accounted for."

"Yes. Leaving seven more. Where Farslayer is now, we just don't know. And Woundhealer lies on this road ahead of us, or so we fondly hope."

"That's seven."

"Right. And Hermes once took Dragonslicer from my hand, and as far as we've been able to find out, no human eye has seen it since."

"And Hermes, a moment after taking Dragonslicer from you, also seized Wayfinder from Baron Doon . . ."

". . . so Hermes ought to have been carrying those two Swords when Farslayer struck him down. But none of the three blades were there when you and I came upon his corpse. D'you know, Mark, I've wondered about that. I mean, maybe Farslayer wouldn't have killed him if he hadn't been carrying the other two Swords with him when he was struck. Three Swords at one time! I've touched two of 'em at one time, and so have you. You know how it is."

Mark was shaking his head doubtfully. "You think just touching three Swords would be too much for a god?"

"Hermes wasn't the god who forged them."

"Even so, I think it damned unlikely that he was just overwhelmed by magic. No, I think the simple truth is that Farslayer killed Hermes, regardless of any other Swords, just as we both thought when we found him dead. As the Sword of Vengeance could kill anyone else in the world, god or human being.''

''I don't suppose it killed all of the gods.''

''No. Not most of them.'' Again Mark rode for a time in silence before he added: ''I think that their time was simply over.''

''That's not really an explanation.''

But now Mark had turned his head and was looking at his son. The small boy had appeared briefly to be listening to the men's conversation. But now Adrian had tired and wanted to be carried, mewling almost like an infant and holding out his arms toward his father's voice.

Mark picked him up and held him briefly before his own saddle. Presently that grew awkward too, and the march was halted while the litter could be unlimbered and put together. The people handling the assembly had not yet performed the task frequently enough to be accustomed to it, and the process seemed, to Mark, endlessly slow.

Eventually the litter was ready, and the procession could forge on.

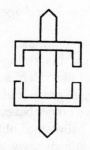

CHAPTER 6

EVEN as Zoltan watched, the reflection of dark hair, in an eddy where the surface of the stream was almost still, turned into an image of black twigs and branches.

He raised his head; there were the branches, part of a dead bush on the other side of the stream, as real as any objects could be. But no, something was wrong. The color of the vision in the water had been slightly different. And he had seen white skin, too. Hadn't he?

Zoltan jumped to his feet and waded in without bothering to remove his boots, keeping his gaze fixed on the reflected twigs. He reached the other bank in half a dozen splashing strides.

He bent over the leafless bush and examined it closely. What must have happened was that she had been hiding in the other bushes just *here,* and had leaned out . . .

He plunged into the streamside vegetation, searching diligently, ignoring the thorns that clawed at him. But he looked in vain for a clue that anyone had ever hidden there.

Zoltan was about to wade back to the other bank and reclaim Swordface when a changed note in the burble of the water downstream caught his ear. For the space of many heartbeats he stood motionless, listening. It had sounded like a trilling laugh. . . .

He started downstream along the bank, on foot, then made himself go back and get his riding-beast. He stroked the animal's head to keep it quiet. Here near the south bank there was almost a pathway, a game trail of some kind, Zoltan supposed. He had now come beyond the area where the marks of recent cavalry patrols had obliterated all other trails.

The path beside the stream grew easier, and he mounted Swordface again and rode. Before he had ridden fifty meters he arrived at another pool. This one looked deeper, and its depths were even more clear.

Something else caught Zoltan's eye. A few long, dark hairs were caught on a rough bush at one side of the pool. Zoltan dismounted and picked the delicate filaments from the bush. He stood there running them through his trembling fingers; the repeated touch of his hands made the hairs turn into threads of common spiderweb and vanish.

Enchantment. If only—

At a sound he spun around. This time he caught a glimpse of movement along the water's edge, thirty or forty meters downstream, as of pale flesh again, and some tight, silvery garment. This time he did not really see her hair that clearly— what he saw next was more like a pure burst of sunlight, as it might leap back from moving water.

Unthinkingly he shouted: "Come back! I won't hurt you!"

No answer. She was gone. There was a faint sound from somewhere even farther downstream.

He swore and splashed and waded. Then he went back to get Swordface again.

The next rapids were steeper, and the path descending beside them was so steep that Zoltan had no choice but to dismount and lead the riding-beast along.

Presently he was forced to leave the animal behind him, tethered lightly to a bush. The way down through the little rocky gorge had simply become too precipitous. It was easy enough for an agile human to clamber down, using both hands and feet, but the hoofed animal would never have made it.

Beside the next little space of flat land there was no solemn pool, but a continuous sinewed rush of water. Zoltan stood beside it listening, watching, holding his breath as if even that faint sound might interfere with his catching the clue had to have. *She,* being an enchantress after all, might be able to hear his breath above the rush of water. He thought it very likely now that he would be able to hear hers.

If only he had been able to tell old Karel about her. Karel could have helped him in this search . . . but no, that wouldn't have been right. Because no one else was meant to find her, only he, Zoltan. A deeper understanding of that point was slowly growing in him. And he was going to find her, now. She couldn't be that far ahead of him.

Zoltan went on. Always forward, always beside the rushing, babbling stream, and down.

Presently he came to a place where the stream was behaving queerly. First, without any apparent cause, there were wide swirls across its surface. And then came a much more serious departure from the normal. The whole baby river meandered for several meters sideways across a slope, a steep place where it should have plunged straight down. Staring at this phenomenon, Zoltan pulled out his dagger and looked about him suspiciously. But then he felt foolish and put the useless knife back into its sheath. Probably one of Karel's elementals had really taken shape two days ago and still existed in the form of this disturbance.

Ordinarily Zoltan would have been fascinated and somewhat frightened on encountering this phenomenon. Now it made little impression, except that thinking of the elemental recalled Karel once again to Zoltan's thoughts. But there was some reason, some important reason, why he should not even think of Karel now. . . .

Anyway, it was more enjoyable by far to think about the girl. To speculate on why she had signaled to him so enticingly, and what secrets—and perhaps other things—she might have to share with him when he had won this game by catching up with her. Zoltan no longer supposed that she might be a prisoner of the bandits, or really in need of rescue. She was just being playful with him, that was it.

There were things about that explanation that puzzled him— but somehow it would be inappropriate for him to think of puzzling things just now. Now was a time for action.

He had followed the stream yet a little farther—just how far was not important—when he actually caught a glimpse of the girl again, her head and arms and part of her upper body. This time she was trying to hide from him among the inter-twined branches of two fallen trees, right at the water's edge, and holding herself so still that for a long moment or two he could not be sure that he was really seeing her at all. And when, without shifting his gaze away for even so long as a heartbeat, Zoltan had come right up to the place, still by some enchantress's cunning she had managed to slip away, so cleverly that Zoltan had never seen her go. All he could think of was that she must have let herself slide into the water and drift away, gliding downstream beneath the surface.

And then he found one of her garments. The girl must have discarded it when she plunged into the water. But, when Zoltan came up to it and took hold of the fabric, it turned into brown moss in his fingers. Moss, grown long and tinged with gray, as if it had been growing here upon this log and rock for years. But though the cloth was no more than moss when he touched it, and seemed to be fastened in place, Zoltan could not be fooled.

The trouble, he decided, was that he simply wasn't moving fast enough to catch her.

Having reached this conclusion, he began to leap and run.

All went well for a little while. Then halfway through a steep descent he slipped, stepping on a slippery, angled rock, and fell, striking his chest on another flat rock with a thud that sent a shock of pain all through his rib cage. The breath was knocked clean out of him before he splashed into the next pool down. If the pool had been much larger he might have drowned. As it was, the rushing water deposited him like driftwood upon a narrow fringe of beach.

It seemed like a long time to Zoltan, lying in the grit and mud, before he could be sure that the pain in his ribs was going to let him breathe again.

Now something really strange was happening. Where was all the light?

Then he realized that the sun was going down. In fact it had gone down already. What light there was came from the full moon rising over the highlands, from which he had spent all day traveling.

Some animal off in the distance howled. It was an unfamiliar sound, as if Zoltan might already have reached some part of the world that was completely strange to him.

Groaning, he dragged himself up into a sitting position and decided that, after all, he was probably going to be able to go on breathing. Even though pain shot through his chest every time he drew in air.

It was, of course, impossible for him to get lost here—all he had to do was to follow the stream back up into the hills. Not that he was ready yet to turn back. He would rest here for a little while, and then he would go on. She couldn't be far away.

Something made Zoltan turn his head. There, illuminated by the last sunlight of the western sky and the rising moon high in the east, he saw the top of the girl's head, no more than ten meters away. Her gray eyes, fixed on Zoltan steadily, were looking over the top of a pile of brushwood.

Another white spot, at a little distance, might be the top of one of her shoulders. He was much closer to her now than she had ever allowed him to get before.

The last light of day was dying quickly, and for the first time Zoltan began to be afraid.

He thought the gray eyes laughed and beckoned, but still the girl moved away from him, going somewhere farther beyond the brushpile, and disappeared.

He had to go after her. It was simply that he had no choice. Zoltan managed to stand up and follow her. Not only his ribs but his leg hurt, as he discovered when he tried to walk. He went on, with great effort and some pain.

After only a little distance, on an easy slope, he came to a larger pool than any he had encountered yet.

On a flat rock just at the side of the pool he saw her eyes again, and the black hair. But *that* object ought not to be her body. The shape of it was wrong, completely wrong. It altered further as he looked at it, the bones and skin alike becoming something different. And then Zoltan saw her scaly length, her flicking tail, go writhing across the rock, plunging down into the riverbank slime beyond.

But there were still eyes—other eyes—looking at Zoltan, from another direction.

He turned, raising his own gaze to meet them.

The dark, winged shape, almost man-sized, perched amid shadows on a high ledge of rock. It looked as much like an illusion as the girl had looked like reality. But the eyes that looked down at him from the winged shape did not change. Gradually, heartbeat by heartbeat, he came to believe that they were very real.

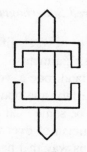

CHAPTER 7

THE full moon that Zoltan saw above the hills had waned to dark and waxed to full again when a column of about twenty riders approached within a few kilometers of the White Temple of Sibi.

At midday, a mounted scout, the first member of the advancing party to actually come within sight of the Temple and its compound, hurriedly surveyed the scene from a slight elevation nearby, then wheeled his riding-beast and sped away to make his report.

Less than an hour had passed before the scout was back, and the column with him. Halting atop a small hill that gave them a slightly better vantage point than that of the first reconnaissance, they looked over the situation more thoroughly.

At the head of the force as it arrived there rode a bulky, middle-aged man at whose belt hung a Sword, the symbol on the black hilt turned inward toward his body so that it could not be easily seen. Besides the Sword itself, appearances suggested nothing very remarkable about its owner. He was outfitted more like a bandit chieftain than an officer of cavalry, and indeed the clothing worn by his followers was very far from uniform. The men in the group—and the few women who were among them—made up an ill-assorted but well-armed gang, with no sign of any livery or colors, though pieces of the uniforms of several different armies could be distinguished among their garments.

At the leader's right hand rode a woman dressed chiefly in animal skins, and whose face and body were painted in ways that suggested she must be some kind of a minor enchantress. That she was not a magician of overwhelming skill could be deduced from the obvious way that her youth-spells struggled with the years to preserve her own appearance.

From their hilltop these leaders looked out over a dozen buildings and an extensive compound, mostly garden, all centered on the white stone pyramid, at least ten stories tall, that was the Temple itself.

The enchantress was the first to speak. "The Sword, if it is there, is lightly guarded."

The bulky man beside her turned his head. "Are you sure? Do your powers tell you that?" His voice was skeptical.

"My eyes tell me. I cannot be sure."

"Then use your powers," the man grumbled, "if you really have any. And make sure. As for eyes, I have two good ones of my own."

"I have powers," she flared, "and one day I'll make sure that you respect them."

He only grumbled again. Even that answer sounded as if it were merely as a matter of form. His attention had already moved back to the Temple, and the woman's threat, if it had really been that, was disregarded totally.

The enchantress dismounted and got to work. From a bag she carried she extracted fine powders of various colors and blew them into the air in different directions, a pinch at a time, from her hardened and somewhat dirty palm. The men around watched curiously, but for a time no one had anything to say.

Presently the woman was able to promise the bulky man—who waited expressionlessly for her report—that the magical protection of the treasure he had come here to get would be trivial at best; she would be able to set it aside easily. "That last prisoner we sacrificed," she assured him, "was a great help."

The man beside her nodded calmly. He had really not expected much in the way of magical tricks and traps from the White Temple; nor much in the way of armed force, either. His only real worry on his way here to take the treasure had been that someone else might have beaten him to it.

Now he motioned to his other followers and raised his voice enough to be sure that they all heard him. "We'll ride in, then. We will take what we want, but no more than that. And let there be no unnecessary killing or destruction."

Hard-bitten lot that the troopers were, they received that last order without protest. Indeed, there came in response a murmur or two that sounded like approval. There were many people who considered any move against the White Temple to be unlucky. Those who still believed in gods—and what bandit did not, at least on occasion?—were vastly reluctant to risk making enemies of Draffut and of Ardneh.

The Temple people inside the compound, and those few who were outside near the front gate, noticed the approach of the bandits when the riders were still some distance off, but their entrance was unopposed. The two White Guards at the entrance retreated rapidly, not bothering to try to shut the gates.

Extending from just outside those gates into the foot of the pyramid itself, there stretched a line of people who had come here hoping to be healed—the sick and injured, some of them accompanied by their attendants.

With the last admonition of their leader still in mind, the intruders cut through this line almost courteously, giving the lame and the halt time to scramble out of their way. The bandit column halted just inside the compound walls, where, at the sharp orders of their leader, its members dismounted and were rapidly deployed, some to guard their rear, a few to hold the animals. Most of them moved on foot against the pyramid.

The pyramid had one chief doorway, at ground level. Half of the small handful of White Guards who were now assembled in front of that doorway decided at once to take to their heels. The other half were not so wise, and the attackers' weapons, already drawn, had to be used. Blood spilled on the white pavement and on the chalky stones of the pyramid itself.

The bandit leader and others went into the Temple, and shortly afterward another Sword was brought out of the small interior room where it had been enshrined. When the bandit leader had satisfied himself that the object he had just acquired was indeed the genuine one he had been expecting, he left it in the hands of his chief lieutenant—in the case of this particular Sword he was willing to do that—and turned his attention elsewhere.

The Sword that had been at the leader's side when he arrived at the Temple had come out of its sheath, briefly, while the fight was on, though there had been no need for him to use it. Now it was again sheathed firmly at his side; this was one blade that he was not about to hand over to anyone else.

The leader looked about him now. "You, there!" he shouted, and gestured imperiously.

An ashen-faced, white-robed priest came forward, trembling, to learn what the next demands of this robber and murderer might be.

"Bring out some food and drink for my people here. Enough to make them happy. And there's someone I'd like to see. I've been told that she lives here now."

*   *   *

Eight years had now passed since anyone had called her Queen, and when she heard that title spoken by one of the servants chattering and whispering in fear and excitement outside her bower, it required no very quick thinking on her part to suppose that she had at last been overtaken by someone or something from those old times.

Listening to the voices more carefully now, she soon recognized a familiar, careless booming that broke in among the others. No need to guess any further. She could tell that the tones of the familiar voice, even as loud as they were, were intended to be soothing; he already had what he wanted, obviously, and he was trying now to set these harmless white-robed folk at ease. Panic, she had heard him declare many times, was always undesirable, unless you wanted to make things unpredictable.

Now the familiar voice outside said: "Tell Queen Yambu that Baron Amintor would speak with her."

The woman who had been listening from behind a leafy screen arose and went to the entrance of her bower, so that her caller might be able to see her for himself.

"Amintor," she called out softly. "I had heard that you were still alive."

He turned toward her in the open sunlight, showing her a face and body changed by the eight years, though not nearly so much, she knew, as she herself was changed. He bowed to her, not deeply but still seriously, she thought.

He said: "And I had thought, my lady, that you were dead. Only quite recently did I learn that you were really here."

"And so you have come here to see me. Well, you will find me altered from the Queen you knew."

"Aye, to see you. And I had one other reason for wanting

to come here, which I thought it better to make sure of first. Now we can visit at our leisure. But you look well.''

"Always gallant, Amintor. Come in.''

Amintor followed the lady among her trellises into what was more a garden than a house, but even so, apparently her dwelling. Cultivated insects hummed musically among some flowers. In the silence of his own mind the Baron was thinking that she looked about sixty years old now, or fifty-five at the very least, although he knew that in fact she could hardly be much more than forty. Her hair had turned from raven black to silver since he had seen her last, and her face bore deep lines that he had never seen before. Her step was firm enough as she moved ahead of him, but without energy. Her body was still straight and tall, but he could tell little more than that about it because of the loose gray clothing that she wore. That, too, was a considerable change.

They had now reached a roofed portion of her dwelling where there was simple furniture. Here the lady gestured her caller to a plain wooden seat.

"I know what I look like,'' said the former Queen, seating herself across from him, and in her voice he could hear for the first time a hint of the old fire and iron. "Hold Soulcutter in *your* hands throughout a battle, man, and see what you look like at the end of it. If it were not for Woundhealer, of course, I'd not be here now to talk about the experience. . . . I suppose you've got that one in your possession now; Woundhealer I mean. I thought I heard some clash of arms out there. Well, I could have told them that they'd need more guards. A child could have told them they'd not be able to keep such a treasure here without defending it. But they're impractical, as always. Never mind, tell me of yourself. That's not Woundhealer at your side, is it—? No, it couldn't be. What is this one that you have, then?''

Her visitor had been waiting for an opportunity to reply.

When he was sure that his chance had at last arrived, he said: "My lady, you amaze me as always. How d'you know it's not the Sword of Mercy that I wear here? You've not touched it, and I wear the symbol on the hilt turned in."

"Amintor, Amintor." She shook her head a little, as if to rebuke him for his slowness. "The Sword you wear at your side is the one you're going to grab when danger threatens. No fear of your relying upon the Sword of Love for that— you'll want to make some wounds, not heal 'em. What then? It can't be Shieldbreaker, not unless your fortunes have risen higher than the rest of your outfit indicates."

Amintor smiled. His hand brought the bright metal a few more centimeters out of its scabbard and turned it to give the lady a better look at the black hilt. Now she could see the concentric circles making up a small white target.

"It's only Farslayer, my lady. Nothing for you to wince at when I start to draw it in your presence."

"*Only* Farslayer? And I may be your lady, but I'm Queen no longer; now I can wince whenever the need arises. I'm afraid that any of the Twelve would be likely to make me do so now."

"Even . . . ?" Her visitor inclined his head slightly, in the direction of his own waiting troops. There was some laughter out there; apparently they were being fed and somehow entertained.

"Oh, the one you've just appropriated has kept me alive when otherwise I would have died. But I've had all the help from it now that it can give me. And I won't be sorry to see it go, for it reminds me of all the rest. But never mind all that. While we have a little time here, tell me all that you've been doing. Gods and demons, Amintor, listen to the way I'm babbling on. Seeing you again awakens in me a craving that I had thought was dead. A craving for information, I mean, of course." There was the hint of a twinkle in the lady's eye. "Now that you're here, and no one seems to be pursuing you, sit with me for a while and talk. If one of the servants ever dares to stick her head in here, I might even be able to offer you a drink."

Amintor smiled, gestured to show that he was at her disposal, and settled himself a little more solidly in his seat.

The lady demanded: "First tell me what happened to you on the day of that last battle."

His smile broadened. "Well, to begin with, I was locked up in a closet."

That closet had made him a dark and well-built prison, on the ground floor of the House of Courtenay, within the city of Tashigang. By the time Amintor was thrust into it and the door barred shut on him, the fighting had already broken out inside the city and was getting close to the house. Something even worse impended also—the wrath of Vulcan, more terrible than any simple human warfare. Or so it was considered at the time.

After Amintor had spent some time in a useless trial of his fingers' strength upon the hinges of the closet door, he found himself unable to do anything better than curl up in a corner and try to protect his head from falling bricks. The level of the noise outside his prison was now such that he fully expected the walls to start coming down around him at any moment. The battle had definitely arrived in the vicinity of the house, and the building appeared to stand in some danger of actually being knocked down.

Still, there were some voices out there that occasionally were able to make themselves heard above the tumult. There was one in particular whose roaring the Baron thought could only be that of an angry god. Then, just when it seemed that the din could be no worse, it somehow managed to redouble. Only when part of one of the closet walls actually came down in a thundering brick curtain was Amintor able to do anything to help himself.

When that opportunity arrived at last, he did not waste it. In an instant the Baron had scrambled his bulky body out over the pile of fallen masonry now filling the space where the lower part of the wall had been. Gasping and choking in a fog of dust, he caught dim glimpses of a scene of havoc.

What he had last seen as two rooms on the ground floor of the House of Courtenay had been violently remodeled into one. In this large space there were now a mob of people scuffling, men and women together surrounding the figure of a giant and trying to bear it down. The plain physical dimensions of that central figure, which struggled to maintain its feet, and laid about it with a Sword in its right hand, were little if at all beyond the human scale. But there was something about it all the same that made Amintor at once accept it as gigantic, more than human.

That fact was accepted by the Baron, but it was not of much immediate concern to him. What concerned him first was his own survival. In that first moment of his freedom from the closet the immediate danger that he faced was the mass of staggering, tumbling, rolling bodies, coming his way and threatening to bury him again.

Despite that immediate threat, Amintor's eyes in the next instant became focused upon the Sword in the giant's hand. That Sword, generating from within itself a sound of thudding like a hammer, went blurring about with superhuman speed and power, smashing furniture and knocking down sections of the remaining walls whenever it touched them. But it did no harm to the bodies of the unarmed folk who found themselves in its path.

Unless Amintor's eyes were lying to him, that blade passed through their bodies as through shadows, leaving them unharmed.

But when one man came running with a mace to join the wrestling fight against the god, Shieldbreaker turned in its arc with a thud, shattered his weapon into fragments, and in the same stroke clove him gorily in half.

Only later did the Baron have the time to puzzle out some meaning from all this. At the moment he could only do his best to get himself out of the fighters' way. Doing so was far from easy. He was in a corner with only the ruined closet behind him, and it appeared that he was trapped.

He dodged as best he could.

Just when the crush of struggling bodies was at its nearest to Amintor, threatening to pin him against the wall, he saw at the giant's waist a swordbelt that carried two sheaths. One of them was occupied, and momentarily the black hilt that sprouted from it was almost at the Baron's hand.

Again he did not hesitate. The tempting second Sword came out of its scabbard into his grip. It was still in his hand as he made his dodging, running, cowering, crawling escape from the building. He came out of the place through what had been the back door but was only a jaggedly enlarged doorway now, from which fragments depended on wrecked hinges. Evidently the fighting had indeed been fierce in and around the building even before that little mob of madfolk, whoever they were, had decided that they were going to wrestle a god. The fallen were everywhere, in the street and on the floor, most of them uniformed in the blue and gold livery that meant Blue Temple guardsmen.

Outside, a large quantity of smoke hung in the air, and Amintor could see that the house he had just got out of, though built mostly of bricks and stone, was trying to burn down.

The other buildings nearby were largely intact, but still there were signs of war down every street. Nearby, the Corgo flowed stained with blood, and rich with debris, including bodies. The whole city of Tashigang was reeling under the combined assaults of human armies and of gods.

While Amintor was still inside the house, the thought had briefly crossed his mind that he might try out his newly acquired weapon in the melee there, against one side or the other. But the Baron had rejected that notion as soon as it occurred to him. None of the humans in that house were likely to be his friends, whether he helped them now or not; and a god's gratitude for any kind of help was certain to be chancy at best. He did pause, now that he was outside, and look at his Sword's hilt, anxious to learn which weapon he had seized.

Farslayer itself! He almost dropped the weapon when he saw the small white target on the hilt. Instead he looked around him quickly to see if he was being pursued, and ran on when he saw that he was not. Right now, he thought, Sightblinder would have been a luckier acquisition, almost certain to mean a safe passage out of all this. He was uncertain of the exact limits on the powers of the Sword of Vengeance, and not at all anxious to have to try them out in open combat. As matters stood, the only playable move for him right now was a quick retreat, a maneuver which Amintor proceeded to carry out with as much dispatch as possible.

Fortunately for himself, the only folk he encountered directly in the streets of Tashigang were refugees, even more frightened and certainly more disorganized than he. They all gave a wide berth to the great bare blade that he was carrying, whether any of them recognized its magical potential or not.

At each intersection that he came to, the Baron paused, and he looked carefully down each street before he crossed it. He avoided anything that looked like the colors of any army, and anything that even suggested the live presence of organized troops.

Now and then the Baron would pause in his course to squint up at the sun. Frequently it was obscured by one column of smoke or another, but he could estimate the time. Many hours would have to pass before darkness came to help him make his way out of the city. It was now no later than midafternoon, and the dust and smoke of the city's suffering still hung over everything in an evil fog.

The walls that completely surrounded the city were everywhere too high, and the gates too few, to encourage casual passage at the best of times. These times were not the best. The Baron's first objective was the Hermes Gate, but when he came in sight of its inner doors he could see that they were still closed and defended.

Breaking his way into a tall building through a poorly barricaded rear window, he went up many stairs. Looking down from the high rooftop, he thought he could see soldiers of an assaulting army massing on the road just outside the gate, with reinforcements coming up. He was going to have to find another exit.

Back in the street again, Amintor chose a route that roughly followed the curving course of the great, ancient walls, that went uphill and down like the Great Worm Yilgarn. He was looking for a way out, but discovered none until he had come back to the river, the same broad stream that flowed beside the House of Courtenay.

Even after all he had already seen today, the Baron was astonished by what he now beheld. One of the huge watergates guarding the approaches to the city by river had been torn down. Very little was left of its gigantic frame of magically rust-proofed iron and steel. Later the Baron was to learn that the gate had been wrenched from its granite sockets by the hands of Vulcan himself, before the Sword of Force had had the chance to work its strange weakening doom upon him.

Amintor was on the point of committing himself to the

river as a swimmer when he was presented with what he perceived as yet another opportunity to better his condition; he seized this one as quickly as he had the other two. This one appeared in the form of a tall, fat pilgrim wearing the white robes of Ardneh, who came wandering through the streets toward the docks and declaiming against the horrors of war around him.

With Farslayer's long blade in hand, Amintor had little trouble in getting the man's attention and urging him into an alley. There, away from any likely interference, the man was persuaded to divest himself of his fine white robes before they should become stained with blood; such stains would have detracted from the pilgrim image that Amintor wanted to present. As matters turned out, no bloodstains anywhere were necessary—once stripped of his dignity, the pilgrim sat down in a corner of the alley and wept quietly.

Trying on the white robes over his regular garments, the Baron confirmed to his satisfaction that they were long enough to let a man carry a long Sword under them almost inconspicuously.

Now, to the river again. After the earlier evacuation, and this much fighting, there were no boats available at any cost, in money or in blood. Wrapping up his newly acquired Sword in his newly acquired robes, Amintor floated the resulting bundle in front of him upon a sizable chunk of wood. In this mode he plunged in and went splashing strongly upstream through the open gateway and was not killed, though for some reason someone's soldiers who were now manning the flanking defensive towers decided to use his bobbing head for target practice with their slings. Fortunately for him, they were still out of practice when he was out of range.

The Baron did not pull himself out of the river until he had made a long kilometer upstream. Luckily the river was almost free of traffic, military or otherwise, upon this martial afternoon. When he did get out of the water he took shelter in the garden of someone's abandoned suburban villa, from which vantage point he was able to observe developments around the city itself. He gathered more information by intercepting and questioning a lone refugee or two who passed the villa.

Amintor found some food that others had overlooked, and remained in his suburban garden until the following morning. By then he had seen and heard enough to feel sure of who was going to win, or had won, the battle, and therefore the war that so heavily depended on it.

As soon as he was sure that his side had lost, the Baron, thinking it would be a long time, if ever, before he laid claim to that title again, melted away into the countryside, as did a thousand others who had found themselves in more or less the same predicament.

During the next few days, foraging for survival as best he could, he saw a great many of those thousand others. Many of them were his own former comrades in arms, from the army of the Silver Queen. His new white robes saw little use. Amintor's appearance, his reputation, and his ability to assert leadership, even without the great Sword now at his side, would have let him recruit as many of these people as he wanted to follow him. But he was very selective in his recruiting. Right now he did not want an army of followers, all of them hungry and poorly organized. He foresaw the scouring of the countryside for such bands that was sure to come as soon as the victorious armies had enjoyed a breathing spell in which to care for their wounded, bury their dead, and put out the fires that were still threatening the city.

That scouring, that hunt for escaping and reorganizing enemies, came just as the Baron had foreseen it would. But by the time it came, he and the handful of new followers he had recruited were well away.

* * *

"It is a very remarkable tale," said she who had once been Queen Yambu. "But no more than I would have expected from you. And a long time has passed between that day and this; I should like to hear more of what you have done."

But Amintor got lightly to his feet and bestowed another bow upon the lady. He caught himself as he was about to offer thanks for her hospitality; the servants had never appeared, and he had never been given the wine he might have taken. He said: "Your Majesty is kind. I only wish I could stay long enough to tell you the rest."

"No more of that, no titles. So, you have gained the weapon that you came here to get."

"If the Sword of Mercy can really be called a weapon."

"Hm. You'll find a way to make it one. I could think of one or two methods myself if I were any longer interested in weapons . . . what will you do with it now?"

He gestured lightly. "The great game goes on, my lady, even if the gods themselves no longer play. I for one have not finished my turn."

"All right, don't tell me, then. I still wish you well. You are a great rogue, Amintor, but I still wish you well."

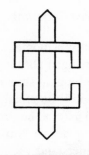

CHAPTER 8

IN the gathering dusk, the dark, winged shape that sat on the shadowed ledge of rock above Zoltan was all but invisible, except for its eyes. They were almost like human eyes, he thought, except that he could feel as well as see their gaze as they swept over him. One pair of eyes, and what looked like wings, and behind them movement in darkness, and that was all he could see of what or who was on the ledge.

Abruptly he discovered that he could not move. His booted feet felt as if they had taken root in the bottom of the stream. His arms were numb and hung down limply at his sides. Enchantment. Zoltan tried to cry out and could utter only a feeble croak. It might be magic that had disabled his voice too, or it might be fear.

As Zoltan stood paralyzed, ankle-deep in flowing water, another figure came as if from nowhere into his field of vision, standing on the far bank of the stream. This new shape, visible in the unshadowed moonlight and the very last of the fading glow of day, appeared, in the circumstances, startlingly ordinary. It was that of a man of indeterminate age, dressed in a soft robe and slippers, as if for lounging in a palace.

The man stood in an arrogant pose facing the stream, and he appeared to be inspecting Zoltan. That was a trivial task and occupied him for only a moment. Then he turned away and his whole attitude changed abruptly. With the submissive air of someone approaching a superior, he made his way quickly along the bank until he stood just below the winged shape on its high rock. There he bowed deeply and addressed a few words to the being above him in some language that Zoltan was unable to understand.

Up on the rock there was a stir of movement in the depth of shadow. Now it seemed to Zoltan that two forms were there, one the size of a riding-beast, the other of a man, and it seemed to him that both of them were winged—but even beyond that, there was something grievously wrong, unnatural, in the shape of both.

Now speech came from the man-sized shape, which was standing, or crouching, slightly in front of the other one. It was answering the man below and spoke in the same tongue that he had used, and Zoltan listening could still understand nothing at all.

He thought that the voice of the thing on the ledge did not sound fully human. There was something too whining and catlike about it. But even so it conveyed a royal firmness.

The man standing on the riverbank replied, bowing repeatedly as he did so. He was working harder and harder to acknowledge his inferiority with regard to the other.

The two of them in their incomprehensible conversation moved across the edge of Zoltan's consciousness like figures in some dim, cloudy dream. There was a roaring in his ears, and he had to struggle desperately to keep from fainting. All he could think about now was his own paralyzed body, his helpless situation.

Now that it was too late, Zoltan was able to understand clearly that for the past several days, from the time when he was inside the cave—*from the exact moment when he had looked out of the cave and seen the girl*—he had been under some form of evil and dangerous enchantment. The spell had not only compelled him to come alone on this mad expedition, but for days it had prevented him from seeking help from Karel or anyone else who might have helped him.

Zoltan did not faint. Perhaps fainting was not allowed.

Now the strange man on the riverbank and the even stranger being who sat above him were debating between them what was to be done with Zoltan. He could tell, because they were both looking his way now, and the man gestured in his direction.

Again Zoltan tried to cry out, but he could not.

And now he saw, with a sense of nightmare, that a third being had joined their conference. This newcomer was a dim figure, a human male in hat and robes. He stood on the same bank of the stream as the other two, and he faced Zoltan from a position between and somewhat beyond them.

Now this third presence became more distinct, and even after all that he had seen already, Zoltan blinked. In the moonlight the newcomer appeared like a caricature, a sketch based on the popular idea of what a wizard should look like, even to the conical, wide-brimmed hat and the robe speckled with strange symbols.

The figure on the high rock and the man standing on the riverbank below each glanced once in the direction of the new arrival when he first appeared. But after that, to Zoltan's surprise, they totally ignored him and went on with their mysterious dialogue as before. And the new arrival was content with silent observation.

Zoltan's capacity for surprise was pretty well exhausted. It scarcely seemed odd to him at all when he found himself suddenly capable of understanding what the creature on the rock and the man below were saying to each other.

". . . what I must have was lost," the Shadowed One above was saying to the obsequious man, "eight years ago. I am convinced now that you know nothing of that Sword's whereabouts. Nor do I think that it is near this place. But it is possible that you will learn something about it; and anything you learn of it must be communicated to me as soon as possible.''

"I understand that, Master." Again the man below bowed deeply. He hesitated, then added: "You can trust me to do so. Such knowledge would only be a burden to me—he whom I formerly served, the Dark King, would be able to testify to the dangers of that weapon, were he still alive—and I am thankful that you stand ready to relieve me of it, if it should ever come into my possession." The man paused, then added blandly: "I am sure that you are aware of the dangers, and can deal with them."

"The Dark King?" said the shape perched on the ledge, managing in the three words to express a great deal of contempt. "Be assured that *I* can deal with it, or with any Sword, and still accomplish my own purposes while doing so. If indeed you are worried on that score, Burslem, you may set your mind at ease."

Burslem. Zoltan could not remember ever hearing the name before, and it meant nothing to him now.

"Then I think," said Burslem softly, making obeisance once again, "that you are more than human."

"Whether I am or not is a point of no particular importance, as far as you are concerned. Think of me either way you like." But Zoltan, listening, thought that the creature, whatever it was, was pleased by the suggestion.

The man below raised pleading hands. "Forgive my ignorance, Master—but are you then one of the gods?"

This time the thing that sat above him was not pleased. "The creatures that you called the gods," it whined in irritation, "were merely artifacts of the collective imagination of humanity."

And meanwhile the silent observer in the background continued to do nothing but watch, and listen. It was as if he, like Zoltan, were paralyzed.

"They were real, the gods," said the man on the riverbank. He was agitated, and again he made obeisance, as if trying to excuse the contradiction even as he uttered it. "Possessing a certain reality, surely. Consider the Swords—"

The smaller shape on the ledge above him waved something that emerged from the deepest darkness looking like a wingtip. "The gods could kill you, if that's what you mean. They could do horrible things to you—to most people—if they bothered to try. But remember that I am of a much higher order of reality than were those you call the gods, and I can do worse."

The man below went down upon one knee. "I shall not forget," he murmured rapidly, his voice quavering.

"Let us hope that you do not. Now, I see no reason not to approve of your plan of action as you have outlined it. This one you have caught"—here again something like a wingtip came briefly out of shadow, gesturing in Zoltan's direction— "and can hold for ransom. But that will not be enough. You should take other hostages, or take some other action of equivalent force against the ruling house of Tasavalta. It is my wish—my command to you—that they be neutralized, lest they eventually interfere with my plans elsewhere. I am going to be occupied elsewhere for a long time. For months or years, perhaps."

"I hear and obey."

There was more to the conversation, but Zoltan heard very little of it. His understanding of the strange language was failing again, the words becoming gibberish in his mind once more. His mind was reeling, and the murmur of speech that sounded only partly human was like that of the stream that flowed around his ankles, going on and on and meaning nothing.

He was only vaguely aware when both of the shapes on the high rock departed, rising up together into the night sky. Together, the large and the small, they made a winged form of shadows that was much larger than a man, but still hard to see against the stars. Soon the composite shape was out of sight altogether.

Now, with that departure, it was as if some strain had been relieved, and Zoltan was free to become fully aware of his surroundings once again. He realized vaguely that at some point during the last few minutes the third figure, the silent onlooker, had disappeared.

He and the man named Burslem, who still stood on the riverbank, were alone.

Burslem was no longer bowing and scraping, but again standing arrogantly erect. Now he made a wizard's gesture at the starry sky, then turned toward Zoltan and stepped into the shallow water. He was coming to look his prisoner over at close range. Even as he approached, there was a splashing in the water some meters behind him, a pale, leaping shape. And now the dark-haired girl, her misshapen body half silver and half shadow in the moonlight, was sitting on the bank behind the approaching magician.

The man must have been aware of her arrival, but ignored her. He approached Zoltan closely and prodded his arms and ribs as if to see whether his paralysis had reached the proper stage. He looked into Zoltan's eyes and ears. Then he moved around Zoltan's immobile figure, his magician's fingers busy, weaving some additional spell into the air around his captive.

Then the wizard turned his head, suddenly taking notice of the girl on the far bank. He snapped his fingers at her, and she vanished, splashing into the water with a movement more fishlike than human.

And then the wizard himself was gone, without a splash, without a sound of any kind. Zoltan was alone.

He waited for one of the strange presences to return, but none of them did. It was as if they had all forgotten him. The moon looked down, the water gurgled endlessly around his ankles. He stood there like a statue and could not fall, but he could grow tired. His injured leg, with his weight steadily on it, hurt like a sore tooth. His ribs stabbed him with every shallow breath.

The moon was down, and dawn was approaching, and he had begun almost to hope that he had been forgotten, before the magician returned, as silently and inexplicably as he had gone.

Burslem stood again on the riverbank, looking more ordinary now in the light of the new day, but not less terrible. Now for the first time the magician's face was clearly visible to Zoltan, and it was startlingly human, only the face of a man.

Zoltan tried to say something, but he could not speak. Now he thought it was magic that sealed his tongue, though by all the gods his fear was great enough.

The other smiled at him. "Well. So, you must be kept in storage, somewhere, somehow. For some undetermined time. How shall it be done?"

Still Zoltan could not answer. At some moment soon, surely, he would wake up. Suddenly tears were running down his cheeks.

The wizard paid no attention to any of this, but stood back, making controlled, decisive gestures. Zoltan's legs, abruptly moving again, though still under alien control, turned him around and marched him through the water to the high bank that ran along the other side of the river. Able to look at that bank for the first time in twelve hours, the boy could see that there was a deep hollow there, really a cave. The entrance to the recess was curtained naturally by a growth of vines that hung over it from above, and screened by tall reeds that grew from below.

His own muscles moving him like alien hands, Zoltan was turned around, then cast down inside the muddy, shallow cave like a discarded doll. Then his position was rearranged, once, from the unbearable to the merely uncomfortable.

"Might want those joints to work when I take you out again." The magician's voice was genial. "Of course, on the other hand, I might never take you out."

There was a silent arpeggio of magic. Mercifully Zoltan was allowed to sleep.

Zoltan awoke, suddenly, to a realization of his physical surroundings, which were apparently unchanged.

It was late at night. The moon was high, and there was something strange about it. Eventually he understood that it had waned for several days from full. He stared at the gibbous shape for a while, trying to comprehend the implications. But in a moment the moonlight falling on the earth outside his cave showed Zoltan something that distracted him from other thoughts.

The same figure he had seen before as a silent listener, that of a little old man, a caricature of a wizard, was standing on the far side of the stream. But this time, after the first moment of confrontation, the witness was far from silent.

Speech burst from the little old man, a torrent of childish abuse that seemed in a way the maddest thing that Zoltan had experienced yet. "What are you doing in there, you stupid? You shouldn't be there at all. Come out!" The tone was one of anger and relief combined.

The man came closer, and as he neared the stream his aged, dried-apple face was plainly visible in the moonlight.

Zoltan could not recognize it, but for a moment he thought that he should.

"Come out of there! Out of there, out of there! Ooooh! Why are you in there at all? There, now you can talk, answer me!" The voice was gravelly and phlegmy most of the time, but on some words it squealed and squawked. In general it was hard to understand.

"I want to come out," croaked Zoltan, suddenly discovering that he was able to talk again. His own voice, after a week of silence, sounded not much better than the old man's. "I can't move, though. Help!"

"Help? Help? I've been trying to come back here and help. You think it's easy?" the aged wizard-figure shrieked like a madman. The body in the strange robe bent and twisted, gesturing. Now he seemed to have hold of the landscape, and twitched and tugged at it, heaving until the land, stream and all, was shaking like a rug. Water rose up in a thin, foaming wall, and for a moment Zoltan feared that he was going to be drowned.

Not only the mundane landscape was affected. Invisible walls went shattering, impalpable bonds were torn apart. It was a painful, fumbling process, but Zoltan at last popped out of his cave, like a bug shaken from a carpet, to splash into the stream again. The water was a cold shock that assured him he was at least fully awake. Moving again, he felt amazingly better than he had feared he would. His arms and legs were full of pins and needles, but they were functioning. And his ribs were only lightly sore, as if the long enforced rest had healed them.

The world was quiet after its purging. The new wizard stood on the riverbank, bent over with hands on knees, peering at him.

Zoltan cleared his throat and demanded, almost prayerfully: "Who are you?"

The other straightened up and answered in a rapid voice that sounded stranger and stranger the more it chattered: "Names are magic. Names are magic. That one who flies would like to grab my name and bonk me, but he can't. He knows your name already, but not mine. Couldn't even see me when I was here before, so there, ha ha!" And the old man laughed. It was a mad and disconnected sound that wandered up and down the scale of human voice-tones.

With something of a chill, Zoltan realized that he could see moonlight through the edges of the figure, as if it were not really, solidly, there at all.

But after everything else that had happened, he wasn't going to quibble about that. "I still need help, sir. Can you help me get home?"

The wizened wizard shook his head. "No, no, no! You are supposed to be out adventuring, Zoltan. You're big, you're all grown up, and you can't go home yet."

That was a shock. "Why can't I?" He wiped his eyes, his face. He was almost sniveling.

"Why? Don't you know? I turned the words around so you could understand them, when those two were talking. Your—your uncle Mark needs help." The wizard stood with fists on hips and glared.

"Oh." Zoltan, feeling shamed, squelched his way out of the water and sat down on the bank. "How can I help him? What can I do?" Then, without waiting for an answer, he jumped up again. "Uncle Mark or whatever, I've got to get out of here before they come back—and how did you do that, just now? Get me loose, I mean?"

"I know tricks. I found out some pretty good tricks, to get things loose. Good old Karel, he put together some great elementals." The wizard chuckled and slapped his bony thigh. Mere image or not, the impact sounded solidly.

"Are you a friend of his, sir?"

There was a pause. "We've met a few times." And the old man, mouth slightly open on his snaggled teeth, squinted sharply at Zoltan, as if to see whether Zoltan had got the joke.

Zoltan, who could see no joke, once more asked for help.

"You've got to go and help your uncle first," his rescuer repeated relentlessly.

"If—if Uncle Mark really needs me, I'll do what I can." Zoltan swallowed. "I'll help. But you've got to tell me where to go, and what to do, and—and how to do it."

The other stood with his fists on his hips, nodding his head sharply. But his speech, just at first, did not sound all that confident. "I don't know if I can tell you all that. But I think I know what I can do—I think. Oh, fuddle-duddle, I can do it. Tell you what, Zoltan. Right now you look very tired, so why don't you go to sleep?"

That was alarming. "I've been asleep. Don't make me go back again. I thought you were going to help me."

"You are tired. Good sleep this time. Go back to sleep."

And Zoltan did.

When he awakened again he had no idea of how much time had passed, but he could see that it was still night—or maybe it was night again. This time he could not find the moon.

At least he had not been stuffed back into the cave. He was in motion—somehow. He was in a sitting position, and his legs were resting, floating, with his knees bent and raised to the level of his chin. He was sitting on something—or in something—but he was moving.

He was really moving. That brought him fully awake. He was in the stream, submerged in water with only his head and shoulders and knees above the surface, but he was not cold or wet.

When he looked down to see what was carrying him, Zoltan discovered that, as far as he could tell, he was being borne up and along by the river itself. Bits of small driftwood ringed him around almost like a gentle fist, urged by some invisible power to offer him support, but it wasn't the wood that kept him floating. It had to be some invisible power because there wasn't enough wood. In this stream there should hardly be enough water.

And when he looked ahead he saw that the land itself was making way for him, trees nodding and swaying as if they walked, rocks bending out of his path where the rapids ordinarily ran swift.

He was borne upstream, through the rapids, easily and safely.

Then came a long stretch of almost level flow. He felt no fear. He was beyond fear now.

A giant fish came to splash beside him, and leap, and splash again. The reality of the night supported him, and once more he slept.

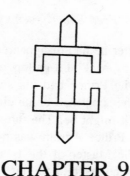

CHAPTER 9

MARK kept a log of distance traveled every day, and after several weeks of the journey he began to watch for certain landmarks, hills of a peculiar configuration that had been described to him in Sarykam. The borders between Tasavalta and the land of Sibi were as a rule not defended, or even sharply defined, but at length he was satisfied that he had crossed them. The clothing of the few people who came into sight was different from that of Tasavaltan villagers, and the only dwellings now in sight were of inferior construction.

When the landmark hills at last came into sight, the Prince felt sure that he was near the Temple that he sought, and he sent a human scout ahead as a routine precaution. His beastmaster of course had birds in the air already—they made faster scouts than human riders, particularly where the terrain was difficult, and often brought back vital information. But there were relative subtleties in things observed, sometimes even things as important as the color of uniforms, which remained beyond the capabilities of the birds to perceive and describe.

The scout received his orders and cantered off, soon leaving behind the main Tasavaltan body that continued to travel at a more modest pace.

Within an hour after he had disappeared the lone rider was
in sight again, coming back at a gallop.

Barking orders, the Prince had his small force ready for
action well before the scout had come close enough to shout
his news, whatever it might be. The ranks had closed around
the litter—in which Prince Adrian was now spending almost
all his time—and the Master of the Beasts had sent all but
one of his flying creatures into the air, where they circled,
keeping a high lookout.

The rider, clattering up at last to the head of the column,
delivered his message out of breath.

"I found the Temple, and there's been some kind of
trouble there, Your Highness. They've scraped up some kind
of extra barricade at the front gate, and there's what looks
like a triple funeral in progress. There were three coffins. If
three people have died suddenly in a Temple that holds
Woundhealer, well, I thought something strange must be
happening. I didn't go in, just took a look and came right
back."

"A wise decision. Any signs of fighting?"

"No sir. Nothing I could see. But I thought you'd best
know as soon as possible what's going on."

Mark nodded, and considered. "All right. We'll go on to
the Temple. But with double outriders, on alert."

With the scout leading the way, the column proceeded at
the same pace as before. Within the hour the Prince had
come near enough to the Temple, which lay in a small flat
valley, to see the signs of trouble for himself. The funeral
was over now, but the black bands that meant White Temple
mourning were still in evidence, stretched across buildings
and strung between them. And there, as the scout had described it, was the extra barricade built from piled-up timbers
and sandbags and even furniture, and looking more a sign of
panic than of determination. The space inside the Temple's

outer wall was thick with people, standing or sitting or milling about, but there was no sign of military activity.

The Prince motioned his own people forward. Within a few more minutes, the column had reached the outer barricade, traversed the passage through it, and arrived at the gate proper. There the single White Guard on duty, his teeth chattering, was brave enough to ask them what they wanted.

Mark, who had already halted his column, now raised his right hand in a sign of peace. "We mean no harm. We have come only to seek a healing from the Sword of Mercy."

The man on guard appeared to be in a chronic state of shock. He looked back at the Prince as if he could not understand what Mark was talking about. Then at last he replied: "It's g-gone."

"Gone? Where? You mean Woundhealer has been stolen?"

"Yes sir."

Mark looked past the guard, into the compound. Now he understood the mournful look of the swarm of invalids who occupied most of the courtyard inside the gate. A White Temple was generally a hospital as well as a place of worship, but this one appeared grievously overcrowded with patients. And a faint moaning in many voices, as of some general sorrow, went up into the pleasant sky. A few nurses and physicians were going slowly and tiredly about their traditional job of trying to alleviate the sufferings of the sick and injured. The air of defeat hanging over the Temple was almost palpable.

Mark turned to Ben. "Set up our camp here, outside the walls. Post guards as usual. We will remain here for a little while at least."

Now priests were approaching from inside the compound, looking as tremulous as their guard had been at first. When they observed that the guard was still alive and armed, they drew courage from the fact and approached the gate more boldly, crying out their grief that the Sword of Mercy had been stolen from them.

Quickly Mark began to question the white-robes, probing for solid information. "Who was it that took the Sword from you? When? How many were there? Which way did they go?"

He was provided, willingly enough, with times and descriptions. Witnesses' accounts differed somewhat, but were alike enough for the Prince to feel that he was getting a fair idea of the truth. Once the priests were sure of Mark's identity, their faces brightened and they began to look at him hopefully.

One of the older white-robes said encouragingly: "They were in no hurry to get away, Your Highness. Only bandits. If you are quick you ought to be able to overtake them."

Mark shook his head. "You say they are many hours ahead of us. My people and my animals alike need rest before we can undertake a long pursuit. And I hope that you can spare us some provisions."

"We can. We can. We will do everything we can to help you, if you can bring us back our Sword."

Mark dismounted, then turned back to the priests with another question. "Why do you say that the bandits were in no hurry?"

"Because, Your Highness, their leader dawdled here. He delayed and spoke for a long time with one of our long-term guests—she who was once Queen Yambu."

Standing just outside the leafy doorway, looking into the bower's cool interior, the Prince said: "I thought perhaps that you had vanished with the Emperor."

"No," replied the dim figure seated at a table inside, and let her answer go at that. When Mark appeared at her doorway she had raised to him a face so changed by time and events that for a moment he did not recognize her at all.

After a moment, she who had once been the Queen got to her feet and asked the Prince to enter. When he was inside she began at once to speak of trivial matters, the weather and the timidity of her servants. She felt a great reluctance to talk about the Emperor, who, on that last battlefield, had asked her for the second time to marry him. For the second time she had refused. Only he, the Emperor, would have made such an offer to a defeated enemy. And only she, perhaps, would have rejected him as she did.

What had kept her from accepting was the fierce need to assert her independence, a need that had been with Yambu all her life. It still ruled her behavior.

With an effort she brought her attention back to the man who was now standing in front of her.

Mark was saying: "I think that some of the white-robes out there are already angry with me, as if it were my fault that their Sword was stolen. They expect me to gallop after it at once and bring it back."

Yambu roused herself to be hospitable.

When her guest was seated and some refreshment had been brought for both of them, she said: "Well, servants of Ardneh or not, there are idiots and worse in the White Temple, just as there are in the other Temples. Or anywhere else. I've lived here long enough now to know that."

Mark sipped from the mug that had been placed in front of him, then took a deeper draught. "You have chosen, then, to live eight years among idiots?"

"Oh, they have their good qualities too. They tend to be peaceful idiots, and for the most part it is soothing to live among them. When I came here I wanted nothing but to be soothed—I made them a large donation—a very large donation—and I expect to get my money's worth in return. But never mind them. Have you now come at last to kill me? Or arrest me?'' She sounded more interested in the answer than afraid of what it might be.

"I have no particular wish to do either. Who stole the Sword of Mercy?''

"Ah, of course. It is the Sword that brings you here, too; I should have known that at once. Well, I can tell you without hesitation that it was Amintor who took it—you'd find out soon enough anyway. He sat where you are sitting now, and took some time to pay his respects to me, in token of the times when we were together. And then he recited to me something of his own history during the past eight years.''

Mark's mouth moved in a faint smile. "An exciting tale, that must have been. Perhaps some of it was even true. What hints did he drop, or seem to drop, about his plans, now that he has Woundhealer?''

Yambu thought back. "Why, he said nothing at all about his plans. I didn't ask him about that.''

"Not that you'd want to tell me if he did.''

"On the contrary, Prince. I think I might well tell you. I suppose I like the two of you about equally well, though you were once my enemy, and he was once my officer—and more. I'll answer any questions you may have, if they are decently put, and if I can find the answers—why not?''

Mark looked at her, and she could see him taking note again of the extreme changes in her since he had seen her last, and thinking about what must have produced them.

Then he asked: "Where is Soulcutter now?''

Her aged eyes searched him in turn, as if she were disappointed in him. She asked: "Why d'you want that? Can't you see what it's done to me?''

He shook his head. "It's not that I want it particularly. But

I'll use it if I can. If I have nothing else to use. I'm ready to use anything.''

"Then give thanks to all the surviving gods you haven't got it.'' The former Queen sat back in her chair.

"You don't know where the Sword of Despair is now? Or you won't tell me?''

"Even Amintor didn't ask me about that one. Why should you?''

"Maybe Amintor is not as desperate as I am. Where is it?''

The lady shrugged. It was a gesture that conveyed sadness and weariness more exquisitely, Mark thought, than any extravagance of behavior could have done.

Then she said: "I really don't know. My belief is that the Emperor took it with him, when he . . . withdrew.''

"Withdrew?''

"From politics. From war. From the affairs of humanity in general.''

"And where is he now?''

Again the lady shrugged, even more delicately than before. "I don't know. But I don't suppose you're going to find him and Amintor in the same place.''

Mark talked with the lady once more, on the following morning, just before he and his people departed on Amintor's trail. But he learned nothing useful from her.

Among the people in Mark's small force were a couple of trackers of some skill. But as matters turned out, their skill was not really needed. Amintor, and the score or so of riders he evidently had with him, had left a trail that would have presented no real problems even to the most inexpert eye, even though it twice forded streams and in several places crossed long stretches of hard ground.

The bandits' trail at the start led straight west from the

Temple, or as near to that direction as the local difficulties of terrain allowed. The land here verged on wasteland, harshly configured but in its own way beautiful. There were signs that grazing was sometimes practiced upon the scanty vegetation. But once the precincts of the Temple were left behind, along with the roads that approached the complex from north and south and east, all signs of human habitation soon dropped from sight.

Mark was not minded to contemplate nature, or beauty of any kind. He had undertaken the pursuit of Amintor because he saw no real alternative, but he was gloomy about the chances of success. To begin with, his riding-beasts and loadbeasts were still tired from the long journey they had already made. But to bivouac any longer in front of the White Temple would give the Baron too great a start.

Secondly, Mark knew that he could expect no help. The few scattered inhabitants of the territory through which he was now passing obviously were not going to provide any; and nowhere did the White Temple have any respectable armed force of its own. They had only the White Guards, best suited for keeping order in a waiting line of invalids, and with some effort usually able to repel the sneak thieves and vandals that might pester any Temple. As an army in the field, or a bandit-hunting posse, the White Guards were nonexistent.

But Mark's greatest difficulty now was that he was compelled to bring his son with him on the chase. It would have been unthinkable to leave Adrian at the Temple, where he would be prey to kidnap or murder by the next set of desperadoes who happened along. Mark had the idea that there would almost certainly be more of them. Word of the Sword's presence there had gone out far across the world, and many would be scheming to try to profit from it. Nor would the Prince have been able to leave any substantial number of guards at the Temple to protect his son—the band he was pursuing was comparable to his own in size.

But the presence of an invalid child inevitably slowed down the pursuit. Even under the best of conditions, Adrian was unable to ride swiftly, and the best of conditions seldom obtained. Nor could the litter, slung between two beasts or strapped to one, make anything like the speed that might be necessary in war. The boy could be carried in front of someone's saddle for a time, but that was awkward and in combat it might prove fatal to child and rider alike.

Still, Mark did not consider the pursuit hopeless. Amintor's people were only bandits. And by delaying to chat with his former Queen, the Baron had shown himself to be in no breakneck hurry. Furthermore, the Baron would have no reason to expect any close and determined pursuit; he ought to have no cause to believe that Mark was on his trail.

During the first days of the chase, Mark had scouts, both winged and mounted, out continually during the daylight hours. Camps were dry and dark, and were broken before dawn, as soon as the light was good enough to allow the following of an obvious trail.

The young Master of Beasts who accompanied the column—his name was Doblin, and he was an intense youth, though he tended to be plump—got little rest by day or night. The birds in his care were sent out on one mission after another mission with a minimum of rest. Two of the messenger-scouts were of a nocturnal, owllike species, friends of humanity since time immemorial.

On the third day of the pursuit, one of the birds that flew by day came back with multiple wounds, as if from an encounter with a leather-wings—one of the more savage types of flying reptiles, which the Dark King and his old allies had frequently used as their human enemies used birds. The wounded bird was in no shape to be sent out again, and the beastmaster kept it in its cage and practiced upon it what healing arts he knew and then enlisted the help of the accompanying physicians. The creature rested on a confined perch as best it could, jouncing along upon a loadbeast's back. It could not or would not communicate the nature of the attack that had disabled it.

Meanwhile the night-flying birds brought back strange reports of something large and terrifying that passed them in the sky and from which they had fled in terror, escaping only with great difficulty. The Master of Beasts was not sure how much of this story to believe. Certainly his creatures had encountered something out of the ordinary, probably some kind of winged dragon; in any case, there was little that he or anyone else could do about it.

Meanwhile, Adrian's condition remained essentially unchanged. Mark observed with mixed feelings the stoic indifference—or so it seemed to him—with which his son bore the increasing discomfort of the long journey. The father feared that it was not courage that sustained the child, but only an ever-deeper withdrawal from the world around him.

Somehow, father and son were exchanging even fewer words than usual these days.

Adrian would—sometimes—eat food when it was put into his hands. He would drink water when someone held a cup or a canteen to his lips. He would let himself be led to the latrine pit and back; but sometimes at night he still wet his bed. He would sit when asked, stand when told to stand, usually hold himself in a saddle for a time when he was placed astride a mount. Eventually, after being put somewhere, he would change his position, and if he was in a saddle when that happened he would very probably start to fall out of it. So far someone had always been at hand to catch him safely when he toppled.

*   *   *

For a day now Mark had given up altogether trying to put his son into the saddle because all signs agreed that the enemy was now not far ahead. There were the wounded birds, and the trail was obviously fresher. The column had to be constantly ready for action at a moment's notice. If Adrian was bothered by being confined to his litter almost constantly, and separated from his mother and the other people of the Palace, he gave little sign of it. He put up with everything, with a cheerfulness admired by those who did not know him as well as his father did. To Mark it seemed like sheer infantile indifference to the world.

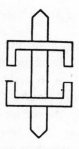

CHAPTER 10

A LL hope vanished that Amintor might not know that he was being followed. The Tasavaltans' only surviving nocturnal scout came in exhausted at dawn to report that some of the human enemy were hiding themselves in a place of ambush ahead, overlooking the trail on which their pursuers could be expected to pass. Meanwhile the main body of the Baron's force, perhaps about fifteen riders—birds were notoriously poor at counting—pressed on. This morning the bird had nothing further to report of the leather-wings, or whatever the mysterious aerial nighttime presence had been that had earlier attacked and disabled its mate.

Mark considered what he knew of the lay of the land ahead, taking into account his scouts' reports in addition to what he could see for himself. To avoid the area of the reported ambush completely would take a discouragingly long time. Besides, the fact that Amintor had divided his force opened opportunities that he was reluctant to pass up.

Ben was evidently thinking along the same lines. "If the Baron knew that we have Shieldbreaker with us he might not be so eager to risk a fight."

The Prince shook his head. "Or, on the other hand, he might know. He might be ready to take the risk. He probably knows how to fight against my Sword if he can get close enough to me. Well, we'll give him what he's looking for. We appear to have some advantage of numbers.''

The morning was chill, with a sky that soon developed a good crop of low, scudding clouds. Driven by gusty autumn winds, the rack reduced the chances of successful aerial reconnaissance, though two birds went up to try. Mark wondered if the turn in the weather might have been brought about at least in part by magical interference. His own magicians could not be sure on that point, but offered to attempt counterspells. He wished silently that Karel himself were here. But wishing was pointless. The people he actually had with him were skilled, or Karel would not have sent them on this journey. Smiling at his magicians as if he really had the highest confidence in them, Mark told them to conserve their powers until later. There was no way to be sure what quality of opposition they might be facing.

As matters stood, the weather continued to make scouting difficult for anything that flew. Since Mark knew of the ambush already, he decided that this situation was more likely than not to be favorable to him, and preferred to act before it changed.

He turned command of the column over to Ben.

Then the Prince selected half a dozen of his best riders and fighters, people he judged outstanding even among the already elite group who had been chosen for this march. With this handful of troops at his back, he set out to surprise the ambushers.

Meanwhile the remainder of the little Tasavaltan column proceeded as before, with the litter protected at its center, following the broad trail left by the Baron and his people. Ben had saddled the six spare mounts and brought them from the rear up into the regular formation of riders. Lances and bedrolls tied to the saddles of the riderless beasts might, Ben hoped, deceive any flying reptiles or birds that might be able to get through the weather on scouting missions for the enemy.

Mark and his half dozen shock troops moved away from the trail that the main group continued to follow. The seven plunged into a thicket of scrubby trees on a fast and difficult ride.

If the birds had been accurate in their description of the topography and the enemy dispositions, all should now be well. If not, the Prince and the people riding with him would have to take what came.

As Mark drew near the place where the birds had located the ambush, he slowed the pace of his advance. Very slowly he climbed what ought to be the last hill. When he was almost at its crest, he dismounted and crept up the last few meters on foot. Wind howled, and rain spattered him from the clouds close above his head.

Peering over, he allowed himself a small sigh of satisfaction. As seemed to happen so rarely in war, things were as he had hoped and expected them to be. There, half a kilometer away now, beyond and below the place where the enemy should be, wound the broad, faint trail along which moved the blue-green uniforms of his own party. Among them he could pick out Ben's imitation riders; once the bandits who were waiting in ambush saw those, they would be likely to understand the reason for them, and anticipate a counterattack.

After this hasty glance at his own column, Mark fastened his gaze on the place, much closer, where the ambushers had to be, if the birds were right. It was a cluster of eight or ten trees, with surrounding lesser growth. The enemy were well concealed, if they were really there, and Mark could not see them yet. They would have their animals hidden in the small grove with them, but if the scouting report was correct the enemy were too few to mount a cavalry charge against the Tasavaltan force. Rather, they would be planning to loose a volley of stones and arrows and then beat a quick retreat, after having inflicted what casualties they could upon the column as it passed beneath them.

Mark had seen enough. He turned and scrambled down to where a soldier was holding his riding-beast for him. In a few words he outlined the situation to his companions. Then, remounting, he drew Shieldbreaker and with one swift silent gesture commanded a charge.

From the moment he aimed the Sword forward he could feel the magic of it thudding softly in his hand and wrist. As yet the noise that always accompanied its magic was not loud, as if the Sword could understand that its possessor now wanted silence.

The seven Tasavaltan cavalry mounts, smelling war and eager for it, thundered down one short slope and up another. The enemy among the trees a few score meters distant had not much time in which to be aware that the charge was coming, yet they were not taken totally by surprise. Slung stones sang out, passing Mark with invisible speed, and he had one momentary impression that the air around him was full of arrows.

With the first appearance of enemy weapons, Shieldbreaker's voice became a heavy pounding. The Sword was controlling itself now, moving into action with a force and speed that must certainly have pulled it from the Prince's grip had not an equal force appeared to weld it to his hand. Its rhythm went tripping into syncopation. A slung stone, which Mark never had the chance to see, was shattered in midair upon that blade. He heard the fragments whine. Arrows—one, two, three of them, faster than he could count—were wiped aside by the Sword of Force before he could well comprehend that the first shaft had been about to hit him.

Mark's picked troops were keeping up with him so far. He himself, in the center of the charging line, had been the chief target for the enemy. But he had come through the hail of missiles unharmed.

The moments had already passed in which the enemy—they were indeed dressed as mere bandits, Mark saw now—might have decided to retreat, and managed to escape. Some of them did want to flee at the last moment, when, perhaps, they had already recognized the Sword. But by then it was too late.

A few of the people who had been hidden in the little grove were now trying to mount their riding-beasts to meet the Tasavaltan charge. Others dodged on foot among the trees, ready to strike at the Prince and his riders as they passed.

By now Mark's powerful mount had moved him a few strides ahead of the others in his party. For a long moment he fought alone, almost surrounded amid the enemy. The Sword of Force went flashing right and left, pounding like a pulse in some great climax of exertion. The blade dissected enemy armor, flesh, and weapons, all with razor-sharp indifference. Clamped in its user's hand, it twisted the Prince and his riding-beast from side to side together, meeting one threat and then the next, or two simultaneously. Whether by sheer speed, or perhaps sheer magic, Mark thought he saw his own right arm, with the Sword in it, on both sides of him at once.

That first shock of combat ended in the space of a few heartbeats. Only now did Mark have time to realize that there were more bandits here among the trees than he had expected, perhaps ten or a dozen of them in all. Without Shieldbreaker, this counterattack of his might well have proven a disastrous mistake. As it was, no more than half of the enemy had survived their closing with him. And the survivors, those who had so far stayed out of the Sword's reach, were now simply trying to get away.

The Prince and his comrades-in-arms gave chase. His pow-

erful mount, a truly royal animal, was gradually overtaking
the fastest of the fleeing mounted bandits. At the last moment
the fellow twisted in his saddle to fight, aiming his long-
handled battle-ax at Mark in a despairing two-handed swing.
Shieldbreaker had fallen silent, but now it thudded again,
twice, as fast as the sun might flicker from its blade. Mark's
own mount pounded on, slowing as he reined in gently and
steadily. Behind him on the ground there lay a broken ax,
a fallen and dismembered rider, a wounded riding-beast struggling to get up.

Mark turned his own animal and rode it slowly back. The
fight was over; only two of the enemy had not been killed,
and they were prisoners. The Sword was quiet now, and he
was able to let it go. He wiped it—in an instant, as always, it
was perfectly clean—and put it back into its sheath. Then he
flexed the numbed cords of his right hand and wrist. His
whole right arm felt strange, as if it might begin to swell at
any moment. But it was functioning; and, all things considered, the Prince was not going to complain.

The action away from the Sword of Force had been savage
also, and the Prince saw that two of his own people were
down with wounds, though it appeared that both of them
would survive, and, almost as important, be able to ride if not
to fight. Matters were under control.

He rode back to the hill from whose top he could easily be
seen from the old trail below and waved his blue-green
column on, giving them the agreed-upon signal for a victory.
He heard a thin cheer go up, and the column started. Ben had
halted it, just outside the effective range of missiles from the
ambushers' original position.

The Prince added another signal, summoning one of the
physicians to hurry ahead; then he rode quickly back to
where the two enemy survivors were now being held.

Leaving Shieldbreaker in its sheath, he dismounted and

approached the captive men. Here were two who had been ready to rain stones and arrows from ambush upon his son. Without stopping to think about it, Mark drew his dagger as he came.

"Mercy, Lord Prince," said one of them, a haggard, scrawny fellow. "You are known as a good and merciful man."

He looked at them intently, one after the other. He knew that they served Amintor, so there was no point in questioning them about that, except perhaps to see if they were inclined to tell the truth or not.

Mark dug the tip of his dagger into the nearest man's throat, just hard enough to draw a little blood. No matter how many times he drove a weapon into flesh, it was always something of a surprise to him how little pressure was required.

"Who is your master?" he demanded. "Speak!"

"Uh. The Baron, we call him. Uh."

"Good, you've told me the truth once." Mark maintained the dagger pressure, though his right hand still felt strange and was still quivering from the grip of magic that other blade had fastened on it. "Now try again: What is the Baron's destination, now that he has his new Sword?"

"He never told us that. Oh, ah." The man died almost silently; the point of the dagger in Mark's hand had dipped down to the level of the victim's heart before it plunged in through his shirt.

Even with this example to contemplate, the second man was no more informative before he died. His passing was almost as quick as that of his fellow had been. There was no possible way of bringing prisoners along on a cavalry chase; and no way in which these prisoners could be released. Mark considered that the world now held two less poisonous reptiles, who had been all too ready to strike at Adrian, and at himself.

There was no time to waste; now it was certain that Amintor
knew they were after him. The weather was still too bad to
allow the aerial scouts to bring word of the Baron's current
position, and perhaps allow a shortcut. In minutes the pursuit
was going on as before, following the trail.

That evening the Baron's own flying reptiles did manage
to get into the air for a while, and back to him in his camp,
bringing him news of the failed ambush.

At least, he thought, listening to the reports as his beastmaster
translated them, at least some ground had been gained on
the pursuers. But that gain was certainly overshadowed by
the fact that more than a third of his own total force had now
been wiped out.

When he had gleaned all the information that he could
from the animals through their human trainer, a process that
involved many questions and several patient rehearings, the
Baron's face was grave. He had never believed that a leader
ought to hide his feelings at all times from his subordinates.
A commander in his situation would be thought a madman,
or an absolute idiot, if he appeared to be unaffected by the
loss of so many people. There was no getting around it. The
attempted ambush had wasted nearly a third of his entire
force. And the efficiency with which the ambush had been
detected and crushed boded ill for the survival of the rest.

Amintor was strongly minded to do an ill turn to whoever
was responsible.

There was one ray of hope: his pursuers, whoever they
were, did not appear to be able to travel very fast. The
reptiles reported that the Baron and his surviving people had
been able to gain ground on them since the chase had
resumed.

From the scanty description that the winged scouts had been
able to provide, he strongly suspected that his pursuer was

Prince Mark of Tasavalta. Amintor knew Mark of old, and considered him an enemy, but would have much preferred him as an unsuspecting rather than an active one. And from what the reptiles had been able to communicate about the fight, the Baron had little doubt that the Sword in the Prince's hand was Shieldbreaker, which he was known to possess.

None of this would be good news to Amintor's remaining people, and Amintor had not yet informed them of his conclusions.

He would have to get a look at those who were chasing him to make sure who they were. Much would depend on making sure of that.

Glancing around at the brighter people among his subordinates, the Baron decided that they were probably capable of making the same deductions he had made regarding the opposition they now faced. It would be a mistake to carry honesty too far—one could very easily do that. With an effort he brightened up, told his people what he thought was going on, and began the job of convincing them that they were still going to be able to survive—not only that, but win.

"Well, it can't be any overwhelming army that's coming after us; the flyers couldn't be that far wrong about numbers. And whoever it is, for some reason, is not coming very fast. Very determined, because they broke the ambush—so if they're not moving fast, it's because they absolutely can't."

He looked around him. The faces of his followers still looked grim. Sometimes he wished he could be rid of them all. He added decisively: "We turn east tomorrow. I want to get a look at just what is coming after us, and how many of them."

Amintor's next step was to go into a close conference with his beastmaster and his enchantress to discuss just where the best place might be for this doubling back and observation.

The two aides bickered with each other, as usual; neither of them was particularly competent.

The Baron had already rejected the idea of splitting his force into two or three parts, or even scattering it into single trails hoping to reunite at some distant rendezvous. He suspected that if he tried that, the Prince might have some way of singling out and following his—the Baron's—trail. Still, Amintor might try splitting his people up, if everything else failed—but everything else had not failed yet.

His enchantress, having somehow driven the beastmaster away, told Amintor: "The Prince pursues us because we have Woundhealer."

"Likely enough. Likely enough, but we can't be sure of even that as yet. Unless you have some proof in magic of what you tell me . . . ? I thought not. Tomorrow, as I say, we must get a look at him."

And next day, Amintor, tired from a hard ride, refusing to allow his tiredness to show, did manage to get a look. Lying on his belly on the grass atop a gentle hill, he scanned the hunters' formation as they moved along his trail. They were less than a kilometer distant in a direct line, though if they continued simply plodding along his trail they were still many kilometers behind.

The first thing that leaped to the Baron's attention as he inspected the Tasavaltans was the blue-green uniforms, confirming that Prince Mark was indeed his adversary. The second thing was the presence of the litter. Just the kind of all-important clue that the damned idiot reptiles could be expected to ignore.

"Not your usual equipment for a difficult pursuit," he commented to the enchantress, who had crawled up to be at his side. "Considering it in conjunction with the fact that he's trying to get Woundhealer, what is your conclusion?"

The woman said promptly: "That he was coming to the White Temple. That he has come a long way from Tasavalta, bringing with him someone in need of healing. That this person is unable to ride, or at least unable to ride well. That when the Prince reached the Temple, the Sword was already gone. And—"

"Enough, enough. And now I would like to know whether you can confirm something I have heard about the ruling family of Tasavalta, which seems to me quite pertinent to our present situation?"

Magic would not likely be required to answer that. The private affairs of the mighty were a constant topic of discussion among the high and low of all nations.

The enchantress said: "That the Prince's eldest son has been a cripple since birth."

Amintor nodded. He was smiling.

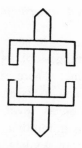

CHAPTER 11

ALTERNATELY waking and sleeping all through the night, never quite sure at any given moment whether or not he was dreaming, Zoltan was carried steadily upstream at the pace of a modest walk. He was still sitting in the water and could feel the movement of it around his body, but he had no sensations of wetness or cold. This bizarre mode of transportation was soft and effortless, and whether he was borne up falls or rapids, or along stretches of the river that were almost level, the speed of it was unvarying.

During one of Zoltan's wakeful periods he was clear-minded enough to realize that the stream had been maintaining an almost level course for an inexplicable distance. This made him wonder if he was still in the Sanzu, which he remembered as an almost endless string of falls and rapids. This stream might well be one of that river's small tributaries— or, for all he knew, he had been translated entirely to some realm of magic where all things, including rivers, were new and strange.

Zoltan was now wakeful enough to take increasing interest in his mode of travel. The stream itself, he saw from close observation, was continuing to flow normally downhill. Only a small localized swirl or eddy, centered on Zoltan's body and perpetually bearing him along with it, moved in a direction contrary to nature. He supposed it was a weakened water elemental; the strange-looking wizard had hinted at something along that line. There were no other signs of enchantment. The trees and rocks and land along the shores were ordinary-looking objects, even though the total landscape that they made was unfamiliar.

Eventually, as the eastern sky began to gray with morning, the forces that were impelling Zoltan upstream appeared to weaken. First his feet began to drag in mud, and then his bottom thumped against a rock. Shortly after that first jolt his upstream progress slowed noticeably. Then it stopped altogether and he sank to the bottom.

Enchantment had now vanished totally. He was sitting in the cold water, little more than ankle-deep, of some stream he still could not recognize in the brightening daylight. He was certainly far from home, and lost. But he was free.

Numbly, Zoltan judged that Karel's river-elemental, which must have been propelling him along, had now died, or dissipated, or whatever such powers did when they reached the end of their existence.

But who had that scrawny, crazy, gibbering wizard been? Like someone out of a dream—but it was no dream that here he, Zoltan, was, set free. Was the rescuing wizard some aide or ally of Karel's? That was hard to believe, from the way the peculiar man had talked. Karel himself, in disguise? That was impossible.

Whoever the strange little magician was, Zoltan understood that he owed him his life.

Sitting in the shallow stream, he became suddenly aware of a great thirst and turned himself over on all fours and drank. Then with a sigh of repletion he got stiffly to his feet and looked about him in the light of early morning. Still, nothing about the landscape looked familiar.

All of Zoltan's limbs were tingling now as if he had hardly

moved them for a week—which he supposed might be the actual explanation. But his legs were still able to support him. He waded out onto the southern shore of the small stream and started walking, his face toward the morning, assuming vaguely that his home must be somewhere in that direction. He looked ahead of him for the familiar hills but could not see them yet. At least the country was open, and progress easy.

The girl came suddenly into his mind—not that she had ever completely left it. He was freed now of the enchantment that had made her an obsession, but he had not forgotten her. He seemed to remember having seen her change into a fish, and back again.

Probably she wasn't human at all, but only a creation of her human master, the man who had bound Zoltan with spells and thrown him into the cave. Or possibly she owed her existence to that harder-to-define and even more frightening presence that had worn small, arm-sized wings and ridden much larger wings up into the night sky. . . . Zoltan shuddered and looked round him warily in the clear morning. It was hard to believe, here and now, that that had been anything but an evil nightmare.

His imprisonment in the mud-cave had been more than a nightmare. His stomach certainly felt as if he hadn't eaten for a week.

Presently he roused himself from speculation to find that the morning's new sun had somehow come around to his left, and he was walking south.

He corrected his course, but in a few minutes, to his renewed surprise, the sun was on his left again.

This time he stopped and stood thoughtfully for a moment. But there was nothing to do but try to go on.

Again he corrected his course, and this time proceeded carefully, paying attention to his directions at every stride.

Soon he realized that he was being guided by a gentle tilting of the ground. Even when the way to the east lay on a gentle downhill slope, the angle of the earth somehow reversed itself where he actually stepped on it. East became a perpetual climb, and south, the easy downhill course. This experience of the tilting earth was similar in a way to what he had felt when he was in the cave; yet in another way this was different, somehow purposeful. South was now always invitingly downhill, though when he walked south he never descended any lower than the surrounding plain. But east was forever uphill, and the slope under his feet became steeper and steeper the longer he tried to persevere in maintaining that direction.

Home lay to the east. If he could be sure of anything he could be sure of that. Zoltan gritted his teeth and persevered. If this enchanted slope got any steeper he was going to have to climb it on all fours. His wet boots were drying now, and his feet had begun to hurt in them, but he plowed on anyway, climbing and climbing. All right, then, he *would* climb on all fours . . .

He had just let his body lurch forward and gripped the earth with his two hands to crawl when a recognizable pair of boots, elongated toes comically turned up, came into view a few meters in front of his nose.

Zoltan looked up to see a familiar figure in storybook wizard's conical hat and figured robe. The wizened face was angrily looking down, the gravelly voice shouted abuse at him.

"Do you want the bad people to have you again, Zoltan? You're a dummy! Don't you ever want to get home to your mother?"

Zoltan stopped, abashed. Slowly he stood up. Still facing east, he had to lean forward to keep his balance. He hadn't realized that this trick was his benefactor's doing also. "Sorry, sir. I'm only *trying* to get home. And my home is to the east of here.''

The magician's face paled; no, it wasn't that, it was his whole figure, becoming faintly transparent. Yes, Zoltan could definitely see through the old man's image, out around the edges. But it shouted at him as loudly and vigorously as ever: ''Zoltan, you dum-dum, Zoltan! I'm trying to help you! I brought you as far as I could through the water, but now you have to walk. You can't go right home. There's something else you have to do first. Didn't I say that? Didn't I say?''

None of this sounded at all to Zoltan like the sort of thing that any respectable wizard, or any elderly person, ought to shout. But Zoltan, above all, did not want to meet the bad people again.

''Yes sir,'' he said. And with slumping shoulders he turned and walked on, in the way that he was being guided. It was easy walking that way—it was all downhill. When he looked around with another question, the figure of the wizard was gone again.

Much of the morning had passed. Zoltan's boots—after he had paused to take them off, drain them thoroughly, and dry them as well as possible—were becoming wearable again. Walking south continued to be easy. He thought, from time to time, about trying to turn east again, but so far he hadn't quite dared. So he hiked on through an open but inhospitable landscape, going he didn't know where, and he was getting very hungry. The provisions he had stuffed in his pockets on leaving home had long ago been reduced to watery garbage.

The pins and needles and the stiffness had worked out of his arms and legs by now. But now all of Zoltan's limbs, his whole body, were beginning to grow weak with hunger.

He looked about him hopefully for fruit on the strange low bushes, or for any of the kinds of plants whose roots he knew were edible in a pinch. He had not yet reached the starving stage, where he would be willing to go grubbing after insects, but he wasn't sure that stage was far away. Nothing more appetizing than insects had appeared. And already his thirst was coming back. The land around him did not promise anything in the way of water.

Except—yes. He was coming over a low rise of ground now, and straight ahead of him, perhaps a kilometer away, a short, straight line of fresh trees were just coming into view, like the boundary of an oasis.

Maybe this was why the wizard had insisted that he go south. Keeping the trees in view, Zoltan held a steady pace.

Presently, having crossed what seemed like several extra kilometers of barren landscape, he began to approach the supposed oasis closely. When Zoltan actually came within a stone's throw of the line of trees, he found them low and thick, making up a formidable thorny hedgerow a straight half kilometer or so in length. Their sturdy freshness certainly indicated a nearby source of water.

Zoltan turned at a right angle and walked beside this tall hedge until he came to a small gap, where he cautiously pushed his way through. The barrier was not as thick or difficult as he had expected, and he discovered that he had just crossed the boundary of a surprisingly well-kept farm. The border hedgerow was much more pleasant to look at from inside. From this angle it was a flowering hedge, thick enough to keep livestock from straying, but he could catch glimspes of the desert outside. The barrier did not appear to be at all difficult for a human to push through, once you made up your mind that you really wanted to do it.

Within the outer boundary of trees, the land was divided into fields and plots by shorter, thinner hedges. The entire farm, Zoltan saw, peering around him, extended over at least a square kilometer; it included pastures, orchards, cultivated fields planted in several kinds of crops, and, in the distance, a cluster of farm buildings. There were enough trees near the buildings to partially obscure them.

Zoltan started walking in the general direction of the buildings, along a path that wound gently between the bordered fields. Meat-cattle grazed contentedly in a lush pasture. Then the lane that Zoltan was following broadened, leading him between more short hedges toward the small house and the farmyard. Even more surprising than the cattle and the pasture were the bountiful crops in the well-cultivated fields. Here and there he could see small irrigation ditches, which explained some of the difference between the land of the farm and that outside its boundaries.

At a little distance he beheld a single human figure moving, hoe in hand, working its way methodically down a double row of some kind of vegetables, just where a plot of garden bordered on an orchard.

Zoltan hesitated briefly, then turned aside from the cowpath and entered the field where the lonely worker labored. Treading carefully between the rows of vegetables—noticing in passing how healthy they all looked—he approached the man cautiously and saw nothing in him to be alarmed about. He was a bent figure, somewhat gnarled, with calloused hands and a sunburnt neck. Whether he was landowner, serf, or hired hand was not obvious at first sight; the man was dressed in rough clothing, but Zoltan had plenty of experience with powerful people who were disinclined to wear finery.

The man, intent on his labor, did not notice Zoltan's approach. His back to Zoltan, he kept at his hoeing, the implement in his rugged hands attacking weeds, churning the rich black soil with a regular chuffing sound.

Remembering his manners, Zoltan kicked a clod of earth

when he was still a few meters from the man, making a slight noise. Then he cleared his throat and waited.

The man looked round at him with only minor surprise. "Well! What be you doing here, then?" he asked mildly enough. His words came in what was certainly a country dialect, though Zoltan could not place its locality.

"Trying to get home, sir." The *sir* was something of an afterthought; but the man's tone had certainly not sounded like that of a serf or slave.

"Home," said the man, leaning on his hoe. "Ah, home!" he cried, as if now he suddenly understood everything. Then with an air of profundity, he said "Ah!" again and turned away and shot up a long arm. Pulling down a waterskin, obviously his own supply, from where it hung on the stub of a treelimb in the shade, he offered it to Zoltan with a quick gesture. "You've come a far way, then. What's your name?"

"My name is Zoltan. Thank you," he said, wiping his mouth with the back of his hand after the most delicious and invigorating drink he'd ever had in his life. For a moment he'd wondered if it was something more than water.

"Zoltan—good old Tasavaltan name." The man nodded judiciously. "I am called Still, young sir. Just plain Still is quite good enough for me, though it's Father Still that some folk call me. Appears that old age is starting to creep up. But I keep busy and I hardly notice, most days." The old man laughed heartily—Zoltan decided that he must really be an old man after all, despite the vigor of his gardening. "But you'll be wanting food, too—and I've already finished off the last of my lunch. Go on to the house, go on to the house, and she'll take care of you." He accompanied this advice with violent gestures, as if he thought that Zoltan might after all not be able to understand his words.

Zoltan obediently turned and started for the house, then paused uncertainly to look back. He was reassured when the farmer, already hoeing away industriously, waved him on with a motion of his hand and went on working. There was apparently no time to waste.

Back on the cowpath, Zoltan realized that the house was farther off than it had appeared at first—indeed, the whole place now looked even larger than it had at first glance.

As he moved on toward the house Zoltan kept looking for other laborers. He looked to right and left, in one field after another of beautiful crops, but he could see no one. Probably, he thought, most of the hands were still taking their noontime rest under one of these rows of trees. Certainly there had to be a large force of people at work to keep the place in the magnificent condition that it was.

Tall, multicolored flowers of a kind that Zoltan had never seen before surrounded the perfectly kept patch of short lawn right at the front door of the house. Bees were busy here; and the perfume of the flowers was as different as could be from that of the pale blooms along the river. The front of the house was flanked by two shade trees, their foliage starting to turn orange and yellow with the onset of fall. The door was wood, solidly built and painted white, and it stood ajar just slightly, in a hospitable way. Somewhere out of sight, toward the rear of the house, dogs were starting to bark to signal Zoltan's arrival—it sounded more a mindless welcome than a challenge.

There was no bell or knocker on the farmhouse door. Zoltan rapped firmly on the white frame, and immediately the white door, perhaps jarred slightly by his knocking, swung open farther as if in welcome. A sunlit parlor was revealed, furnished with enough chairs and tables for a large family, though at the moment it was unoccupied. Then footsteps, soft but brisk, were coming down a hall.

The woman who emerged from the interior of the house was silver-haired and generously built, garbed in a flower-

patterned dress of many bright colors, which was half-hidden
by an apron. She looked at Zoltan with an expectant smile, as
if she might have been anticipating some messenger who
bore good news. Zoltan could not guess whether she was the
mistress of this house or only a servant, and for the moment
at least it hardly seemed to matter.

He said to her: "The man out there in the field—Still, he
said his name was—sent me here. I need—"

He never did get the chance to spell out what he needed.
Perhaps his needs were all too obvious. The woman, talking
much faster than Zoltan in his present state could follow,
swept him in with great gestures of the straw broom in her
hand. He followed her to the kitchen, where in a moment the
broom had vanished, to be replaced by a plate of small cakes,
and then another of sliced melon. Next thing he knew, he
was seated in a sturdy wooden chair at a broad wooden table,
with plates in front of him. The kitchen was a huge room—
the house, he realized, must be a little larger than it had
looked from outside. A small fire crackled in the huge cooking hearth, and the air was full of magical vapors, of a kind
that the visitor had sometimes experienced in the kitchen at
High Manor. Here—he had never been so hungry—the aro-
mas were of doubly concentrated magic.

Mother Still was a large woman, much bulkier than her
good man out in the field. But like him she was hard to place
in terms of age. Now she was bustling everywhere. For a
moment Zoltan thought that she was in two places at once.
"Call me Goodwife Still, or Mother Still—it's all one to me,
my laddie. Have some cheese; it goes well with that melon."

Zoltan, his mouth full, discovered that it did indeed. Experienced people had told him that if you were really starved it
was a mistake to stuff your belly to its limit as soon as you
had the chance. But, by all the gods, this was a special case.
Maybe starvation that occurred under enchantment wasn't the

same as the more dreary, ordinary kinds of the affliction, and required special treatment.

Meanwhile he observed that his hostess was starting—what else?—to cook dinner. The carcass of some small four-legged animal, pale and plump, was being adroitly skewered on a spit.

That Zoltan—he got the impression that it would be the same for anyone else in her presence, or in her house—might have the bad luck to be attacked by hunger appeared to strike the goodwife as a personal affront. The boy, with arrays of dishes growing on the table before him, was bombarded with offers of cold milk to drink—drawn up in a stone crock from some deep well—and a clean fork appeared on the table in front of him, and yet another plate, this one holding a slab of fruit pie that Zoltan, after the first bite, was prepared to swear was the most delicious thing that he had ever tasted.

"A little something to keep you going until dinner's ready." For all the incomprehensible amount of work that she was somehow getting done, Mother Still never seemed to hurry. Now she had joined Zoltan sitting at the table, a mug of tea in her large, roughened hand; and now finally she allowed the talk to shift away from things that he might like to eat or drink. "Is someone chasing you, child? How do you come to be here in this condition?" She was still indignant that the world had treated him so poorly.

Zoltan, who had not realized that his condition was quite so obviously bad, told her the story as best he could, beginning with the strange experience he had shared with the younger children in the cave. Mother Still made appropriate sounds of sympathy as she heard about that and about the magical events that had afflicted Zoltan later on, but he wasn't sure that she really believed him—given the nature of the story he had to tell, he was prepared to understand anyone's not doing so.

But Mother Still asked questions as if she might believe him. When he mentioned the name of Burslem, she frowned and shook her head. The two of them sat there in the kitchen talking for some time, and they were still sitting there when from outside there came the lowing of cattle, a sound that in Zoltan's experience usually accompanied the animals' being driven back to the barn.

He got to his feet, loosened his belt a notch, did his best to suppress a belch, and offered to help bring the cattle in.

Mother Still smiled at him approvingly. "The old man'll be glad of help. Just trot out, then."

He went out the back door and pitched in to help. Still, unsurprised, welcomed the assistance and sent Zoltan out to another field where there were more milk cows that needed prodding. All the animals were fat and healthy; by now Zoltan would have been surprised to find otherwise.

There was a well just outside the kitchen—a cool, stone-lined shaft complete with windlass and bucket—and when the cattle had been brought into the barn Zoltan hauled up two pails of water and carried them into the kitchen and set them beside the big stone sink. It was the kind of thing he hated doing when at home, but he'd plenty of experience of it for all that. There weren't always a lot of servants ready to wait on you at High Manor.

Presently dinner was announced, and Zoltan, after a thorough washup, reached the table right on the heels of Still. He was hungry again—it was as if all the food that he'd eaten since his arrival had already packed itself away into his bones and blood and muscles, leaving his stomach ready for more.

Dinner was roast meat, with delicious accompaniments—bread, vegetables, pickles, more pie—and conversation.

"Just the two of us here now. Children all grown and gone."

Zoltan had seen enough farms to recognize that this place

was a gem, and he said so several times. It was obvious to him that there had to be more workers around somewhere, a bunch of them, but somehow he didn't want to come right out and ask where they all were. He just wanted to get through the rest of this day without any further complications.

An oil-lamp was lighted, making the parlor almost as cheery as it had been during the day, and Mother Still—somehow, incredibly, she had managed to clean all those dirty dishes already—sat down with her knitting.

Meanwhile Still had reached up to a high shelf above the mantel and brought down some kind of a board game with pegs; he challenged Zoltan to a game and started to explain the rules even as he set up the board for play. Zoltan, trying to make sense of it, could hardly manage to stifle his yawns.

"Better sleep in late tomorrow, young one. Then, soon as you're able to get up and about, we'll set you some chores."

"I'll do chores. I'll do them"—yawn—"for you tomorrow. But I don't see how I can stay here any longer than that."

No one reacted to that statement. It was as if they might not have heard it. Mother Still suddenly uttered a wish that she were back on what she called the big farm; "but then we have to do as best we can."

Struggling to stay awake, Zoltan indulged his curiosity. "Where's the big farm?"

A hearty laugh from Still. "It's way out in the country, laddie. That's the best place for them. But, it's a little harder to get to than this one. And we thought there might be visitors."

His wife shook her head, as if her husband had made an objectionable joke. Or, more like it, as if he had repeated an old one once too often. Then she smiled at Zoltan and changed the subject. "So, your uncle Mark is Prince of Tasavalta now."

"Yes, ma'am. He has been for the last eight years," Zoltan acknowledged, wondering. "Do you know him?" Zoltan thought that would not be strange. His own father had died as a low-ranking soldier, and he could remember something very like poverty in his early childhood. Uncle Mark had not always moved in royal circles, and to his nephew those earlier years of his uncle's life had always seemed the most interesting.

"Must be the same Mark that Andrew knew," the old man commented abstractedly while taking another of Zoltan's painted game pegs off the board.

"Well, of course, Father!" Mother Still sounded patiently and mildly exasperated. "I do wish you would try to keep up, where there's family connections and all."

Family connections? Zoltan thought. But he was too sleepy to think about it much.

"I keep up, Mother," Still grumbled. "I keep up pretty well. Andrew's the one that Yoldi married. Rest her soul."

Andrew, in Zoltan's experience, was a fairly common name. Yoldi was not, though. In fairly recent family history—things that had happened after Zoltan was born, but when he was still too young to remember them now—there had been Dame Yoldi, the almost legendary sorceress and companion of Kind Sir Andrew. Could these two simple old farm people be talking about that Yoldi and that Andrew? Zoltan didn't really believe they could, and anyway he was too tired and too confused to ask.

But now, incredibly, Mother Still was talking about her late sister, who, it seemed, had unfortunately got mixed up in being an enchantress, and all that kind of thing. And it sounded as if her sister were Yoldi. Zoltan couldn't credit it. He was half asleep and knew he was getting into some kind of hopeless muddle.

"And in the end it killed her." Mother Still shook her gray

head, knitting furiously. She looked at Zoltan as if he was the one arguing with her. "No, laddie, that kind of a life is not for me. I'm too plain for that."

Father Still, squinting into the yellow lamplight that fell across the gaming table, nodded patient agreement.

Then he put out a gnarled hand and deftly cleaned the last of Zoltan's pieces off the board.

There was a steep stair and a small upstairs room at the top of it; Zoltan was sure before he saw the room and bed that they would be clean and warm and comfortable. In the moment before sleep came, he had just time to ponder whether he would be better off starting for home right after chores in the morning, or resting here another day. And eating one or two more meals of Goodwife Still's cooking . . .

In the morning, Zoltan slept comparatively late. On awaking, in the broad daylight of a fully-risen sun, he jumped up, feeling somewhat guilty for having stayed so long in bed, and hurried downstairs. Mother Still was in the kitchen, and he asked to be given chores.

"That's fine, laddie. There're still eggs to be picked up in the henhouse." Mother Still added that her good man was already out in the fields.

After bringing in the eggs and polishing off a gargantuan breakfast, Zoltan got directions from Mother Still as to where to find her husband and went out to join him at his labors. Zoltan felt he could hardly refuse at least one full day's work to these people who had saved his life.

This morning, as it turned out, the job was harvesting gourds and pumpkins, which grew intermingled in the same field. A small, phlegmatic loadbeast pulled a cart along while Still and Zoltan cut the fruit from vines and lifted it into the cart. As before, there were no other human workers to be seen. Zoltan felt his scalp creep faintly. All right, some kind of magic was at work here. He should have realized it yesterday; he would have realized it if he hadn't been exhausted and half-starved when he arrived.

The great wizard Karel had told him that it was easy to tell good magic from bad, provided you could get a good look at all of the results. The results here, as far as Zoltan could see, were anything but bad.

It didn't seem right to simply ignore the situation. Straightening up to stretch his back, Zoltan remarked: "Seems to me awfully unlikely that two people could manage to run a farm this big without any help."

The man grunted, lifting a big pumpkin into the cart. "Can always use some help."

"But you don't really *need* any?"

Still appeared to be faintly amused. "Laddie, I live in the real world, and I expect to work. Long as there's work here, I expect to get it done. My share of it, anyway." He rapped the loadbeast on the rump, getting it to move along.

Zoltan didn't push the subject any further. Maybe there were kinds of beneficial magic that were spoiled if you talked about them.

As he and Still were returning to the house for their noontime meal they were both surprised to see a traveling wagon, with two riding-beasts in harness, parked on the grass immediately in front of the house. The animals were lean and worn, as if they had been hard-driven. Two people, a middle-aged couple in clothing that had once been expensive but was now worn and stained as if from a long journey, were standing beside the wagon, talking to Mother Still. The goodwife had evidently just come out of the house because a kitchen towel was still in her hand.

She turned her head and called out cheerfully: "Father, Zoltan, we have more visitors!"

The newly-arrived man and woman looked around. Zoltan

saw that the man was holding an elaborate leather swordbelt
and scabbard out in front of him, supporting it awkwardly in
both arms, as if he did not quite know what to do with it and
was ready and eager to give it away. A large black hilt
projected from the scabbard.

Now the man, still holding out the black-hilted weapon
and its harness, approached Zoltan and the farmer. When he
came closer Zoltan could see that he looked as worn as the
team that drew his wagon.

"Your good wife here," the visitor said hoarsely, "doesn't
understand. We have been commanded to bring this weapon
here. So here it is. It's your problem now." And he thrust
the weapon toward Still with a commanding gesture.

Still, however, was in no hurry to accept the present, but
stood with arms folded as if he did not yet understand what
this was all about.

Zoltan was now close enough to the black hilt to get a very
good look at it, and he could feel his scalp creep. He had
been allowed, once or twice, to enter the royal treasury in the
Palace at Sarykam, and he had seen Swords before. The
white symbol on the hilt of this one was a small, winged
dragon.

"You've got to take it." The man from the wagon sounded
agonized. He shook the swordbelt at the farmer so that the
massive buckle jingled faintly. "We've put up with all we
can. You people must be wizards, warriors, something. You'll
know what to do with this. I've been assured that you won't
hurt us. I'm only a trader, myself. My wife is only my
wife."

"Why do you bring us this weapon?" Still asked, sounding suddenly not so much like a farmer. "Wasn't just by
chance you came here, was it?"

"No. No. Because of him. He drove us to it." The visitor
looked around, as if hopeful of being able to see the person

he referred to, but not really surprised when he could not. "I mean the little old man. A little old wizard. In peculiar clothing, as if he were made up for some part on the stage. He's been driving us crazy, hounding us for days and days. He wouldn't accept the Sword himself when I wanted to hand it over to him. Oh, no, wasn't able to carry anything himself, he said. I wasn't about to argue with him, not after the way he picked up the road under our wagon and shook it like a clothesline. So he told us where to find the Sword and made us dig it up and bring it here. And now it's yours, because I'm giving it to you whether you want it or not." And the man glared at Still and Zoltan with a courage obviously born of desperation.

"Little old wizard, hey?" Still grimaced as if he found that description distasteful. And very puzzling. "Did this feller tell you *why* we were supposed to get a Sword?"

The man's arms, holding out the swordbelt, sagged with exhaustion. "He said we had to bring it here because Prince Mark needed it. I suppose he means Prince Mark of Tasavalta, that's the only one I ever heard of . . . and someone here would take the Sword on to him."

Still continued to take thought. He stroked his chin, almost like a rustic considering an offer for his pumpkins. Almost.

"It's taken us weeks to get here!" the man holding the Sword agonized.

"Prince Mark needs it?" Zoltan asked.

The visitor, with new hope, switched his attention to Zoltan. "Yes! That's what the wizard tells me!"

"Then I will take it to him." And Zoltan reached out for the Sword. He had handled weapons before, but still somehow the weight surprised him; no wonder the man's arms were tired.

The man babbled with gratitude; his wife, in the wagon, urged him to get in and drive. "Let's get out of here!"

But they were not to be allowed to leave that quickly. Goodwife Still had them in charge now. They could, and did, protest that they wanted to depart at once, but protesting got them nowhere. Visitors to this farm could not be allowed to go away hungry—that was some kind of a law. And besides— this was undeniable—their team needed attention. "See to the poor animals, Father!"

Mother Still led the couple, who were still muttering objections, into her house.

Zoltan stood holding the Sword in its belt while Still, who had already started to unharness the team, paused to watch him.

Zoltan's right hand smothered the white dragon. The sheath, wherever it had come from, was beautiful. But then its beauty, that of merely human work, was eclipsed as the bright blade came slowly out of it.

Seeing the Swords in the Tasavaltan treasury was one thing, but drawing and holding one was something else.

After a few moments Still asked him: "You'll be taking that to your uncle, then?"

Zoltan nodded.

"Reckon you're grown-up enough to do your duty, if you be grown-up enough to see what it is."

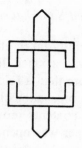

CHAPTER 12

MARK raised his right hand abruptly, and the dusty, weary column behind him reined in, some of the animals stumbling as they came to a halt.

The single, small shape in the late morning sky, approaching from dead ahead, was not one of their own Tasavaltan scouts returning. Already it was possible to see that the set of the wings was wrong for that.

It was one of the reptilian enemy scouts. But this one was not content to circle high overhead and observe.

The creature flew straight for Mark, and from an altitude of about fifty meters—so close that stones and arrows were on the verge of being loosed at it—it dropped something, a small packet that came plummeting down almost at the feet of the Prince's riding-beast. In the next moment the messenger was spiraling upward to a safe altitude, where it drew wide circles in the sky, as if waiting to see how the communication it had brought might be received.

"Why do the bastards always use reptiles?" Ben asked of no one in particular.

"Because," said the chief magician, "reptiles have a certain affinity for demons." He gestured to an assistant.

" 'Ware poison, Highness! Let me look at that present first!" The aide cried out and in an instant had swung down from his mount and carefully taken charge of the object that had been dropped. It was a small leather packet, not big enough to hold much more than a folded sheet of paper.

When all due magical precautions had been taken and the packet was opened, the contents proved to be exactly that. And when the folded paper was opened, it revealed a neatly lettered message.

> Salutations to Prince Mark, from an old acquaintance:
>
> I am prepared to trade Swords with you. Yours for mine, Woundhealer for Sheildbreaker, even up, fair and square. Consider that it is impossible for you to overtake me now, and that we should both benefit from such a trade.
>
> There has been fair dealing in the past between the two of us personally, and there is no reason why that cannot continue now.
>
> Look atop the next cliff to which my trail brings you. Someone will be there to talk about a truce and a conference.
>
> Amintor

Mark read the message through once more and then read it yet once again. As he read he knew a sinking feeling located somewhere near his stomach because he recognized that he was seriously tempted by the offer. Whatever the worth of Shieldbreaker might be, it was never going to heal his son.

By this time Ben had ridden up beside him and was openly reading the message over Mark's shoulder. Others had crowded around, and the Prince let them have the paper to pass around among them and read. Already Ben was profaning gods and demons, and a murmur of derision was beginning among the others present at the idea of Amintor's even proposing such a trade.

But Ben perhaps realized the true state of affairs. He was not smiling, and he was watching Mark closely.

Mark said: "It won't hurt us to look atop the next cliff, as the note suggests."

An old soldier was openly surprised. "It won't?"

At once a lively discussion sprang up among Mark's aides as to what kind of treacherous ambush the former Baron was likely to be preparing for them now.

The beastmaster advised: "The best you could possibly say for this note is that it's an effort to delay us."

Mark thought that as such it would be unnecessary. If Amintor was already somewhere beyond the next cliff, as he must be, then he had gained high ground; and if he was not actually as far ahead as Mark had feared, he certainly had the advantage of terrain. There was no way the Prince was going to catch him now—not unless Mark were willing to leave his son's litter behind and set out with picked riders at full speed. Then it might be possible.

He nodded, listening to the ongoing outrage of his friends at the suggested trade. Then he said to them: "And yet—I can remember times in the past when the Baron *did* deal fairly."

"When he thought it was in his interest to do so!"

"Of course." The Prince looked at the trail ahead, squinting into the bright sky. "But I think that I will talk to him anyway. We'll be on guard against another ambush. And a few words cannot hurt."

One of the magicians muttered some words of doubt about that. But it was not a reasoned objection, even in terms of magic, and Mark ignored it.

The column advanced again. Presently, as the designated

cliff grew near, a lone figure did appear on its low crest. The man was well above the advancing Tasavaltans and so out of their likely range of success with bow or sling; yet he was not too far away to conduct a shouted conversation.

Mark might not have been able to recognize that figure at first glance had he not been expecting it. Baron Amintor, never thin, had bulked fatter in the past eight years.

The figure waved, and called in a powerful, familiar voice. "Halloo! Do you have my message?"

The Prince rode a little closer before he shouted back. "Why should I trade anything with you? How do I even know what you're carrying in that scabbard?"

And even as he uttered the words he realized that the man before him was wearing two swords, one on each side.

The Baron, right-handed and therefore a little awkward with the motion, drew the blade at his right side and held it up. The hilt remained all but invisible, smothered in his grip; but the sun caught on the blade, and even at that distance his claim to have one of the Twelve Swords became quite convincing.

Again his voice came firmly to Mark across the gulf between. "As to why we ought to trade, Prince, I think I can leave that up to you to answer. Surely you can think of at least one good reason. Why is your elder son not riding at your side today?"

Just behind Mark, Ben's voice, sounding like a rumble of distant thunder, began to swear.

Amintor had paused for a shouted reply that did not come. Now he called: "If you are worried about what I plan to do with the Sword of Force when it comes into my possession, be assured that I have no ambitions ever to be anything more than a minor brigand. Not at my time of life. I will do nothing that might inconvenience in any way the royal family of Tasavalta—or their armies—that is the farthest thing from my intentions. Still, the Sword I hold is mine now, and I do not propose to give it up for nothing."

"How much gold do you want for it?" Mark heard himself calling back.

"No, Prince. Not gold. I don't think you can be carrying enough of that in your little train there. No, I have told you what I want, and I do not intend to bargain."

"If Your Highness is minded to do business with that man," said the disapproving voice of one of Mark's magicians, "then let him come into our camp alone, with the Sword, under a flag of truce. And let him loan us its power, for as long as it will take to treat Prince Adrian. You might ask him what price he will accept for that."

Mark, shouting, put the proposition to the Baron.

"Why I might do that," the answer came booming back. "I might. I should warn you, though, that my price for such a loan will be exactly the same as for the Sword itself. And if I am there in your camp, alone, how is our trade to be carried out?"

"How is it to be carried out in any case?"

"I have some ideas on that subject," yelled Amintor, "that I believe you will find satisfactory. And let me repeat, after the trade is made, I have no plans to do anything that will disturb you in any way. My modest ambitions will take me in another direction entirely."

Mark and his aides now fell into a low-voiced conference. There was of course no reason to think that the rogue wouldn't lie, and the Prince's advisers were unanimous in rejecting the idea of trying to conclude such a trade as the Baron proposed. At the same time, they had to admit there was a certain plausibility in what Amintor said.

The vision of Adrian was in Mark's mind when he turned back to face Amintor; but he could feel at his back the uneasiness of those who could not see that vision with the eyes of a father. He knew they were wondering why he didn't reject out of hand the idea that such a trade might be possible.

Yet still the Prince hung back from complete acceptance. At last he shouted back: "I must think about it!"

The Baron's distant figure nodded, a generous gesture visible at long range.

"Think wisely, and well," his return shout counseled, "but do not think too long. My business, such as it is, requires that I depart these regions as soon as possible. Let your shadow lengthen by only a hand, and I'll expect an answer. Shout again when you are ready."

With that, the figure on the clifftop turned round nimbly and disappeared. Mark supposed that a riding-beast might be waiting just over the crest.

The first move the Prince made was to redeploy his own troops so they should not be where Amintor had just seen them. Then Mark set out a double guard and again called all of his chosen advisers into a council. He was disregarding the deadline of a hand's change in his shadow's length; shadows were starting to disappear altogether as clouds gathered for what might well be another afternoon of rain and difficult aerial scouting. Anyway, Amintor was the one who had suggested a truce and proposed a trade. That meant the Baron was truly interested in such a deal and was not going to ride away while a chance of it still existed.

The people with Mark were still unanimous in their opposition to the idea.

His magicians, having now investigated the matter in their own way, advised him that the Sword the Baron offered was indeed Woundhealer—the conclusion made matters no easier for Mark in making up his mind.

The cavalry officer pressed him: "With neither side trusting the other, Highness, how could it be arranged, assuming you were willing to go through with it?"

"There's probably some way to manage that."

"You will pardon me if I speak frankly, sir."

"Go ahead."

"I think you cannot be serious about wanting to give away such an advantage in war."

Ben had perhaps the most powerful argument. "It may be true that our friend over there is only a brigand now. Probably he is. But if he had Shieldbreaker at his side, to go with his smooth tongue, who can say what he might become? I don't believe for a moment all that about his 'time of life.' "

A magician chimed in. "And, once he has the Sword of Force, he might be able to trade or sell it to someone else. Someone who does have an army, and ambitions."

"What was that other sword that he was wearing, I wonder? An ordinary blade, maybe, or—?"

"You are the magicians, not I. Discover the answer if you can, and tell me. If you cannot, I must make up my mind without knowing."

Mark had answered firmly, but he felt a chill. Complications, unpleasant possibilities, were piling up. Things he hadn't thought of before, in his absorption with the problem of his son. Still, he remained stubbornly unwilling to give up the idea of the trade.

He could think of at least one argument to put in on the other side. "We know how to fight against Shieldbreaker."

Ben scowled. "Aye, and so must many others. Including Amintor himself, even if he hasn't yet shared the secret with his followers. Are you trying to say the Sword of Force is of little value? Consider how well it served you yesterday."

There was no arguing with that. But Mark would not let himself be argued out of trying to make the trade. He said: "It's vital to the whole realm that Adrian should be healed. It's not just that he's my son."

The others were silent. But he could see in their faces the grudging admission that the point was valid.

Ben was not through arguing. "Is there any reason to think that Amintor does not know how to fight against the Sword as well as we do?"

"Those troops he left to ambush us—"

"When he set up the ambush I'll bet he didn't yet know who was following him, and he didn't have any idea that he was up against the Sword of Force. You'll find he deploys his people differently the next time he tries it. There'll be two men, at least, unarmed so the Sword can't hurt them, ready to jump on you and drag you from your mount. Others, well-armed, close around those two, to protect them from your armed friends."

Mark forced himself to smile. "You make it sound easy."

Ben shook his head stubbornly. "Not easy, but it would be possible. If Vulcan could be overcome that way, you're not too tough."

The Prince and his old adviser argued on while the rest of the council, though agreeing still with Ben, sat by in stubborn silence. The more the arguments went on, the more Mark favored trying to make the trade. None of those who objected to it were able to suggest another way in which he might obtain the Sword of Healing for his son.

Ben got up angrily at last, turned his back on the Prince, and walked away.

Mark glared after him in black anger. But he did nothing about the snub. Instead he mounted and rode back to the approach to the cliff where he had last communicated with Amintor. Reining in his mount, he called out in a great voice.

There was no answer. He called again, roaring in a voice even louder than before.

Stung by a sudden apprehension, he rallied his people to him and spurred up onto another rise of land nearby.

There, in the distance, through oncoming mist and rain, he could see a group of riders that must be Amintor's band, traveling at good speed along a road.

Even as Mark was getting his column slowly into motion again, a flying scout came in to report that the enemy were making good time into the distance and gave no sign of wanting any more conferences.

"After them!"

But within the hour it became apparent that as long as Mark's troops were hampered by the litter, he had no hope at all of overtaking the other party.

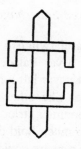

CHAPTER 13

NEAR midnight in a high tower of the Palace at Sarykam, Karel, the chief wizard of the house of Tasavalta, dreamed.

Karel's dreams were often very much stronger and stranger than those of other men, and the visions he endured this night were no exception.

He saw the small Prince Adrian lying as still and pale as death in his small bed inside a tent. He saw Prince Mark riding into battle, surrounded by a furiously spinning profusion of Swords, all the Swords there were in the universe and more. And in his dreams the wizard Karel heard the roaring of an unseen river in flood and saw young Prince Zoltan struggling against strange monsters.

Then came darkness and silence. Not the cessation of the dream, but an interval of empty night contained within it. And then, presently, as if he were emerging from deep shadow, the powerful wizard Karel beheld huge trees, of a kind that even his waking eyes had never seen; and now he could see the river that had roared in flood, and the serpent Yilgarn that lay in wait for everyone at the end of the world to swallow gods and men together. The serpent in the dream was trying to swallow the mightiest river in the world, and in turn the river tried to strangle the serpent and kept on running always to the sea.

That scene faded. Karel twitched in his bed, in his high lonely chamber in the royal Palace of Tasavalta; and the benevolent guardians that never left him by day or by night, the invisible powers that he, like other wizards good and evil, relied upon against his enemies, tried to keep the worst of his dreams from gaining too much hold over him. But there were limits on how much his powers could do.

The wizard, as helpless in his own sleep as ordinary men might be in theirs, dreamt on. Against a sky aglow with fantastic stars and comets, he saw the griffin that flew by midnight, and he saw who rode upon the griffin's back.

Karel woke up when his dream showed him that. His body jolted upright in a moment, and he was screaming like an abandoned child.

For a long moment he did not know who he was or where he was. Fear had dissolved everything. He sat there in his narrow bed, trying to control his sobbing breath and listening to the night wind that howled around the high stone corners of the Palace tower that held his room.

It had been only a dream. Only a dream. But the wizard was still afraid, still terrified, because he knew what the dream meant.

Once upon a time it had been possible to confine the worst things in the world in a dungeon under the world. But no one, not even an Emperor's son, could do that now.

Princess Kristin, too, was wakeful on this night. There were no dreams for her unless they came in the mere sound of the wind as it moaned around the carven stones. To keep her thoughts from being snatched away by the wind she listened to the surging surf of autumn crashing remotely in the darkness. As a child she had loved falling asleep to the sound of that autumnal surf.

But tonight sleep was far away. She got out of bed, went to

look in on little Stephen, and found him sleeping peacefully, as ever untroubled by what the night side of the world could do. On her way back to her own chamber the Princess paused to glance at another small bed, this one empty. The scrolled-up storybook that everyone had forgotten to pack for Adrian lay on the bedside table. His mother, gazing at the bed and book, was mortally certain that Adrian, wherever he and his father might be at the moment, was having a seizure. And she was not there to hold and comfort him.

That was a foolish thought. How could she be there?

She had just returned to her own room and was about to get back into bed when a familiar tap came at the door. One of her maids was there to tell the Princess that her uncle Karel was at the door of the royal suite saying it was vital that he see her now.

Suppressing her fears, Kristin quickly put on a robe over her nightdress and went to greet her uncle in a sitting room, where the servant had already brought out an Old-World lamp.

By that mellow and steady light, a signal that the world could somehow be controlled, the old man first hastened to reassure her that the things she must fear most had not happened—it was not irredeemable disaster to her husband or her oldest son that brought him to her door at such an hour.

The old man sighed. "Still, certain things have happened. I have had visions, and I decided that the telling of them had better not wait until morning."

"Then tell them to me. I am ready to hear them."

He sat opposite her, on the other side of a small table, with the lamp turned to a subtle glow, almost between them. "Kristin. I am going to say some names. Tell me if any of them mean anything to you."

"Say on."

"Deathwings. The Master. The Ancient One."

She considered each name carefully, as seemed to be her duty, then signed that they were strange to her.

"He has gone by other names as well." Karel rubbed his sleep-tousled hair. "He has at least one other name, very powerful, that is very much older—and I would give much to know it. But I know now that he is still alive, and actively our enemy."

"The Dark King?"

Her uncle shook his head. "Would that it were only he."

"Only? Who is it, then? Tell me! What is the danger?"

Karel seemed almost at a loss to explain. "The danger is himself, and that he must be our enemy," he said at length. "I am talking about an incredibly ancient and evil—and powerful—magician. I had thought that he was dead, many centuries ago. Everyone thought so, as far as I am aware. But he has somehow—I do not know how—managed to survive into the present. It would take me all night to tell you all I know and suspect about him, and the telling would help you very little."

"I see," she said, and wondered if she did.

"I am afraid you don't see," her mentor told her sharply. "You cannot. Perhaps it was foolish of me to wake you in this way. I can see only a little, and . . . you think I mean that he is merely old. That would not disturb me so. There are others who have achieved centuries."

Something prickled down the back of Kristin's neck and then went on down her spine. "What do you mean, then?"

"If the Beastlord Draffut is still alive," said Karel above the howling wind outside, "he will be able to identify this man—if the one of whom I speak can still be called a man. Probably no other being on the planet except the Great Worm Yilgarn has survived so long."

"So, what are we to do?" the Princess asked.

"What we can. Get your husband back here, to begin

with. We must contend now with greater problems than a healing.''

She said: "I had word upon retiring—I was going to tell you tomorrow—Zoltan's riding-beast has been found, unharmed. It was grazing along the Sanzu, not twenty kilometers from the cave.'' There could be no doubt of which cave the Princess meant. "The saddle was still on it.''

"But no clue to where the boy himself might be?''

"Nothing.''

"I will want to look at that riding-beast tomorrow,'' said Karel abstractedly. Suddenly the Princess noticed that he looked very old. "About the Ancient One of whom I spoke—I am sorry that I woke you tonight; there is nothing we can do immediately.''

"It doesn't matter. I couldn't sleep.''

"I must warn you, though. He is truly abroad in the world again, and there is no way that I can match him. Nor can any other magician who lives today. Only the Swords themselves, perhaps, will stand above his power. My hope is that the Ancient One will busy himself with other matters and not turn against us directly yet. That he will attack us only through his surrogates, Burslem and others.''

"As you say,'' said Kristin, "we will do what we must and what we can. Beyond that it is all in the hands of Ardneh.''

"I would,'' said Karel, "that Ardneh were still alive.''

He arose from his chair, slowly and heavily, and turned as if to depart. Then he faced her again. "Tell me about Rostov. What is the General planning to do tomorrow?''

"Working on ways to use the army more efficiently in hunting for Zoltan, and patrolling the frontiers. Our army is not very large these days, as you know. I'm considering the idea of sending reinforcements after Mark. The news his birds have brought in has not been reassuring.''

The wizard nodded. "Let me talk with you again in the

morning before you issue orders. I am going to sleep no more tonight.''

"Nor I, I think. Good night.''

In the morning there was more news by flying messenger, none of it particularly good. Certain other units of the army were still being deployed into the area beyond High Manor and the surrounding hills, where Swordface had been found. A renewed and expanded search was being pressed in that area.

And then a message came in from Mark, informing his wife that the Sword he had sought was stolen from the Temple—and he was taking their son with him and going after it.

The Princess passed on the news to her advisers. And then she tried to pray to Ardneh.

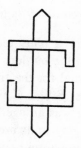

CHAPTER 14

ON the evening of the day on which his hand first drew the Sword of Heroes from its sheath, Zoltan told his hosts that he intended to leave the farm in the morning, taking the Sword with him. "My uncle needs it, if what we have been told is true. As I must believe it is. I don't know where to find him, but I must try."

He was half expecting the old people to try to argue him out of that course of action—to tell him that the news about Uncle Mark, like the Sword itself, had come to him in a strange way and ought to be distrusted. Zoltan had his own argument ready: he couldn't take that chance. But the Stills did not argue. They only promised him, calmly, such help as they could manage.

Early in the morning Mother Still called Zoltan into her pantry, where from a shelf devoted to remedies she took down several small jars and packages for him to carry with him on his journey. These medicines she labeled carefully and packed into a bundle. Meanwhile Father Still was making preparations of a different kind. He said he thought he knew where there was a saddle in the barn, and he expected he could spare one loadbeast from the harvest.

Saddlebags and a roll of blankets appeared from somewhere. And in the kitchen, Zoltan was loaded down with food until he had to cry a halt, fearing that his loadbeast would be staggered with the burden.

Approaching that animal for the first time, Zoltan thought he could see why Father Still had been so sure it could be spared from the farm. It was an aged and bony beast, with a considerable amount of gray in its brown coat, and the farmer had to expend much tugging and swearing just to get it out of the barn. Under ordinary conditions the appearance of this mount would have been enough to discourage Zoltan from starting even the simplest journey. Even the finest farm animal was not the kind of beast you could ride out on thinking seriously of adventure, and this creature was not the finest. Once he was mounted, the thick shaggy hide and hard rib cage under him felt as if they might be impervious to beatings, if and when he should have to resort to that method of obtaining greater speed. And the saddle, now that he got a good look at it, was an old one and a poor one, with the additional drawback that it had doubtless been designed for a riding-beast. It seemed in some danger of sliding from the animal's back at every jarring step.

But Zoltan accepted as courteously as he could the gifts that were meant to help him, and at last all was ready for his departure. With his new Sword hung from his waist upon its fancy belt and Farmer Still walking ahead to show him the way, Zoltan rode to the gate, ready to push on.

The farm, Zoltan discovered, had one real gate to the outside world. He had never seen that gate until now because it was on the opposite side of the farm from where he'd come in.

Mother Still, too, had ungrudgingly taken time out from her work to come as far as the gate with Zoltan and bid him farewell.

Father Still, on parting, gave Zoltan directions and advice.

His uncle Mark ought to be somewhere between here and Tasavalta—especially if, as seemed likely, Mark was out in that area searching for his missing nephew. And, if Mark truly was in need of Dragonslicer, it stood to reason that he was, or was about to be, in some kind of trouble with a dragon. Large dragons, the rare few that survived to grow into the landwalker stage, were the only kind that meant real trouble, and one thing large dragons always needed was plenty of water. The only way to get plenty of water in this country was from one of the relatively few streams that crossed it. Anyone who had trouble with a dragon would have it near a stream.

"Simple enough? Hey?" The farmer grinned at his own logic.

Zoltan had to admit there was a certain sense to it.

Now Zoltan's route, according to this scheme, was also simple. Once outside the gate, he had only to follow the boundary hedge of the farm around its perimeter until he came to running water, the stream that was here partially diverted for irrigation purposes. Then, if he followed that tumbling creek downstream, he'd find that it flowed into the Sanzu. Following that river upstream, in turn, would bring him back at last to Tasavalta. If Zoltan went that way and still failed to encounter his uncle Mark, he would have done the best he could, and he ought at least to be able to find his way home again with the Sword-treasure that he'd been given.

The main gate of the farm, pulled easily open now by man and wife, was a high and sturdy construction of wood and twisted iron with decorations of what looked to Zoltan like ivory and horn. Vines with shiny green leaves grew over all. Only when the portal was opened to let Zoltan out did the road on the outside become visible. The couple who had brought the Sword to Zoltan, once more greatly impatient to leave, had this morning followed him to the gate in their wagon. Their team, after one night of rest and food, looked ready to go again.

The road outside the gate led straight away from the farm, and the man in the wagon whipped up his team and sped that way at once, without looking back.

Zoltan's path immediately diverged from the road. The gate closed promptly behind him, at which time his loadbeast decided to stop so suddenly that it nearly pitched him over its head. He kicked the animal in the ribs and got it to amble forward.

The Sword at his side swung as he rode, banging awkwardly against his leg and the animal's flank. Zoltan could wish he had been required to carry Wayfinder or Coinspinner instead. From what he had heard of the powers of those two, either would be able to guide him in short order to Uncle Mark. But Dragonslicer told him nothing as to which way he should be going or what he should be trying to do. Its powers were very specialized.

He wondered what sort of dragon Uncle Mark was going to have to fight. Until now Zoltan had never even seen a dragon at all, except for contemptible small-fry, the almost froglike early stages. And even those he had glimpsed but rarely.

There was no problem in finding the stream he was to follow. Leaping down from one small tumbling rapids to another, it looped close to the farm's hedge-fence and then away again. From the quiet intermediate pool at the exact boundary, a ditch, barred from the outside world by its own grating—a simple barrier to keep cattle from wandering out—drank from the stream and led some of its water away inside the hedge. The volume of the little river did not appear to be much diminished by this drain and remained considerably larger than the Sanzu was near its source. Why, Zoltan wondered, couldn't the river-elemental have delivered him here?

But there was no point in wondering about that. He kicked his loadbeast in the ribs again and journeyed on, now following the river downstream.

Twice before nightfall he stopped to eat, using up some of his excess baggage of provisions. During his second rest stop he scanned the sky and realized that he was now under the surveillance of an aerial scout. The creature was too far away when Zoltan first saw it for him to be able to tell whether it was a friend or an enemy. Its presence was not accidental, for it kept him in sight, but did not come any closer.

When darkness overtook Zoltan he continued riding for a while, hoping to shake off the hostile observer. Progress was difficult, and he lost sight of the flyer in the night sky. After an hour Zoltan gave up and pitched camp, letting his loadbeast drink from the stream and then tethering it to a bush. He unrolled his blankets nearby and forbore to make a fire.

Suddenly he felt very much alone. He wished for Uncle Mark and the search party. Failing that, he wished that the crazy magician would reappear, even if it was only to favor him with another lecture.

The voice of the tumbling stream provided a kind of company. The stars had turned through several hours above him when a more purposeful splashing woke Zoltan up.

He knew somehow what he was going to see even before he turned his head. He could just perceive the fish-girl, or rather part of her. One eye, some hair, part of a bare, white shoulder in the light of moon and stars.

She was about ten meters from Zoltan, and this time he could see with certainty that she was sitting right on the bank of the stream. It was plain, too, that she was swishing not feet but a fishtail in the water. Her dark hair, already drying, fell down over her very human breasts.

The girl only sat there, looking directly at him, but saying nothing.

Go away. He formed the words but could not say them. With vast relief he made sure that he no longer felt a hopeless compulsion to jump up and pursue her, as he had before. He felt a fear of her, contending with his curiosity, but so far the fear was manageable.

Nothing happened. Her eyes still regarded him. He could not read the expression on her face.

Zoltan rose slowly to his feet. "What do you want? Who are you? I'm not going to chase after you anymore."

At last the girl spoke. "You don't have to chase me anymore. And I am glad. I didn't want to make you do that, but I had no choice. I was enslaved to the Ancient One. But now I have been set free."

"The Ancient One?"

"A wizard. A very bad man. You must have seen him, on the night of that day when you first saw me. But he can't use me any longer. Someone helped me to get free."

"Someone?"

She moved one white arm in a graceful, puzzled gesture. "A strange little man. I think he helped you, too."

"Yes. The one who helped me is strange, all right." Zoltan shifted his position. "Who are you, then?" he repeated.

"I don't know who I am." The voice of the mermaid, suddenly pitiful and ghostly, shifted into a strange, unfamiliar accent. It brought a small shiver along Zoltan's spine. It was as if only now had the girl in front of him become completely real.

"But are you . . ." He couldn't quite bring himself to say it.

"Am I what?" It was a tragic whisper.

"Are you a human being or not?" he whispered back.

There was a pause. "I don't know that either," the girl answered finally. "I don't know what I am now. Certainly I was human once—I think."

A few minutes later Zoltan was sitting closer, almost close enough to touch the girl, and she was explaining that although she was no longer subject to the commands of the evil wizard, she still experienced sudden changes of form, from being entirely a fish to this half-human state, and that she had almost no control over them.

"I am no magician. I cannot help you."

"Perhaps no one can." The girl went on to recount something of her earliest memories, of a village beside a much larger river than this one. Something terrible had happened to her there to end that phase of her childhood.

She related also how she had seen Zoltan being set free from the riverbank cave by the same peculiar old wizard who had rescued her—or partially rescued her—from the evil enchantment that had enslaved her.

There was enough moonlight to let Zoltan see plainly the long fish-shape of her lower body, and what ought to have been her legs. The marvel was certainly genuine enough. Starting at a little below her navel, human skin shaded into bright scales. In the back of his mind, the suspicion that this might be only some renewed trick of his enemies persisted, but it was fading steadily.

She was a girl—at least the top half of her was. More than that, she was lovely—at least certain things about her were. Before long Zoltan was quietly moving closer to her again, and soon he moved a little closer still.

As he was reaching out, about to touch her hair, she looked at him with alarm. There was a white streak of movement, a splash, and she was gone.

He returned to his blankets and wrapped himself in them again for sleep. Slowly, half-unwillingly, he drifted into slumber.

When he woke again the sun was up. Zoltan ate some breakfast from his ample stores—catching fish would have taken time, and besides, hooking any fish just now would have given him a very peculiar feeling. Then he resaddled and mounted his loadbeast and went on following the little river downstream.

Looking up at frequent intervals to see if the flying scout of yesterday had returned, he at last received something of a shock when he saw not one winged presence in the sky but a squadron, thin black shapes against bright blue.

As the creatures drew closer, Zoltan could tell from the shapes of their wings that they were reptilian and therefore almost certainly his enemies. Certainly they would not be his friends.

Until now, with one or two doubtful exceptions—yesterday and high in the sky above High Manor—Zoltan had never actually seen an unfriendly aerial scout. But he knew that the enemies of Tasavalta had used such creatures in the past.

The creatures in this current flight were much bigger than he had realized at first. Their true size became apparent as they came closer, landing to rest on logs or rocks that Zoltan had already passed as if they were cautiously sniffing at his trail. And they were certainly reptiles. Some strain of dragon, he thought, of which many more subspecies existed than were usually seen in the vicinity of Tasavalta.

His heart was beating faster, more with exhilaration than with fear. Here was evidence that the crazy-looking little wizard knew what he was doing after all. Dragonslicer appeared to be the very Sword that Zoltan was going to need today. He rested his hand on the black hilt but, somewhat to his surprise, could feel nothing there but its solidity. So far, the Sword of Heroes was quiet in its sheath.

Now the reptiles had started diving at the stream, fifty meters or so ahead of where Zoltan was. Something large and white was under the surface there, something that splashed violently, trying to escape the onslaught from above. A silvery fish that looked too big for this small stream.

Zoltan suddenly tried to kick his loadbeast into greater speed. When that effort failed, he jumped down from the saddle and ran at the reptiles, yelling, challenging them to fight. He had drawn his Sword now, and with each stride that brought him closer to the enemy he expected that the power in it would be activated. But nothing of the kind occurred.

The creatures, not at all unwilling to fight someone who wanted to interfere with their own hunt, turned on Zoltan. The flashing blade in his hands did not appear to impress them in the least.

The Sword of Heroes remained silent and lifeless in Zoltan's grip as he lifted it on high. The enemy came at him in a black swarm.

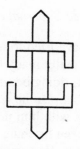

CHAPTER 15

EARLY on the morning following his parley with Mark, the Baron received a disquieting report from one of his flying scouts. As interpreted by its trainer, the animal reported that their pursuers were now gaining ground on them again, despite the fact that Amintor was now driving his own people and animals at a faster pace.

Amintor scowled, and demanded: "How can they be gaining ground while they have that litter in their train?"

The beastmaster tried, with little success, to put that question to his charges. As before, the animals were unable to tell, or at least unable to say, whether the pursuing force still included a litter or not. All the beasts were sure about was that the enemy were getting closer.

While his aides, knowing it was time to keep silent, watched him closely, Amintor thought the situation over. He could, of course, send back a human scout to see what was really happening. But unless the Baron slowed down his own retreat after that, a rider might have a hard time catching up with him again to deliver his report. Whereas the flyers, as long as the weather was tolerably good, brought back their news within an hour.

Breaking camp, getting ready to move out again, he pondered on Mark's motives. "Still really interested in my Sword,

155

is he? Maybe I should have tried to make the trade with him after all. Maybe he was really ready to go through with it.''

Amintor's enchantress, riding beside him now, complained that she did not know what plan he really had in mind, and it was hard for her to work with him under such conditions.

The Baron, who had been listening to her snore for most of the night, ignored her now. He summoned his beastmaster to him again and briefed the man carefully on what he wanted to find out.

An hour or so later the new report came in from the flying reptiles: Yes, there were now two groups of mounted people in pursuit. One of these formations progressed quite slowly and was thus falling ever farther and farther behind. But the other group, as previously reported, was gaining ground, and therefore seemed more important to the scouts; it was the only one that they had mentioned in their previous report. Humans had long tried to impress upon them the need to report the nearest and the swiftest-moving of the enemy.

The Baron recalled to mind the configuration of the last few kilometers of land that he and his people had passed over. Then he acted swiftly.

He picked out a dozen or more of his best troops, grimly aware that he was undoubtedly going through a very similar process to the one that the Prince must have followed on being forewarned of Amintor's attempted ambush. With this assault force set aside, the Baron ordered the remainder of his people, with all of the spare mounts and the meager baggage of his train, to continue their retreat in the same direction as before. Sniffing the wind and scanning the sky, he could hope that the Prince's aerial scouts would not report his splitting his force and doubling back with part of it. Clouds and wind were both increasing now, rapidly enough to give the Baron hopes of that.

Then, with his dozen picked men following him, the Baron

rode in a wide loop, heading for the place where he thought the litter ought to be now if it had advanced steadily since last reported. At the moment there did not seem to be any of the Tasavaltan birds aloft. He could hope that they would not observe his maneuver, but he could not rely on their failure to do so.

In a matter of minutes, Amintor and the fast riders with him were thundering down an arroyo, heading in a direction exactly opposite to the one in which they had been industriously retreating only a few minutes earlier. He felt reasonably confident that he had now outflanked the rapidly advancing forces of the Prince.

Presently, mounting a hill, he came in view of a small plateau, ahead of him and a trifle lower; the far side of this tableland fell away precipitously. Amintor could see the small Tasavaltan baggage train progressing across the top of the plateau, the litter in the middle surrounded by half a dozen guards. Also beside the litter there rode one white-robed figure, doubtless a physician. That was all. The Baron's striking force had the Tasavaltan Guard detachment seriously outnumbered.

Wasting no time, the Baron maneuvered his people closer, up to the near edge of the plateau where the slope was gradual, then led them breaking into view and charged.

The guards around the litter hesitated when they saw the bandits coming, but then realized they were badly outnumbered, and retreated, galloping to save their lives. The physician, abandoning his patient, fled with the rest.

Now the loadbeasts of the Tasavaltan baggage train, including the one that bore the litter, finally decided that it was time for panic. They started off at the best lumbering run that they could manage, in the general direction of the cliff.

Amintor shouted, kicked his heels into his mount's ribs, and led the chase. In a matter of moments the litter was overtaken. One of the Baron's people grabbed the loadbeast's harness and brought the stampeding animal to a halt. Meanwhile Amintor himself had ridden up beside the litter, ripped open the canvas shade covering one side, and looked in to see—an empty pallet.

Understanding came to him even before he heard the shouts behind him. From nearby woods, along another edge of the tableland where the slope was gentle, there now burst out a wave of Tasavaltan uniforms, a cavalry charge with leveled weapons. In the center of the line rode the Prince himself, with Shieldbreaker brandished high. Meanwhile, the guards who had pretended flight were turning as one rider and coming back at a gallop toward the baggage train.

Amintor's people were now outnumbered and caught between two forces. They had already scattered, beginning their pursuit of the various baggage animals, and the Baron made no attempt to rally them. Not against a disciplined force of superior strength. And most especially not against the Sword of Force. Never that without most careful preparations, none of which had been made. Instead, the Baron instantly abandoned his own comrades-in-arms, even as they were scrambling to abandon him. He fled for his life.

The blue-green uniforms were closing in on three sides of him. A sword—not Shieldbreaker—came swinging at his head. He parried it in a ringing crash with Farslayer, whose own magic still slept. It would be useless to evoke that particular power in the face of a dozen enemies. Amintor rode on, bent low over his mount's neck. His riding-beast was swift but not the equal of the one the Prince was riding, he was sure. The lack of speed would doom him if the cliff ahead did not; but there was still one chance.

The Baron's people were all out of action. His foes in dozens were thundering after him, behind him and on each flank, all closing in. Yet, in midgallop, he managed to replace Farslayer in its scabbard at his left side, and then, awkwardly, he worked the Sword of Mercy out of its sheath at his right. Behind him closer than ever he could hear the Prince's voice, calling thunderously for him to surrender, shouting to him that he was trapped. Ahead the tableland ended abruptly, at the edge of what must be a considerable cliff. Well, Mark was a good fellow and all that, but Amintor was not minded to become Mark's prisoner—not right now. Not just after being tricked into trying to take the Prince's darling son a hostage.

Slung stones and arrows sang past the Baron's head. He tried to dodge them, bending his neck beside the long neck of his steed. The animal stumbled, it was wounded, but it did not go down.

The edge of the cliff ahead was rushing closer. There was no doubt that the gulf beyond was one of deadly depth.

If this desperate attempt should fail, thought Amintor, then still it has been a good life, all in all. Would he want to live it all over again, making the same choices? One thing he did know, he wouldn't trade the life he'd had for one, or two, or three of the ordinary kind. He thought: I have led an army, an army of people who were eager to follow me; and I have bedded a beautiful queen; and I have stolen from a god.

His riding-beast was superbly trained and had never yet refused to do anything that the Baron asked of it in combat. Nor did the animal now betray his confidence; running at full gallop it went high and nobly off the cliff. Only when he was falling did Amintor allow himself to look down, to glimpse the flat hard rock and rocky soil some fifty meters below.

He felt the animal's muscles tense convulsively beneath him in midair and saw its limbs begin to windmill. It tried to turn its neck back, halfway through the long fall, to look a question at its master.

Clutching Woundhealer to his chest with all his force,

Amintor felt the galvanic pang of the silvery blade entering his very heart. Force poured from that enchanted steel, a power that, far from killing him, would have altered him into someone else if he had let it do so. Fiercely he resisted that godlike force, clinging to himself, to being what he was, what he chose to be.

Still in midair, somewhere past the middle of the long fall, he separated himself deliberately from the animal that had been carrying him. Now it was as if he still had an infinitely long time to consider what was happening, to think of things that he might do. With both hands he held the Sword of Mercy by its hilt, keeping the blade inside his body, transfixing his own heart. He saw his stallion moving away from him a little as it fell, its four legs still working, trying to gain purchase on the air.

He did not look down again, never saw the last rush of the ground coming at him. He only felt, beyond pain, his body shatter with the impact at the bottom of the fall, the bones in his legs go splintering away as he came down feet first. Now at last he let himself look down, to see a flash of terrible white sticks, their jagged ends protruding through his leggings.

But his flesh was boiling with the awful power of Woundhealer, an energy that expunged shock and pain. As if he were cutting himself into pieces, Amintor drew the blade of the Sword of Healing, still plunged as it was into his chest, down through his torso to his crotch, then, still not withdrawing it completely from his body, into one leg after the other. The steel knit bones together as it passed through them, restored his flesh, renewed his nerves, set right the hopeless-looking havoc of the fall. Even his skin closed seamlessly behind the bright blade as it passed.

In moments the white of bone was gone. His legs were straight again. Inside Amintor's leggings, which were soaked with his red blood and still torn where his jagged bones had pierced them, he could feel that his bones and muscles already were whole and strong once more.

He sprang up on his feet and carried the Sword quickly to where his riding-beast lay broken, not even trying to get up. The animal was breathing with a hideous noise and endeavoring to raise its head. He pierced the heaving torso with the blade, making sure first of the heart and lungs. Then he sliced at the strangely angled limbs, beholding the miracle, feeling the smooth flow of power in his hands. He kept on using Woundhealer until the animal was standing, quivering and whinnying as he stroked it with his hand, its body whole and ready to run again.

Then Amintor turned at last and looked up at the clifftop above him. There was the silent line of his enemies, some of them dismountd now; all of them balked at that last jump. They were looking down at him with their weapons—even Shieldbreaker—hanging useless in their hands.

And now the Baron could see how the Prince was holding the small form of his son before him, just in front of his saddle. The cloak that had earlier concealed the child had now fallen back.

One good trick deserves another; the Baron saluted them all with the Sword of Healing.

"Now," he shouted up to them, "are you ready to talk about a trade?"

Already, while they watched him heal himself and then his riding-beast, they had had a little time to think the situation over. Almost at once Prince Mark shouted back: "Suppose that I were minded to trade, Baron—how would we manage the exchange?"

"Why, easily enough. You climb down here—make sure you come alone. I'll stand well back, never fear, and give you plenty of room."

The Baron went on to describe how he thought the trade could be managed from that point.

Thinking over the proposed conditions, the Prince turned in his saddle and handed his son over to the senior physician in his train. It was obvious that the hard ride and the combat had been a bad experience for Adrian, and the boy was now in the earliest stages of what looked like a severe seizure. His face was paler than usual, and there were tremors in all his limbs.

Ben drew the Prince aside. "Are you really going on with this mad scheme of trading Swords?"

"I am. Unless you can think of some more certain way to get Woundhealer into my hands."

Ben scowled at him ferociously. The effect would have intimidated almost anyone. "I could hardly think of a more certain path to trouble—but have it your way."

"Thank you."

"You'll have it your way anyhow. And at least let us do something to help you. I'll take one or two people over that way, along the cliff to where those trees hide part of the slope, and come down to the bottom on a long rope. He won't be able to see us."

Mark looked around, wondering if Amintor had any similar trickery in mind. But it was pretty plain that there was no point in worrying any longer about any part of Amintor's force except the man himself. Those who had survived the skirmish around the litter had scattered in flight, and Mark was morally certain that they were fleeing still.

He said to Ben: "All right. I thank you. But once you and the two others are at the bottom, don't do anything unless I signal you. His riding-beast is healed and ready to go, and he'll be off like an arrow if he suspects there's anything wrong."

Ben nodded and moved away. He took the precaution of posting a few of the best archers along the edge of the cliff, though Amintor had already withdrawn to a distance that would make their best shots very chancy. True to his word, the Baron gave Mark plenty of room when the Prince, Shieldbreaker at his side, began to clamber down the cliff.

Since the baggage train, when reassembled, contained enough rope for two long lines, Mark used one to have himself lowered. The descent would have been possible without the security of a rope, but using one increased both speed and safety. Ben had Mark's line secured at the top and took care to keep his own conspicuous figure in sight, in order that Amintor might not wonder what had become of him, Ben had had second thoughts about going down the other rope himself and had delegated that job to several lighter and more agile folk.

Partly through luck and partly by design, Amintor had now placed himself in an excellent position. There was an easy escape route at his rear, and his enemies were all in front of him, in such a position that it was going to be very difficult for them to get at him. From where the Baron was standing now, stroking the riding-beast beside him, it should be possible for him to see Tasavaltans approaching him from any direction when they were still a bowshot away. He would be able to jump on his mount and be gone before anyone coming down the cliff at any point could begin to get near him on foot.

Mark's descent on the cliff, as he was lowered on the rope, could have been quite swift. But he deliberately created minor delays, fussing over knots and loops, wanting to give the people who were using the other, hidden rope plenty of time to get down. Still, he did not want to protract his delays to a suspicious length, and soon he was on the bottom, standing ankle-deep in a small stream that flowed there along the foot of the precipice.

He disengaged himself from the rope and at once turned and began to walk toward the Baron, who stood waiting almost a hundred meters distant. Mark continued to advance until Amintor raised a hand.

Then the Prince halted. He was now about fifty meters from Amintor and approximately the same distance from the foot of the cliff he had just descended.

The voice of his enemy floated toward him. "Let me see if the sword you have brought me is indeed the Sword I want, Prince. If you don't mind—ah." Even at the distance, there was no mistaking what kind of blade it was that caught the light as Mark held it up.

As had been agreed, Mark, having resheathed the Sword of Force, now unbuckled the belt that held it, and cast belt, Sword and all on the ground in front of him.

Amintor in the same manner was unfastening one of the Swords he wore and putting it down on the ground. Mark was sure it was the one he wanted—his magician had already advised him that the other Sword carried by the Baron was Farslayer. If Amintor were to be given a choice between keeping the power of healing and that of vengeance, Mark had no doubt of which one the Baron would elect to keep.

Now, as had been agreed, both men began to walk. Amintor was leading his riding-beast close beside him as he moved. They walked two clockwise arcs of a great circle, keeping diametrically opposite each other. Each could see that another Sword was waiting for him, where his adversary had put it down.

Mark did not look back at the cliff, or at his friends on top of it. But he calculated that the people who were to have come down secretly must be at its foot by now, if all had gone well, and ought to be watching for his signal.

Amintor, as if he might suspect some such trickery, had chosen to walk his circle in the direction that took him farther from any possible ambushers, not closer, and kept them in front of him. If anyone were to try to rush out at the Baron from concealment near the foot of the cliff, the greater speed of his riding-beast would let him scoop up one Sword or the other from the ground and be gone before he could be touched.

But so far no one was rushing out. Mark's people were well-disciplined, waiting for his signal. The situation balanced on a knife-edge. Mark felt the time of the slow walk being counted out in heartbeats. His adversary was almost too far away for the expression on his face to be visible at all, but the Prince thought that the man was smiling.

Now each man was approaching the Sword that his adversary had put down. And now each quickened his pace just a little. Mark came within a stride of the Sword in front of him and bent to pick it up without lowering his gaze more than momentarily from the Baron, who was simultaneously bending to take up Shieldbreaker. Mark observed that Amintor, doubtless mindful of the possibility of treacherous arrows or stones, had put his mount between himself and the clifftop. But once Shieldbreaker was in his hand, he stepped out boldly from behind the animal.

We might, thought Mark now, have shot at the animal and disabled it. Then we might have rushed him . . . but there was no use now thinking about possibilities that had not been foreseen, pondering plans that had never been made.

Amintor now had the Sword of Force in hand.

But Mark had Woundhealer. The hilt of the Sword of Mercy had come into his hand, bringing with it a flow of gentle power; this Sword was one of those he had held before, and the touch of it was unmistakable. It brought back, with a rush of memory, the days when he had first come to know Kristin, when for a time the two of them had been alone against the world, and princely power was far away.

Triumph shone in the face of Amintor as his right hand closed upon the hilt of the Sword of Force. But the Baron did not delay for even a moment to savor triumph. Nor did he deviate in the least from the behavior that had been agreed upon.

Mark had anticipated the possibility of treachery by the other at this point. But the Prince knew how to fight against Shieldbreaker and was ready to disarm himself before Amintor could gallop across the space that intervened between them. And the other would have to consider that Mark might not disarm himself, but might instead wield the Sword of Mercy; what Woundhealer might do in direct opposition to the Sword of Force had never been tested.

But that test was not to happen now. Amintor was keeping to the letter of his agreement regarding the exchange. Now astride his mount, the Baron saluted Prince Mark with his new possession, and now the triumph in Amintor's face was unmistakable. In another moment he was off, cantering briskly toward the line of trees that marked the course of the small stream after it meandered away from the foot of the line of cliffs.

Mark looked down at the black hilt in his own fist and at the small, white, open hand that marked it as a symbol. A moment later he had turned his back on the retreating Baron and had in fact almost forgotten him. The Prince moved quickly to meet the friends who ran toward him.

Adrian's eyes were open when Mark stepped into the tent. The boy was lying on his back but sat bolt upright on his pallet as soon as his father approached with the Sword in hand. Both of the Princeling's small hands came up, eagerly groping, to touch the blade of Woundhealer as his father held it out toward him. The small fingers played freely over the invisible keenness of those edges and came away from them undamaged.

But Mark could feel that no real power had yet gone forth from Woundhealer. The sightless gaze of his son still wandered as before, and Adrian's small voice was silent.

Now Mark, with his friends crowding unheeded into the tent behind him, knelt down beside the pallet of his son and thrust the Sword forward again. It touched the head of Adrian, and that keen point passed across his eyes and through them. But still those eyes saw nothing, and still Mark could feel nothing in the hilt.

"Light," the child said suddenly. "Father, light!"

"Yes!"

But then Mark's son lay back in his bed, his hands still groping in the familiar gestures. His eyes refused to follow the physician's hand when it passed back and forth in front of them. It was obvious that his blindness was no better than before.

Another hour had passed before Mark emerged from the tent at last. He stumbled into the sunlight as if he too were now blind. Ben was at his side, trying to think of words to say to him. But the Prince had the look of a man who could not hear, almost the look of a man who is ready to die.

Woundhealer had done absolutely nothing for his son.

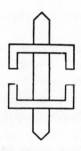

CHAPTER 16

THE mermaid was struggling fiercely if not very effectively against the reptiles that swooped at her from the
air. Her broad, flat tail thrashed up sheets of water, her small
fists struck out at jaws and wings that came within their
reach. She screamed at them in her human voice, using the
wizards' language that Zoltan did not know, and for the first
few seconds the sound of the words seemed to upset their
attack.

But in a moment they came screaming and clawing back at
her, renewing the assault.

The beasts were larger than eagles, with teeth and talons
big enough to kill. All that saved the fish-girl from immediate and serious injury was the water. She had luckily found
an unusually deep pool, though even here she was almost too
big to submerge entirely in her half-human form. The water
could not protect her completely from the diving, reaching
talons. The flying creatures, though reptilian, were not am-
phibious. But they could evidently tolerate brief plunges.

Next time the mermaid came up, she was armed with rocks
in both hands and hurled them at the leather-wings. They
ignored the missiles and dove at her again.

But by now Zoltan was standing on the bank beside the
mermaid's pool. Dragonslicer was a bigger and heavier sword

than any he had used in practice, but it was not too big for him to swing. And never, in practice or anywhere else, had he handled a weapon as keen and deadly as this one. Though no magical power had yet manifested itself as it ought to have done against true dragons, neither were the creatures he was fighting protected by the incredibly tough armor of a dragon's scales. In Zoltan's capable two-handed grip the weighty steel drove razor-sharp through leathery skin, sinew, and bone. Any of the attackers that he managed to hit solidly fell dead or crippled from the air at once.

The human voice of the mermaid gasped and sobbed for breath whenever she had to bring her head above the surface of the water. Apparently she was forced to come up for air like a human. In the hasty glances he could spare to look at her, Zoltan could see that she was wounded and bleeding about the arms and shoulders. But she defended herself as best she could with rocks and fists, and showed no sign of disabling injury as yet.

Abruptly the enemy broke off the attack, leaving three of their number dead or wounded on the ground. Dragonslicer had taken off the head of one of them completely, and two more were crippled. Some of the reptiles still airborne were flying as if they had been wounded too, nicked or scraped by the Sword that had not been quite quick enough to take their lives.

Zoltan, panting, standing ankle-deep now in the water of the stream, rested his weight on the Sword of Heroes, feeling the sharpness of the point cleave its way slowly into the bottom of the stream between rocks. He was still uninjured, and he knew a savage pride. He was fighting off these dangerous and determined creatures without the help of any magic, under his own power.

The girl's head broke the surface of the water in the pool

beside him, and Zoltan looked at her. She was floating on her back, gasping and bleeding in a very human way.

"Can you get away," he asked, "while they are gone? Swim downstream? Is there a deeper pool within your reach that way?"

She watched the circling creatures in the sky. "No. Not close enough. They would have me before I reached it." She floated on her back, resting, tail stirring the surface weakly. "*He* has sent them after me," she added. "I am not worth a greater effort on his part, I suppose."

And then the enemy, whose black swarm had briefly receded, were coming back again.

Once more the mad confusion of the fight descended upon Zoltan and his companion. Fighting, he had no time to think or feel or be afraid, no time to do anything but swing the Sword and duck and dodge to try to make the clawing, biting enemy miss him, and straighten up swinging the Sword again.

Two of the beasts came at him at once. He felt a claw fasten in his scalp, his flesh tearing with appalling pain. He screamed, and twirled the Sword above his head, and felt an impact as the blade bit leathery hide and bone. The talon in his scalp pulled free.

Again the enemy broke off the attack.

And yet once more, before Zoltan had time to rest or breathe, the onslaught was renewed. Blood was flowing from his torn scalp, but fortunately it ran around his ear, not into his eyes. He hacked yet another reptile out of the air.

At last, the four leather-wings who could still fly, dripping their own blood and hissing half-intelligible imprecations, flapped off, making unsteady headway into the northwest.

Zoltan, gasping, leaned on his Sword again and watched them until he was sure it was a genuine retreat. Then he looked around. The nymph, mermaid, whatever the right word for her was, had completely disappeared again. Turned back completely into a fish again, he supposed, and diminished in size, or he'd be able to see her somewhere in the water nearby. He wondered how much control she had, if any, over her changes of form. She might have saved herself some harm by doing the fish-change sooner. Or maybe the smaller body of the fish would have been hooked out of the river on a talon and torn apart.

Moving unsteadily, on shaking legs, he went to one after another of the wounded reptiles on the ground and finished them off with economical thrusts and chops of Dragonslicer while they screamed curses at him. One closed its eyes before the Sword came down. It was the closest Zoltan had ever come to killing a human being.

Now he had achieved a silence that would let him rest.

Zoltan wiped his Sword clean on grass, then knelt down and drank from the stream. Next he tried to stanch the bleeding of his scalp. Tied on his belt was the small medical kit that Mother Still had given him. Inside it he found a small jar labeled FOR BLEEDING. Using the Sword itself, far keener than any other blade he'd ever handled, he hacked awkwardly and blindly at his curly hair until he thought the wound was as exposed as he could safely get it. Then he loaded a finger with the unpleasant-smelling salve and pressed it directly into the flow of blood. Immediately the bleeding diminished, and in a matter of moments the flow was stanched completely.

Only then did Zoltan remember to look for his mount. He was suddenly afraid of what the reptiles might have done to it while he defended the mermaid; but the loadbeast was unharmed. Perhaps the leather-wings had been under orders to concentrate on the escaping mermaid. She had said something about their being sent after her by some enemy.

Zoltan remounted and pushed on. He continued down-stream, paralleling the river.

Hardly was he well out of sight of the place where he had fought the reptiles when a familiar figure reappeared. It was the crazy-looking little wizard again, standing directly in Zoltan's path.

This time Zoltan was treated to praise and concern. "You're a brave boy, yes. Oh my, that was fine. But your head is hurt. Oh, oh, oh, oh." And the wizard, his dried-apple countenance pinched up as if he felt the pain as much as Zoltan, did a little hop-dance of helpless sympathy, mean-while waving his arms ineffectively.

Zoltan felt called upon to be patient. "It'll be all right. The bleeding's stopped already. Mother Still gave me a medicine that worked beautifully."

"Are you sure? I don't know her. Oh, oh."

All Zoltan could think was that this wizard, despite the power that he had demonstrated, did not inspire much confi-dence. Raising a hand, he gingerly explored the area of clotted blood where his hair was now cut short. "Yes, I'm sure."

"That's good. That's good. Then you should go on."

"I mean to do so."

"That's good, Zoltan. You're a brave boy."

"Thank you, sir. Who are you?"

"I don't think I ought to tell you that. Because if I tell anyone, *he* might find out somehow, and—and anyway, whoever I am you still have to go on and find—and find your uncle. No matter what."

"Where is Uncle Mark?"

The wizard gestured nervously again. "I think you should look for the trail of a dragon."

"Oh. If I follow a dragon's trail, it'll lead me to him?"

"Something like that. Yes, I think that would be the best thing for you to do."

"All right. But wait, what does a dragon's trail look like? I've never seen one."

The figure of the wizard hopped from one foot to the other, speaking faster and faster in its gravelly voice. "You'll know. Oh, you'll know it when you come to it, won't you? Go on, hurry, hurry! I can't stay here arguing all day."

And, almost as soon as he had uttered those words, the strange wizard disappeared again.

Zoltan forged on, still heading downstream. He assumed that was still the proper direction, not having been given any instructions to the contrary. If finding his uncle Mark meant trailing a dragon, well, he would never be any better equipped for that than he was right now. Pride was growing in him as he realized how successfully he had fought off the attacking leather-wings. Not that a dozen of them were the equivalent of a real dragon, of course—but he felt ready to fight the dragon himself if it came after him.

At least, almost ready. That was a chilling thought. Well, possibly the creature wasn't very large. The smaller land-walkers, he had heard, were no bigger than loadbeasts.

Zoltan had expected soldiering and adventuring to be painful and sometimes frightening. But now he wondered if such activities were always as confused and filled with uncertainty as this. Somehow this wasn't quite the way he had imagined things would be.

He pushed doggedly on, along the stream.

That night he camped on the riverbank again, and lay awake, watching the surface of the water ripple in the moonlight, and waiting. Before he could fall asleep the girl came back, a splash and then a silvery outline, a dreamlike presence in the moonlight.

Zoltan wasn't sure if he was relieved or worried at her presence, but he moved to sit beside her and talk to her again. He offered his medicine kit but she declined; he could see that her wounds were superficial and were already partially healed, showing rough scabs and crustings on her skin.

The air was colder tonight, and Zoltan brought his visitor one of his blankets as she sat on the rock. She thanked him politely. They congratulated each other on surviving, and she thanked him for his aid against the reptiles.

He told the girl his name and explained to her that he was taking the Sword of Heroes to his uncle, who was going to have to fight a dragon. She said that she had heard of the Swords of Power, and sounded as if she had some idea of what they were.

"But how are you going to locate your uncle?" the girl asked.

"Our friend, the strange-looking little wizard, tells me that I have to look for the dragon's trail first. Then my uncle will be nearby somewhere."

"What is our rescuer's name, I wonder? And why are you so sure you must do what he tells you? If he tried to give me orders, I should be very doubtful about following them."

"So far I don't believe he's lied to me. But I don't know his name." Zoltan went on to tell the girl more of his story than he had told her previously. Then he got around to asking her if she had yet managed to recall her name.

"No. It may be that my name is gone forever. Along with half of my humanity." She flicked her tail, sending up spray.

"I asked the strange little magician for *his* name, but he wouldn't tell me."

"That is not so strange, for a wizard. Names are things of great power in their lives."

"I'm no wizard. My name is Zoltan—I told you that before. I wish you could remember yours."

The girl shrugged, a delicate motion. "There are certain names of power that I remember—ones the Master used to call me by. But I am afraid that if I uttered one of those, I should be completely enslaved to him again. And the other man, the lesser wizard to whom he gave me, sometimes used those names—but I will never say or hear them again if I can help it. You should call me whatever pleases you. I think that I have never had a name I truly liked."

Zoltan's mind was a buzzing blank. "I'll try to think of something." And he went on to tell her something more of his own story.

The mermaid assured him that she believed his story; it was, after all, perhaps not so unbelievable as her own.

Not that she could remember very much. She had been somehow kidnapped from a fishing village—she seemed to remember it as a fishing village, along a river very much bigger than this one—at a very early age, and conscripted into the evil Master's service—she was very vague about the details of how all that had happened.

She hesitated suddenly, in midspeech, staring past Zoltan as if she saw something there that frightened her. Before he could turn, the transformation, which until now he had not witnessed directly, happened before his eyes. There was a large puff and cloud of something like steam in the moonlight, close enough for him to feel it; and he caught one clear glimpse of a large, leaping fish before it splashed into the water.

Late next morning, Zoltan, still following the stream downhill, came upon a trail—he didn't know how to describe it except as a trail—that was unlike anything that he had ever seen before. A vast, shallow gouge in the hard, dry earth, wide as a wagon road, knee-deep in the center and shallowing toward both sides. Desert bushes and other small plants had been uprooted and rocks torn out of the earth and dragged. At least it was easy to see which way the trail led. It looked to Zoltan as if some cylindrical weight the size of a substantial house had been dragged in a gently curving path across the land.

The track went right across the river and away from it again on the other side. Zoltan was still sitting on the bank, around midday, frowning at it, when the mermaid emerged partially from the water to talk with him again.

This time she sat in the sandy shallows instead of climbing out. She frowned at the strange scar that wound across the earth, and announced at once: "It is the track of a great worm."

Zoltan stared at her for a long time before he spoke. "Oh" was all he said when he did answer. Deep inside him, somewhere between his stomach and his heart, a lump of ice had suddenly congealed.

Almost everyone had heard at some time of great worms, though neither he nor the mermaid had ever actually seen one of the creatures. Very few people in this part of the world had ever done so. They were the final phase in the life cycle of the dragon and a thousand times rarer even than the landwalkers.

Immediately after the first shock of fear that Zoltan experienced, doubts began to arise. Certainly this was not what Zoltan had had in mind as the spoor of the dragon. He had been intent on finding gigantic footprints of some unknown shape—but in some vague way, reptilian-looking—showing the marks of great unretracted claws. But this—this looked, he thought, as if an army had passed by, dragging all their baggage on sledges, obliterating by this means all of their own footprints and hoofprints. Such an effort might have wiped out even the tracks of dragons, landwalkers, Zoltan supposed, had there been any.

"Are you sure?" he asked the girl.

"Oh, yes. I am afraid so. I am afraid that this can scarcely be anything else."

He was silent, thinking. Was it possible that any army would march with a dragon, or several, in its train? Zoltan had been reading and listening to martial stories since he was old enough to read, and he had never heard of the creatures being used as war-animals. The beasts were said to be too stupid and uncontrollable for anyone to try to use them—though, now that he thought about it, Uncle Mark and Ben told tales of a dragon, constrained by magic, that had once been set to guard the treasure of the Blue Temple.

Suppose, Zoltan thought, someone could harness a land-walker, a big one, and make it pull a sledge. Maybe, conceivably, it would produce a trail something like this . . . or maybe a gouge like this one would need a squadron of landwalkers. Now, following the trail slowly as it curved away from the stream—there was no doubt of which way it led—he had come to a spot where even small trees were bent and broken. One of the treetrunks was almost as thick as a man's body.

Wide as a wagon road, yet without ruts, the broad concavity went curving gently across the rugged countryside.

If this was indeed the dragon's path, then Zoltan's duty was to follow it. To do so, he was going to have to leave the stream, perhaps for good, and with it abandon his alternate plan of getting back to Tasavalta that way. Also he would miss his sometime companion, but there didn't seem to be any choice. Of course, the wizard's actual instructions had been to stick to the river. But having found something this unusual, it was hard not to assume it was the trail he had been told to look for.

He returned to the place where the trail crossed the river, and knelt to fill his leather water-bottle. The mermaid gazed at him sadly, and Zoltan tried to explain his difficulty to her. "I don't know if this is really a dragon's trail or not. But I suppose I have to follow it."

She was silent. Then he saw with vague but deep alarm that she was starting to weep.

"It is the trail of a dragon, as I have said," she told him presently. "But I wish that you would not follow it. I think that you are now my only friend, in all the world. And it will kill you."

The lump of ice was back, bigger than before. Other sensations, less definable but equally uncomfortable, accompanied it. Zoltan muttered something incoherent, and for some reason he could feel himself blushing.

As if with an effort of will, the mermaid ceased to weep. Brushing hair and tears out of her eyes, she predicted that the trail would loop back to the river again within a few kilometers because of the dragon's great need for water. "Unless of course it should be going to another river. Or some lake or pond."

"I do not think that there are any lakes or ponds near here."

But she was crying again and could not answer.

Zoltan finished refilling the waterskin that Mother Still had given him, and struck out away from the river, following the awestruck track, whatever it was, across country.

He came presently to a place where there were blurred hoofprints that he took to be those of several wild cattle, small convergent trails which terminated at the edge of the purported dragon's track. Here on the barren earth was a spurt of what might be dried blood, and here, nearby, was a fragment of a wild bull's leg, complete with hoof, some hide, and lower bones. But otherwise there were no bones or other debris to be seen in the area.

Zoltan pushed on. Presently he came to a place where there were droppings—what looked like a mound of dung, several days old and high as a man. Sharp fragments of large bones protruded from the mass. There were scales, too, and other products of digestion less identifiable.

He dismounted and poked at the mass with Dragonslicer, and swallowed. He had just felt, for the first time in his life, a stirring of power in a Sword.

Despite the mermaid's warnings, that gave him a shock. Of course there might be tiny, mouse-sized dragons burrowing in that compost heap. He knew it wasn't likely. That small, he thought, they should be living in a stream. Or . . .

The trouble was that a single creature that could make a trail like this and leave a pile like this—that was an alternative that hardly bore thinking about. Zoltan didn't want to believe that something like that could really exist, that he might really have to face it.

He moved on.

Looking back at the titanic spoor, just before he rode out of sight of it, he still couldn't make himself believe that it was really what it looked like. Someone must have gathered together all the droppings of the animals of the whole army, and . . . but why should anyone do anything like that?

No. No one creature could be that big. There wasn't any possibility of such a thing. Besides, how could such a monstrous creature catch anything to eat? Certainly not by stealth. It could of course consume vegetation, he supposed, whole thickets and trees. But there wasn't a lot of vegetation in this country. And in the pile back there, the bones, the evidences of carnivorism, had been plain.

Zoltan felt a little better when he saw that the trail was indeed leading him back to another loop of the river, about a kilometer away. He hurried ahead and found the mermaid already waiting for him there.

"I think you may have been right," he told her, and explained.

"Oh yes, I am right. It is the track of a great worm, Zoltan." She sounded sad, but resigned now, not tearful. "It is very much like an enormous snake. A great worm can move very fast for short distances. It can knock down anything you could put in its way. And I do not see how your uncle can fight it, even if the Sword that you are bringing him is magic as you say. How do you know where, in all that length, to find the heart?"

"How do you know so much about them?" The ice was still in his gut, and now his lips were going dry.

"That is something else that I cannot remember. Perhaps I saw a great worm once, when I was—when the evil people had power over me. Perhaps I saw—" Then the girl was silent, a pause that stretched on and on.

"Tell me more," Zoltan urged.

Her human lungs drew in a deep breath. "There is only one way I can think of by which it might be killed. A creature like this must seek some kind of shade, under trees, and lie still through most of the day. Otherwise the heat of the sun will kill it—it cannot find enough water here to lie in. Or it may be that the Master has given it the protection of his magic, too. Then even the magic of your Sword will do you no good at all. And if that is not enough, there is one more danger. The worm can hypnotize large animals and even sometimes people, and force them to march right into its jaws."

"But I must follow it." He could do that much. That was all he had to think about now, following it. If and when he actually came in sight of it—then he would decide what had to be done next.

Pushing on again, following the trail, Zoltan came to more droppings, and more bones. He found himself thanking Ardneh that the trail was still old. He estimated several days old, from the condition of the uprooted plants.

A thing this size could even gobble a landwalker. Especially if one came along that was not too large.

How do you know where, in all that length, to find the heart?

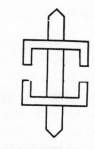

CHAPTER 17

AGAIN the moon was almost full. Baron Amintor, riding alone, observed the off-round shape of it just beginning to materialize in the eastern sky at dusk as he began to jockey his riding-beast uphill around a minor waterfall, which occupied most of the width of a small canyon. The Baron, after a month of lonely travel, was still wearing his two Swords, one at each side.

He had been traveling almost steadily since trading Swords with Prince Mark, and he had come a long way on a winding route. The Baron's goal, a prearranged meeting place, was very near now. It lay just upstream along the river he had now reached. Amintor had never seen this river, the Sanzu, before, but he knew that its headquarters were somewhere deep in the rocky hills of Tasavalta, a good many kilometers to the east and north of here.

It was not the Baron's habit to hurry unnecessarily, but now he was peering somewhat anxiously ahead of him through the dusk, and when his riding-beast began to demonstrate an increasing reluctance to go forward, he kicked it in the ribs to urge it on. Amintor did not want to risk being late for the impending meeting. The appointment he was trying to keep had cost him a great deal of time and energy to set up, and it was of inestimable importance to his future.

The past month had not been unpleasant. As a rule he actually preferred traveling alone. No member of that band who had been with him before he'd taken the Sword of Mercy would have been a suitable companion for the grander enterprise upon which he was now entering; and by now the Baron felt almost grateful to Prince Mark for helping him to be rid of them all. Under the new conditions they might well have proved something of an embarrassment.

Amintor had expected, when he sent messengers to propose this meeting, that he'd be coming to it with Farslayer and Woundhealer at his belt—but as matters now actually stood, he thought he was in a substantially stronger position even than that.

Here, as on the even higher reaches of the Sanzu, none of the individual falls and rapids were very high, but there were a great many of them, which made progress difficult for anyone on foot or mounted who sought to follow the stream closely. When he had attained the next level spot where there was room, the Baron paused to let his mount breathe while he gazed up at the next splashing fall above and muttered to himself—it was a habit that had begun to grow on him during the past few weeks of solitude.

"No sign as yet he's here at all. And I'll not find him at all should he not want to be found. But I'm still convinced he's here and wants to talk to me."

Impatiently he cut short the pause for rest and pressed on. And, rounding the next rugged bend in the stream, the Baron had good evidence that his conviction was correct. Not that he saw the eminent wizard he had come here to meet; but what he did see awaiting him in the dusk appeared to be something even more unusual.

It lay like a fallen log across the earth and made a gently sagging bridge across the stream. And it was a roughly cylindrical, horizontal shape. But it was too thick and far too long—even had it not been disposed across the canyon in great snakelike curves—to be any fallen log that Amintor had ever seen.

At first glance he thought it might be some peculiar earthen bank, showing where the river had once followed a slightly different course. But here in the canyon that would be impossible, and anyway the configuration of the object was all wrong for that. Here and there it rose above the earth.

And then, even as the Baron studied it, the thing, the formation, whatever it was, moved. Shuddering longitudinally in a majestic, large-scale ripple, it shook off the fallen leaves that had begun to drift upon its top, and started up small animals which had been huddling next to it. The thought crossed Amintor's mind that the thing must have been lying immobile for quite some time if small animals had started to regard it as part of the landscape.

But his main, overwhelming impression was of sheer awesome size.

Now another part of the vast length, thirty or forty meters from where Amintor sat his mount, rose up from the earth. Something that had to be a head, though it looked to Amintor as big as a small chariot, reared up at that distance, topping the small trees. Yes, those two bright plates in the dusk were *eyes*. Impossibly huge, round and green as fishbowls, with such a span of shadow in between them that the Baron found he had some difficulty in drawing his next breath.

He looked to right and left along the rugged canyon floor, trying to see where the curves of the titanic body ended. What with the trees, and the shadows of the oncoming night, he couldn't tell. One thing was certain: there appeared to be no way for him to get around the creature, not in the confines of this gorge. Yet his instructions had been plain in the answer his messenger had brought back; this was certainly the way he had to pass if he was going to follow those instructions. And he was sure that this obstruction was not accidental.

The Baron's mount, faithful enough to jump off a cliff upon command, was growing restive in the presence of this monstrous creature, and he had to struggle for control to keep the riding-beast from bolting. He knew what to call the thing that blocked his way—a great worm—though in all his travels he had never actually seen one until now.

It was the terminal phase in the life cycle of the dragon; and not one in a million of those beasts ever reached it.

His two Swords in their metal sheaths clattered with the motion of the terrified riding-beast under him. Neither Farslayer nor Shieldbreaker was of the least good to him now. The one Sword that might possibly be able to help a man against such a creature was one Amintor did not have.

As he struggled with his mount, wondering meanwhile what to do next, a man's voice called to him from beyond the dragon. "Come on, then! Climb over!"

It was an authoritative voice, and though it was completely unfamiliar to the Baron, he had no doubt of who its owner was. Very well, then, he would climb over the waiting dragon.

If he was going to do so, there was no choice for him but to dismount and leave his mount where it was; to his relief the riding-beast quieted as soon as he got off its back—it grew peaceful with magical suddenness indeed, he thought wryly—and let itself be tethered.

Then he approached the scaly wall of the worm's side, trying to look as if this was something he did every day, or once a year at least. As he did so Amintor thought that there were smaller eyes, eyes on a human scale, regarding him from a high ledge of rock beyond the beast. But he ignored that gaze for the time being.

The thickness of the creature's enormous, snaky body was

approximately equal to Amintor's height. He gained a small advantage from stepping on a handy stone on the near side, stepped once more upon a roughly projecting scale—the beast took no more notice of his weight than would a castle wall—and vaulted to the top and over, dropping down nimbly enough on the other side.

"Up here, Amintor."

On a ledge of rock beside the next small cataract—a shelf of stone overgrown with vegetation and several meters above the worm—a figure waited. It was that of one who could only be the wizard Burslem.

Amintor had never seen the magician before, but one who gave orders here could hardly be anyone else. The Baron chose a route and clambered up to where the other man sat regally awaiting his arrival. The other arose from the fine chair he had been sitting in, as if belatedly deciding to offer that much courtesy; and the two men stood in the moonlight sizing each other up.

Burslem was quite a young man in appearance, though Amintor did not allow himself to be deceived by that. Indeed, the magician had the look of a somewhat bookish youth, wearing a soft robe that like his chair would have looked more appropriate in a library than on this desolate hillside surrounded by splintered rocks, grotesquely growing trees, and rushing water.

But the strangest things in the immediate environment were not those, perhaps not even the great worm. Amintor could sense living things whirring and rustling in the dusky air above the wizard's head, but they were almost impossible to see, and Burslem never looked up at them at all. The limb of a tall, dead tree projected through that space, and above the tree, a higher ledge. And, perched on that ledge, where the shadows of several taller trees congealed together, was a solid form, that of something that might have been a reptile—unless it was some kind of creature even less savory. Something in the Baron recoiled from that presence. He did not know what it was, and quickly decided that he did not want to know.

The wizard's youthful face was solemn as it regarded him. Had someone been watching at this moment who had also known the evil emperor John Ominor, of thousands of years in the past, the observer would have been struck by a certain resemblance between the two.

There was, perhaps, also a likeness to that ancient ruler in the brusque way that this man talked.

"What is the purpose of this meeting, Amintor? I am a busy man." The voice was nondescript.

"Indeed, we are both busy men." Calmly the Baron refused to be rushed or rattled by the impressive reception the other had provided for him. "So I will come at once to the point. My thought is that each of us has certain skills—powers—that the other lacks. Therefore we might do very well to form a partnership."

The other, hands clasped behind his back, looked at him in silence for what seemed to Amintor a very long time. It was as if the magician were reassessing an earlier impression.

"Your recent acquisition of Shieldbreaker," Burslem admitted at last, "has increased your status in my eyes, to a considerable extent. I should like to hear the story of how that was accomplished."

"Gladly."

And the Baron retold the story, in its broad outline, as succinctly and truthfully as he could, not omitting his own mistakes along the way. He then returned, without pause, to his theme. "Separately we are both of us strong, but together we will be stronger still. I am a dependable military leader and have a knack for finding the right way to talk people into doing things—not a skill to be sneered at in matters of diplomacy and war. The fact is that I see no practical limits to what we might be able to accomplish in a partnership.''

Burslem at least did not immediately refuse the proposal, or laugh it to scorn. Instead he gestured with his left hand, and what had been a rock became—or seemed to become—another comfortable chair beside his own. There on the small ledge above the little waterfall the two men sat and talked well into the night, with the great worm coiled—or at least looped—below them, right athwart the space that any other physical being would have had to cross in order to approach them from below.

Only the gods and demons, thought Amintor—and my friend here—know what may be blocking the way into this canyon from above. He also found himself wondering, in the occasional pauses of the conversation, how fast the creature below him might be able to move if and when it decided there was a need for speed. He could not imagine anything that a great worm would feel the need to run away from, but it must require enough food for an army, and catching that might well require some quickness sometimes. And, how long had it taken to travel here, from whatever strange place it had been summoned?

"A most formidable guardian," he remarked at one point, indicating the limbless dragon with a gesture.

"I have lost," Burslem muttered, "some of my faith in demons." It was as if the wizard were speaking more to himself than anyone else.

The Baron was not sure that he saw any relevant connection between demons and dragons, but he did not choose to pursue the matter.

The magician turned slightly in his chair to face him. "Let us speak plainly."

"By all means."

"You invite me into a partnership. Between partners, there is always one senior to the other."

Amintor spread both hands, a gesture that caused the Swords at his sides, in their metal-bound sheaths, to chink faintly against rock. The wizard had totally ignored the priceless weapons so far, and continued to do so now.

The Baron said: "I would certainly not claim seniority over one who was the chief of security and intelligence for King Vilkata."

Burslem grunted. "If he had listened to me, he would be alive today. Not only alive. He would have won the war."

In those days Amintor himself, of course, had been at the right hand of the Silver Queen. But he made no claim now to having given advice that, if taken, would have altered the outcome of the war. Instead the Baron said only: "When one of these Swords finds itself in a ruler's hand, there is a tendency for it to dominate his thinking." Vilkata had held the Mindsword, then. "Or her thinking, as the case may be."

Burslem laughed. It was a hissing sound, unpleasant and somewhat labored, quite out of keeping with his ordinary appearance. Amintor found himself thinking he would not be surprised if a serpent stuck its head up out of the man's throat. The great worm had long since lowered its head again, become a silent wall that curved through deepening night. But the eyes of the other thing on the ledge above, whatever it might be, were still there watching.

"Well," the wizard said, "we may hope that the Sword of Love now dominates the thinking of Prince Mark. Maybe it will lead him into trying to do good unto his enemies."

"May it be so indeed," agreed the Baron heartily. "He has done a fair amount of troublesome things to me, though in the end I had what I wanted from him."

"Is it possible that you will want more from him in the future?"

"I should say it is quite possible. By the way, Burslem, I have here a small flask of wine of a certain rare vintage. Would you share a drink with me? A toast, to the future prosperity of both of us?" The Baron stopped short of proposing that they drink to a partnership that had not yet been finally agreed upon.

"Why not?" Burslem reached over with a well-kept, ordinary-looking hand to take the flask. At that moment Amintor was conscious of the faintest throb of power inside the length of Shieldbreaker as it lay along his thigh. Weapons of magic arrayed in opposition meant no more to the Sword of Force than did those of steel. *None stands to Shieldbreaker.* But the Sword's reaction was nothing serious as yet; a preliminary stirring, he supposed, a response to some magical precaution activated by his host when Burslem took the drink into his hand.

Now the wizard was holding up the small flask of wine in both hands and gazing at it, as if he were somehow able to study the fluid inside the leather skin. Amintor, expecting to be able to perceive something of testing at this moment, could just detect, with his mind more than with his senses, the passage of something in the air immediately over his own head. He looked up. He had a sense that it had been of considerably more than human size, but already it was gone. The small green eyes that he had seen, of something perched upon the higher ledge, were now gone too.

As soon as the airborne presence had passed, the wizard heaved a great and human-sounding sigh. Then he opened up the flask and drank, without any hesitation but with little evidence of enjoyment either. Even as the magician swallowed, the Baron felt a mild glow inside his own belly, as if it were there that the wine had landed.

Burslem passed back the flask and wiped his mouth. As the Baron drank in turn, the great worm again raised its head upon the column of its neckless body, just enough so it could turn its gaze at him. The huge eyes still glowed with the faint reflected light of the night sky. The Baron made a little gesture in the worm's direction with the flask, a kind of to-your-health, and sipped again. The Sword at his side was quiet; was the great worm a weapon? Probably not within the logic of Shieldbreaker's protective magic. The dragon could come and kill him and the Sword of Force would be a sword in his hand and nothing more, as useless against such an attacker as against an earthquake.

He understood that at the moment he might well be relatively vulnerable to the wizard's power; but he also thought that for the moment he had nothing to fear from that.

Burslem, as if his mind were running in the same track, suddenly remarked: "You realize that I could take those two Swords from you at any moment."

Amintor, who had dealt with Swords before, realized nothing of the kind. Except for the controlled presence of the dragon, he would have been tempted to laugh at the idea. Even for the dragon to reach him would take time, and he and Shieldbreaker would not be idle in that time.

But the Baron was not going to try to dispute the point just now. "Thereby depriving me," he answered calmly, "of the pleasure of putting them willingly at the service of my senior partner—or am I to take it that our agreement is not yet formally concluded?"

The other laughed again. "Yes, perhaps I do need your skills at negotiation, Amintor. Very well, the agreement is concluded. Keep both your Swords, for now. They are likely to be of the greatest use upon a battlefield, and you are much more likely to find yourself on such a field than I am."

The talk between the two men resumed, now in something of a new key. It soon turned to practical planning.

The magician said: "One of your first duties will be, of course, to raise an army, substantially larger than the mere guard force—about three hundred soldiers—I have at my disposal now. There are times when nothing but a real army will do, if one is to be taken seriously enough in the world."

"Indeed."

"Yes. The worm below us, for example, is capable of taking a city, or defeating an army in the field. But no matter how cleverly it is given orders, it cannot very well collect taxes, or guard an entire frontier."

"Certainly."

"We shall have to discuss the question of what exact size and composition of the force will be most practical. The recruitment, organization, and training will then be left almost entirely in your hands."

"If such matters are to be done properly, they inevitably take a great deal of time."

"Yes, time and patience. But until the army is ready, our greatest plans, as I see them, must be held in abeyance."

Amintor was silent.

"You disagree?" Burslem asked sharply.

"I only venture to suggest that there are some great plans that by their nature do not require an army."

Shortly after that remark was made, and before it could be amplified in discussion, the first conference between the partners was adjourned. There were matters, Burslem said, for which he had to prepare, and the preparations were of such a nature that they had to be accomplished without human company. So far he still had not taken up Amintor's hint about great plans.

*   *   *

The talk between the two men resumed on the following afternoon, in a pleasant camp above the canyon rim. Amintor had led his riding-beast up out of the canyon, and it now cropped grass under a tree nearby the camp. There were a handful of servants in attendance, all of them apparently quite human, who quietly and efficiently saw to their masters' needs. The worm was gone—somewhere. Amintor had not tried to see where its great swath of a trail led.

Shortly after this newest session of talk began, Burslem abruptly asked to see Shieldbreaker. Amintor at once drew the Sword of Force and held it up. He was gritting his teeth, preparing arguments for a refusal to hand it over, but the wizard made no such demand on him, being instead content to gaze upon the blade from the other side of his comfortable pavilion.

"It still remains a mystery to me," the magician commented at last, "how Vulcan lost it."

The Baron, who had been actually on the scene—or very nearly so—when that loss took place, had also been for a long time unable to come up with any reasonable explanation. At last his meditations on the subject had convinced him of what the explanation was; but he offered no answers. He only related what he had seen while his new partner listened to the account with keen interest.

Amintor concluded: "And the giant figure with the Sword in its hand—I am sure now that it could have been no one but Vulcan—was still knocking and slashing about with the blade, in a fair way to knock the very building down, when I got out. But the more I think about what I saw, the more certain I am that, with very few exceptions, the men and women who struggled against him were not hurt by that Sword. Not even though it struck and pierced their bodies again and again."

"We are partners now," said Burslem solemnly, "and you may very well carry Shieldbreaker into combat in our common cause. Therefore I must tell you what I have discovered about it.''

"Which is—?'' inquired Amintor with all the innocent eagerness that he could muster. He felt quite sure that the disclosure would tell him no more than he had managed to deduce for himself some time ago.

"That he who strives *without weapons* against the Sword of Force,'' Burslem proclaimed, "cannot be hurt by it.''

"Ah.'' The Baron blinked three times. "That may well be so. That would account for the exceptions.''

"I tell you that it is so. Think back on what you saw that day, and tell me if I am not right.''

Amintor did his best to look as if he were thinking back with great concentration. "You are right,'' he said at last.

The other nodded. "Also, the wielder of the Sword of Force is well-nigh powerless to resist, by any other means, such an unarmed attack as you say these people were carrying out against Vulcan. Because the Sword, so long as he holds it, draws most of his strength into itself; nor will it allow him to let it go, as long as his enemies still confront him.''

That was an idea that Amintor had never worked out explicitly for himself. Yet now that he heard it stated clearly, he thought that it must be so; otherwise, how could that gaggle of struggling humans ever have overcome even a weakened god?

"A strange imperfection, that, for the ultimate weapon to have,'' the Baron meditated aloud.

"Ah, yes. But do not forget that it *is* the ultimate weapon, when it is set in opposition to any other.'' And the wizard was looking at him sternly now, as if he might be thinking: *I see I shall have to do more of the mental work in this partnership than I had hoped.*

In fact those identical words were running through Amintor's mind. Well, great skill in magic did not necessarily mean great wisdom, or even an efficient practical intelligence.

The Baron said: "I will not forget it." Then, not wanting to overplay his effort to appear somewhat inferior in intellect, he added: "That is one reason why I never tried to use Farslayer, even as a threat, against the ruling house of Tasavalta, though I consider them my chief enemies. You know, a little old-fashioned blackmail. Dear Princess Kristin, send me ten thousand gold pieces right away, or you'll wake up one morning to find your husband, as he lies beside you in your snug bed, is wearing a new ornament above his heart. Like a half a meter of god-forged blade."

"You were probably right not to make the attempt." Burslem nodded. "Farslayer would very possibly have failed to work against a man with Shieldbreaker in his possession. And, by the way, what was your other reason? You implied that there were two at least."

This time Amintor allowed himself to display an intelligent smile. "I am not a dolt, Burslem. It didn't take me long to realize that Farslayer is not the blackmailer's weapon of choice against any well-loved man who spends most of his time surrounded by his friends. The threat in that case is unlikely to be credible. Of course, for a blackmailer with Shieldbreaker in his possession, matters may be somewhat different—then he can expect any return stroke to be warded off."

The wizard returned the smile. "You might have tried it against someone else, who had not so many friends around him."

The Baron laughed heartily. "I'll certainly never try it against a wizard of your caliber, either. Though I have turned that idea over in my mind, in reference to a magician or two other than yourself."

"Indeed? Just who are these other wizards, of my caliber?'' It was very hard to tell from Burslem's voice whether he was ready to admit the possibility of the existence of such folk or not.

Amintor shrugged. "To a blade of grass, like myself, all trees look about equally tall."

The other grunted and gave him a long, considering look over the rim of a golden goblet of light, bubbly wine. Then Burslem said: "Now you have both Farslayer and Shieldbreaker in your hands. Are you ready now to attempt to blackmail the house of Tasavalta?"

"I also have a partner now. I must find out what you think of the scheme first."

"That is a good answer," said Burslem, leaning forward, setting down his wine. "And there remains Woundhealer to be considered. And other things . . . Let me tell you of my own most recent contact with the house of Tasavalta. I, too, thought that I had a kidnapping arranged, a number of most valuable hostages in my grasp. And my plans, too, were unexpectedly upset."

"Tell me," said Amintor with genuine surprise.

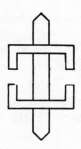

CHAPTER 18

FOR several days now the Tasavaltan party had remained camped in the same spot. Mark was struggling with himself, unable to bring himself to give the order to begin the long march back to Tasavalta.

As he saw it, his only other choice besides starting for home at once was to pursue Amintor again. But neither could he bring himself to order his people to fight against the Sword of Force. Especially not after he, the Prince, had traded it away.

An alternative would be for him to pursue Amintor alone, leaving it to Ben and the rest of the escort to see Prince Adrian safely home. It would be easy for Mark, in a way, to run off after Amintor and postpone the full acceptance of responsibility for what he had done.

But two things held Mark back from any pursuit of the Baron. The first was uncertainty. Was the Sword's failure to heal Adrian somehow a result of something Amintor had done, deliberately or not? The Prince could not be sure of that. The second difficulty was that Mark knew he was needed at home—the birds had brought him word that Zoltan was missing, and there would be other problems demanding his attention.

The Prince could not make up his mind. Never before had

he known the power of any Sword to fail when called upon under the appropriate conditions. There were moments when he was convinced that the Baron had somehow cheated him deliberately, had done something to the Sword that rendered it powerless to help Adrian—or else had created some magical imitation of the Sword and traded that to Mark. The Prince had seen a similar trick performed once in the past.

But all of the magicians in Mark's party had examined the Sword in his possession, and all of them had testified that it was genuine.

Most convincing of all, the Sword with the white hand on its hilt could work its healing magic as powerfully as ever upon the wounded in his camp. Except for its failure to help his son, there was no reason to doubt that it was genuine.

But Mark could not fathom the meaning of that one exception.

Anyway, Amintor was no magician, nor was a bandit leader likely to have a great enchanter in his employ. And why, supposing the Baron had the power to do so, should he have directed such an effort against Adrian? As far as Mark knew, the pointless infliction of pain had never been one of the Baron's traits. He had no objection to the happiness of other people—as long as they did not dare to deny him anything he wanted.

The fact was undeniable: the Sword of Mercy could cure the hurts of everyone except Adrian.

Why?

Could its magic be somehow blocked by the only equally powerful force Mark knew of, that of another Sword? He could not see how.

Or might there be some other source of power that was even stronger than the Swords?

Whatever the answer, he could not sit here indefinitely in

the middle of nowhere, bemoaning his fate. Mark at last, reluctantly, gave the order to start for home.

But scarcely had the march begun when a group of riders came in sight, approaching from dead ahead. There were three white-robed figures in the group, and when they had come closer Mark could be sure that they were priests of Ardneh. At least one of them was of high rank, to judge from the way the others deferred to him. These were accompanied by half a dozen armed servants and attendants.

Mark called a halt and exchanged greetings with the priests of Ardneh. A conference began, and all of the White Temple people were overjoyed to learn that the Prince had indeed been able to retrieve Woundhealer.

"We will erect a statue and a shrine in your honor, great Prince, above the new repository where we keep the Sword."

Mark gave the speaker back a black look in return. "You may erect my statue if you like. But there will be no such repository."

The others gazed at him mystified.

"I mean I am not going to return the Sword into your care. I am taking it home with me to Sarykam."

The ones in white robes were aghast. "It is ours, Prince; it was stolen from us. What can we do to persuade you to give it back?"

"You can heal my son."

"The Sword cannot heal him?"

"Can you? With the Sword or without it?"

The priests looked at one another. "We will do what we can," the leader announced.

Ordering their servants to establish camp, they set up a tent and brought the patient into it. After a lengthy examination, the white-robes declared that they could do nothing for him. They were as mystified as Mark by the Sword's failure.

One of the priests offered the opinion that Adrian's condition might be the result of some punishment inflicted by Ardneh himself.

It was not a wise thing to say. The Prince was enraged.

"And you want me to return the Sword to you? What for? So that the next bandit gang that comes along can take it away from you again and sell it to the highest bidder? Then you can all weep and wail some more and accuse me of not being there to defend you. And accuse this child of having offended the kind gods . . . I want to hear no more of gods, or of you, either. Get yourselves out of my sight."

"But, our Sword . . ."

"It belongs to me now, if it belongs to anyone. And it can cure just as many folk in Tasavalta as it can in your oasis in the middle of nowhere. More, for we'll retain it."

The priests of the White Temple were accustomed to courtesy, if not respect, from almost everyone whom they encountered. This outburst surprised and offended them. But, observing the black expression of the Prince, they withdrew with no further protests.

Hardly had the Tasavaltans resumed their progress toward home when a handful of lame and diseased folk, having materialized seemingly from nowhere out of the barren landscape, appeared in the path of the column. These approached the Prince, crowding around his riding-beast, pleading to be allowed to benefit from Woundhealer's power. Somehow they had already learned that it was in his hands.

Mark called a halt again and gave orders to the physicians that they should use the Sword to help the sufferers. And all indeed were healed.

Ben, observing the process, commented: "If we stay in one place very long, Prince, we're going to find ourselves surrounded by an army of 'em."

"And if we move, I expect we may find more waiting

wherever we arrive. Well, we'll do the best we can. I'll not deny Woundhealer's help to anyone who asks for it.''

For several days the Tasavaltans' march toward home continued without further incident.

The fundamental question about the Sword's failure would not cease tormenting Mark.

"Why, Ben? Why?"

Neither Ben nor anyone else could answer that.

Ben mumbled and scowled and was glad when he could find some excuse to turn away. The Master of the Beasts turned his head also and scanned the skies, as if suddenly hopeful that one of his missing scouts might yet return. The magicians and the doctors scowled when Mark questioned them yet again, and said as little as they could.

Once, one of the magicians answered: "Perhaps Karel can tell us the answer, Highness, when we are home again.''

And through all the puzzling and the questioning, Adrian lay for the most part wrapped in his own dreams, enfolded in his own blind world. He spoke sometimes to his father, who in turn said nothing to his son of Swords or illness or danger, but tried to tell him that they were going home and cheer him with thoughts of friends and toys and good food waiting there. The condition of the young Prince was apparently no different than it had been before the Sword of Mercy was brought to him. No seizures had assaulted him since then, but often in the past, periods of many days had passed without an attack.

Meanwhile, Shieldbreaker continued to be much in his father's thoughts. Once Mark said to Ben: "Gods and demons, why didn't you bind and gag me before you let me give that Sword away? I think that, after all, the scoundrel's swindled me somehow.''

And Ben could give no answer.

*   *   *

Mark had ridden out a little in advance of the small column, scouting the way ahead. He was gazing into the distance when, quite near, a strange figure appeared to him. It was that of a wizard, a caricature that gabbled a strange childish warning, cautioning him that he ought not to return home yet. He was able to see the figure only indistinctly and could understand only a word or two of what it said.

The Prince was suspicious of this warning and hesitantly decided not to heed it. He reported it to Ben and his own magicians when the others rejoined him, but they could make nothing of it.

"Had you seen this figure anywhere before, sir?"

"I . . . I was about to say no. But yet . . . there was something familiar."

On the next day, a certain man appeared among a group of other feeble travelers intercepting the column. This man was young and would have been robust and active except that he suffered with an infected wound in one arm, which came near to driving him mad with pain. He was also terrified that any ordinary surgeon who treated him was certainly going to amputate his arm.

The fear was well-founded, thought Mark, looking at the injury. But when Woundhealer had rested on the limb for a few moments, the smell of gangrene was gone. A few moments more and the man sat up, flexing his biceps and proclaiming himself ready to draw a sword.

He drew no blade, however, but rather, in the relief of being healed, made a confession.

"I must tell you, Prince—I was one of the bandit band of Amintor who fought against you. I was wounded in the fight on the day that he attempted to kidnap your son."

Mark stared at him, feeling a sullen hatred, knowing that its indulgence would bring him no peace. "Well," he said at last. "That is over. Here you are, and here I am. And my son is as well as he has ever been. Go your way."

"First, Highness, I would pay my debt to you—and also to him, who deserted me on the battlefield and saved himself." And the man spat on the ground.

He went on to relate his knowledge of Amintor's plans, including the time and place for meeting Burslem. This man claimed to have dispatched the flying messengers that carried word between Burslem and the Baron as they planned their meeting.

Mark had learned enough to bring him to the point of a new decision. Ben and the others who had listened to the story agreed that the man was probably telling the truth.

"So, Amintor is taking Shieldbreaker on to Burslem, trying to form a partnership—I'm sure of it now, Ben. The answer to our problem with Woundhealer lies somehow with the Baron . . . that smooth smiling devil has swindled me somehow. I gave him the Sword I promised. Now there's nothing to keep me from taking it away from him again. He has no more than three days' start, on a long journey. With my mount I can catch him before he meets Burslem, since I know now where he's headed."

Someone, one of the mounted troopers spoiling for another fight, let out a whoop of triumph.

But Ben waited soberly for what was coming next.

Mark strode to the tent in which his son was sleeping, put back the flap, and looked inside. "Take him home for me, Ben. I leave you in charge of magicians, doctors, soldiers, everything. Much good have they done me, or Adrian. Take them all, and see that my son gets home to his mother safely."

"Yes, Your Highness. Immediately, sire. And where in all

the hells of the Blue Temple did you say that you were going? I don't think I could have heard it properly.''

"After Amintor.''

"You're going alone? As he goes to meet the great magician?''

"I was alone in giving my Sword away, was I not? If what our informant told us is true, I should be able to overtake the Baron while he is still alone as well.'' Mark went into the tent to speak to his son.

"And what if our informant, as you call him, lied after all?'' Ben's question outside the tent went unanswered.

Inside, the Prince bent over the small pallet. "We'll win out, son. Or we'll lose. But we'll not lose by staying home and waiting for the sky to fall on us. Are you with me? I have the feeling that you're with me.'' And Mark gently squeezed the painfully thin hand and arm that lay within his grip. "Not that you can ride with me. Not yet. Ben will see you safely home. I'll be home when I have Shieldbreaker back.''

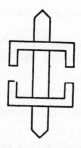

CHAPTER 19

MARK, once he had gripped Ben's hand and had formally left him in command of the Tasavaltan force, did not look back, but completed his hasty preparations and rode out in pursuit of Amintor.

He was barely out of sight of his own column when again he heard a strange, crabbed voice calling him: "Prince! Prince!" But the next words, though conveying a sense of urgency, were garbled.

Mark turned quickly in his saddle and caught a glimpse of the strange little figure, as of a caricature of a wizard. But, as before, he could not get a clear look at it. And in a moment, both voice and image were gone.

Ben, left in command of the Tasavaltan column, angrily issued orders to continue the march home. He disapproved of what Mark was doing now, even as he had disapproved of trading off the Sword of Force in the first place. Of course, he was not the sprout's father, nor was he Prince.

With the column in motion again, he rode along at the head of it, grumping steadily. The other people in the train left him alone as much as possible. It was unusual to see Ben of Purkinje in a foul temper, and it was all the more ominous for that.

He thought he heard a faint cry behind him. Ben turned his mount to ride briefly beside the litter. Pulling aside the canvas cover, he saw that the Princeling's eyes were closed. The small body turned stiffly under a light cover. To Ben, who would have admitted he was no expert, it looked more like restless sleep than a real seizure.

A physician looking over Ben's shoulder sighed. "Should we call a halt, sir?"

Ben frowned at him. "To what purpose? This doesn't look like a fit to me. And what if it were? The child is always having them anyway, isn't he?"

"Frequently, sir."

"And they never kill him. My orders are to get him home. If you think he needs treatment, do what you can for him while we keep moving. Unless you think it essential that we stop?"

"No sir." The man sounded defeated, almost indifferent. Ben would have discharged him in an instant if he'd thought there was a better replacement available. "I have no reason to believe that it's essential."

Without further speech Ben urged his mount to a faster pace, leading the column on.

The next few hours of the journey passed uneventfully. The crying from the litter was not repeated. Then a keen-eyed soldier reported flying creatures in view, approaching from almost directly ahead. The column was alerted; but as the winged forms drew near, it was plain that they were friendly birds. A faint cheer went up from some of the human travelers.

Three of the birds landed at once, perching wearily on the backs of the loadbeasts that now bore the empty protective cages. One of the arrivals was an owl, flying now in daylight with hooded eyes, relying on the guidance of its diurnal escort. Meanwhile the remaining flyers continued to circle powerfully above. Ben, squinting upward, could make them out more clearly now. He had heard the beastmaster back in Sarykam talking about them, but none had been available yet when the column left the city. They were hybrid creatures, bred of owl and hawk and magic. Grown to a size and ferocity beyond those of any other bird, they were intended by the Master of the Beasts in Sarykam to serve as escorts through dangerous air for the smaller though more intelligent messengers. The new hybrid aerial fighters unfortunately did not tolerate burdens well, even the smallest message capsules. Their brains were not well suited for making observations, or at least for relaying them in ways understandable to humans. Nor were their marginal powers of speech good enough to repeat messages accurately.

The packets that the messenger-birds had brought were quickly opened.

The three message packets—all holding the same information, in deliberate redundancy—came from the Princess herself and were addressed to Mark, but under the circumstances Ben made no scruple about opening them.

He skimmed impatiently through the first short paragraph of personal communication. Kristin missed her husband but refrained from actually urging him to hurry home before completing the mission that he had undertaken. All was well at the Palace except that Zoltan was still missing, though his riding-beast had now been found unhurt. The boy's mother was naturally taking it very hard, as was his sister Elinor. The efforts of the search parties continued and were now being directed more to the southwest. It was quite possible that Mark and his escort on their way home might encounter some of the patrols.

That was about it. Ben, seeing no reason not to do so, passed on the messages for others in his party to read. He ordered the resumption of the march while trying to compose in his mind a reply to send the Princess.

*   *   *

Back in the Palace at Sarykam, Princess Kristin was having a difficult interview with General Rostov.

He could report no further success by the parties searching for Zoltan. Except for one detail—the discovery, many kilometers to the southwest of the place where Swordface had been discovered, of the trail of what had to be a great worm. Such a trail was certainly a remarkable phenomenon in itself, in this part of the world particularly, but it was hard to connect directly with any of the strange and tragic events that had prompted the search.

It had to be assumed that Prince Zoltan had somehow come to grief. The one ray of hope was that as yet no ransom demand had been received, from the villain Burslem or anyone else.

Kristin, when her turn came, had some bad news to report to Rostov also.

A few hours ago a messenger-bird had straggled in, bearing word from her husband. The note it carried identified it as the last bird he had available, and she had sent out additional replacements. That was not the bad news.

The bad news in the message was that Shieldbreaker was now in the hands of the former Baron Amintor. And that Woundhealer, though obtained at such a great price, was doing nothing to help Prince Adrian.

Prince Adrian was not foremost in Rostov's thoughts. On hearing of the loss of the Sword of Force, he raged, though out of respect for the Princess he almost managed to keep his anger silent.

Almost. As he stalked off, announcing that he could not delay a minute in starting to adjust the defenses of the realm to take into account this new catastrophe, he muttered something.

The Princess wondered if she could possibly have heard it

right. She summoned Rostov back to repeat what he had just said.

Standing before her again, the General burst out that the Sword of Force, upon which so much depended, had now been simply thrown away.

"You said something more than that, General. I thought I heard the words *high treason*. Is that true?"

"I am sorry, Princess," he muttered hoarsely.

Color flamed in her cheeks. "If it were anyone but you, Rostov . . . understand, once and for all, that I will allow no such muttering in my presence. Especially when my husband is the object of it. If you have anything to say on the subject of treason, it is your duty to say it to me loudly and clearly. Now, have you?"

"No, Madam." He was almost whispering. "I am very sorry that I said what I did."

"You should be. Now off about your duties." She waved a hand in a gesture of unusual violence.

The General was gone in a moment.

She had no more than a few moments to herself before she was informed that the chief wizard Karel wanted to see her. As soon as she was alone with her uncle, he announced his latest discovery: that Burslem and Amintor had now hooked up in an evil partnership.

What made matters even worse, their partnership was somehow related to a third party, the Ancient One, whose presence Karel had warned Kristin about earlier.

Karel was making preparations to dash off to the southwest, in an effort to forestall the enemy's plans against Mark and Adrian—the wizard thought he could now see those plans taking shape.

Kristin's uncle was still with her when the captain of the Palace Guard came to her with a report that a strange reptile had just dropped a note on a high roof of the Palace. The unwelcome beast was now perched arrogantly upon an even higher steeple, as if awaiting a reply.

The Master of the Beasts seemed to consider this invasion a personal affront.

"Shall we have the damned leather-wings down at once, Your Highness?" he asked angrily. "My owls will rend it as soon as night falls. Or I could call upon the captain of the Guard for archers." He did not seem to find this last alternative so pleasing. The hybrid birds that could have destroyed the formidable intruder by daylight were not yet returned from their escort mission to Prince Mark.

"Wait." The Princess, despite her own jumping heart and nerves, managed to be soothing. "If the intruder brought a message, let us first find out what the message says. It is not impossible that there may be some reply." In her own mind she was certain that a ransom demand for Zoltan had arrived at last.

Karel dispatched an assistant to the roof and presently had the message packet in his own hands. After taking all due magical precautions he opened it, and without reading the unfolded paper passed it directly on to the Princess.

Kristin took it, and read:

> Ask your husband, dear lady, what has happened to the Sword Shieldbreaker that was once given into his care.
>
> If he no longer has with him the Sword of Force, then he must begin to 'ware Farslayer's bite.
>
> I will be glad to send you another message, confirming the continued good health of the noble Prince Mark, but such assurances are expensive and difficult to obtain.

Pray enclose with your reply to this two
of the finest pearls for which the treasury
of the house of Tasavalta is so justly fa-
mous. Such a present will ensure that your
written answer is accorded the close attention that it will undoubtedly deserve.

Amintor

Kristin read the message through twice. She made no
comment, but passed it back to Karel, whose eyebrows went
up as he scanned the neatly lettered lines. Otherwise he
betrayed no surprise.

The Princess's heart rose. All she could think was: *Then
they have captured no one yet. No one. All they can do is
threaten us with Farslayer.*

To her wizard she said: "Catch up with Rostov, who was
just here, and have him read this too. He must know all the
problems that we are facing."

Then she turned her gaze to the Master of the Beasts.
"Meanwhile, spare the leather-wings. Give it some water—it
is only a messenger. I am going to compose an answer for it
to carry back, and I do not want my reply to go astray." She
hesitated. "You may read the message too. There is nothing
in it I want to keep secret."

The two men bowed as the Princess left the room. Then
Karel hastily sent a messenger, on two legs, after Rostov.

Alone in her own suite, Kristin sat at her desk and closed
her eyes for a long moment. Then she took up a pen and a
sheet of her personal notepaper, and wrote:

Amintor—I have learned that you are now
in partnership with one who is, if possible,

more depraved than yourself. It seems to me that only one of you at a time will be able to possess the Sword of Force and benefit from any protective powers that it may possess. Therefore, I think that you and your notorious partner should both beware of sending me, my husband, or any of my friends, the gift of Farslayer, under any circumstances that might cause us to feel unkindly toward either of you.

Kristin, Princess Regnant of Tasavalta

As soon as the ink had dried she carried her reply back into the other room, where the two men were still waiting, and handed it to Karel to read. He scanned it quickly, smiled at Kristin as if he had expected nothing else, and then folded the paper and sealed it with something on his ring. Then he passed it on to the Master of the Beasts to see to its swift dispatch.

Having done all that, Kristin's uncle bowed before her and remained in that somewhat awkward position until she told him brusquely not to be a fool but to stand up and get busy.

The Master of the Beasts, on his way out of the room, paused in the doorway. He was a trustworthy man, but incurably curious.

"My lady," he asked, "is there to be any enclosure with this? Shall I pass the word that you would like the mistress of the treasury to attend you?"

"Don't be absurd," the Princess said, and waved him out.

As soon as the men were all gone, a maid came in and stood waiting for orders. The Princess was standing alone in the middle of the floor and trying to think. She did not want to bother to go to a roof, or a window, just to see the leathery wings climbing like the shadow of death above her Palace.

Instead, announcing that she was tired, she dismissed her maid and went alone to her bedroom, leaving orders that she was not to be disturbed save for the most serious emergency.

Once alone, the Princess cast herself down on her fine bed and wept. It seemed to her that a faint odor of her husband's body still clung to the bedclothes, though they had all been changed several times since his departure. This made her weep the more.

A little later small Stephen, after being put to bed in his own room by a nurse, found his way in, to his mother's side, and tried to comfort her.

Meanwhile Karel was not idle. He confirmed that his messenger had caught up with Rostov. Then he started toward his own rooms in his own high tower, where many tasks awaited him.

Entering the marble-lined, semiprivate corridor that ran the length of the Palace's uppermost full floor, Karel muttered an imprecation under his breath. Someone was waiting to intercept him.

It was Barbara, the diminutive, dark-haired wife of Ben of Purkinje. She was dressed in fine fabrics and jeweled a little beyond the limits of good taste. The wizard groaned silently when he made sure, from her bright, anticipatory gaze, that he was her objective; he simply had too much to do to be bothered with this woman now.

"There you are, sir wizard," she said briskly, putting herself directly in his way. Small she might be, but Barbara was not easily impressed by wizards, or, indeed, by much of anything else. Karel had heard she had been a great hand at twirling a sling in combat when she was younger. Behind her, looking helpless, was a young officer of the Palace Guard charged with keeping these upper corridors clear of those who were not supposed to be here.

Karel nodded sympathetically at the officer, who no doubt lived somewhat in fear of the lady's husband. The wizard prepared to handle this himself.

He cleared his throat impressively, but that was as far as he got. Barbara was not in the least shy about coming out with her problem or the difficulties she had encountered for several days now in trying to see Karel. His underlings always reported that he was too busy, and what was one to do in that case but come in here after him?

"Whatever your problem is, Madam—"

"My little girl. She's afflicted."

"The Palace physicians, Madam, must be available to you. And they—"

"I've tried them. It doesn't seem to fall into their sphere, and besides, I don't think they know the first thing about dealing with children. Despite all the experience they must have had. They listened and looked and threw up their hands. One of them did show a glimmer of intelligence in telling me I ought to consider consulting you. Especially since it seems that you are in some way involved already."

Karel did not rise to that bait. Instead he made a mental note to find out which physician had said that, and arrange some kind of minor revenge as soon as the opportunity arose.

For the present, he gave up. "Very well, then, what is it? As briefly as possible."

Fortunately for his nerves, long-windedness was not really one of Barbara's faults. "My little girl, Beth. She's ten. She was with the other children that day when they were all caught in the cave—"

"Yes, of course. What about her?" Karel could remember the child. He had talked with her, briefly, as he had talked with all the others who had come through that ordeal, not really expecting that he would learn much from them. His expectations in that regard were confirmed. The truth was that Karel did not particularly like children, though on occasion he felt somewhat guilty about his attitude and extended himself to put on a show for them.

"She's been having nightmares ever since that day in the cave. Not just ordinary nightmares."

"Madam, as I'm sure the physicians must have told you, after an experience like that it must be perfectly normal to—"

"Don't waste my time, sir. I'm not here to waste yours. I've been taking care of that child for ten years, and I know what ordinary bad dreams are like. And I know when something out of the ordinary is happening."

The wizard had already started trying to edge his way past the little woman. "I can't spend my time on—"

She maneuvered herself boldly to keep in front of him. "It's the one dream in particular. About a strange-looking little wizard and the commands he seems to be trying to give her. He orders her to tell you about someone riding on a griffin."

"—on children's dreams. If you—" Karel had taken one more ponderous step before his progress slowed to a stop. "On a griffin? What wizard is this?"

"The one who keeps talking to my daughter in her dreams is strange-looking, as I said. She describes him as looking like the painting on the nursery wall, here in the Palace. The one who rides the griffin is more frightening. She can't see him at all well."

Beth's mother, with confidence equal to her determination, had brought her along to the Palace. Zoltan's young sister Elinor had come along too, whether to offer support or receive it. She and her mother were staying at the Palace now, that they might be the first to hear any news of Zoltan that might come in. In a very few minutes, Karel was escorting all three females up into his tower.

Once, on the winding stone stair, Karel stopped so suddenly that he startled all three of his visitors. Confronting the girl Elinor with a fierce glare, he demanded suddenly:

"On the day that you hid in the cave—"

"Yes sir?"

"*Why* did you pick that particular cave in which to hide? I mean, did you think of it, or Zoltan, or what?"

"No sir, it wasn't either of us, really," Elinor decided after a thoughtful pause. "Adrian just kept tugging us along. Not as if he could see, but like there was somewhere he really wanted to go."

"I see," said Karel after a moment. He turned and once more led them up the stairs.

There, a minute or two later, Barbara and Elinor were firmly lodged in an outer room while Beth was privileged to enter a certain chamber that few other human eyes had ever seen. Not that she was aware of the honor; Karel saw to it that there was little or nothing odd in the appearance of the place just now.

He seated her courteously, as if she were an adult visitor, and sat down across from her. "Now then, Beth. Tell me all about the strange dreams that have been bothering you."

Despite Karel's precautions, the sturdy ten-year-old was just a little awed by this place. Certain vibrations could not be quenched. But soon she was talking volubly about the dreams.

"And, you know, he's a funny-looking little old man, and he seems to know me. And he keeps telling me to do things, like tell you about the griffin."

"What about the griffin, exactly?"

"Like someone is riding on it—I don't know, I get scared every time the dream gets that far. This stupid little old man keeps shouting at me, and I don't know what to do." Beth drew a deep breath. It was obviously making her feel better just to have this chance to talk about her problem.

"Do you know what a griffin looks like?"

"I've seen pictures."

"And what does this little old man look like? How do you know that he's a wizard?"

"Well—he just *looks* like one. And I saw him once when I wasn't dreaming." She looked up at Karel with a strange expression. "I thought it was you, sort of. I was really sure that it was you."

"Aha. Why were you sure that it was me?"

"Because you did it for us once before, at Midwinter Festival. You made the funny wizard. It was years ago."

"Ah," said Karel, and closed his eyes. Then he opened them with determination. "Tell me about the day you hid in the cave. What did the funny wizard do then?"

"Oh. The other kids were in the cave already, and Stephen and I were trying to find them—you know, playing hide-and-seek."

"I know the game. I myself was a child once, believe it or not—go on."

"Well, I didn't think we were ever going to find the other kids; there were just too many places to hide. Then this funny-looking little old man popped up, like right out of the rocks on the hillside. He said: 'Go on that way, Beth, Stephen, hurry, hurry.' And it was like he was all excited. And he said: 'Don't tell anybody I told you, I'm not supposed to do this,' or something like that."

"And why didn't you tell me all this before now? That same day, when I was questioning all the children about what had happened?"

"I—I guess I thought then that it was you. Someone said that you were helping us that day. Later, when things got real dangerous. So I thought it was you, earlier. If it wasn't you making the image of the funny wizard, who was it?"

"We will come to that later," said Karel softly. "When I have made sure of a few more things—so, you and Stephen ran on to the cave—very fortunately for you, as matters turned out.''

"Yep.''

"And you found the cave, with the other children already in it, just where the funny-looking old wizard had indicated that you should go.''

"Yes sir.''

Karel sighed. "I think I ought to talk to Stephen, too.''

The conversation was interrupted at this point while Stephen was located, summoned, and reassured.

By now the Princess herself had got wind somehow of what was going on and appeared in Karel's tower, insisting on sitting in on the next round of questioning.

Stephen confirmed Beth's statement, in its essentials.

"Why didn't you tell me, darling?'' the Princess cried.

"I thought the funny wizard winked at me, like to keep a secret. I thought it was part of the magic, not to tell. I thought I couldn't.'' For once the five-year-old looked alarmed.

"It's all right,'' Karel assured him. "All right. But now, now is the time for all of you children to tell us everything else you can remember. I can make it come out all right—I think I can—if you tell me all about it now.''

Beth's ten-year-old brow was creased in a thoughtful frown. "I thought I knew the wizard,'' she said, "because I had seen him before.''

"Where?''

"There's a book, I think,'' she said at last.

The scrolled-up storybook lay on the little bedside table in Adrian's quiet room. Karel held the book up in his two hands and felt of it and looked at it, not only with his two eyes. It had been much used and read and even chewed on, but the linen was strong and durable, and some of his own arts had been invested in the paints. The colors in the painted pictures were still quite strong and clear.

"This is the book?"

"Yes sir."

"Show me the picture."

They found it immediately. The friendly, funny wizard, with some storybook name, helped the children in the story through the jolly adventures that befell them. Beth had read this book when she was smaller, and Stephen read it sometimes now, and Adrian had liked very much to be read to out of it.

The Princess was staring at the worn scroll. "I thought Adrian took that with him. I thought that the maid packed it. But it was probably here, in the bed or somewhere, and didn't show up until they'd left."

She took the book from her uncle's hand and frowned at the pictured wizard. "I've seen that costume before, somewhere. I know, the Winter Festival." And now she stared at Karel.

"That's what I said!" chimed in Beth.

Karel gazed at the picture too. Yes, he remembered now. Years had passed since he'd done anything for the children at the Festival, and this imitation wizard hadn't been a big part of it, even then.

He said: "I'm surprised that you remember that, child. I confess that I'd forgotten all about it myself."

And now Karel was on the verge of beginning to understand.

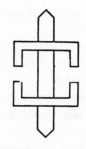

CHAPTER 20

AMINTOR was standing in a tent, trying on his new uniform in front of a mirror. The tent was real enough—or at least he thought it was—but the mirror was certainly not glass, and perhaps it wasn't there at all. Still, he could see himself as if it were. And the splendid new uniform had magic in it too, for it kept changing colors on him, slowly and subtly. Burslem, it seemed, had not yet made up his mind on the proper livery for his army. Right now the Baron was decked out in a plum-colored turban, trousers and boots of ebon black, and a jacket that kept shimmering between crimson and silver.

The uniform looked all right, Amintor supposed, allowing for the chromatic inconsistency, but right now he hardly saw it. His mind was too much absorbed in other matters. The Baron had been forced to put aside, for the time being, the planning and problems involved in attempting to create an army practically from scratch. Burslem was insisting on an immediate advance, and attack in some form, against Tasavalta. They were to march at once, with whatever forces were immediately available.

The wizard had promised to explain his change in plans en route. For the time being, Burslem's three hundred or so armed guards—backed up, of course, by the power of the great worm—were going to have to suffice as an army. It was necessary to move against Tasavalta at once, and Amintor would be told why in good time.

The man who had commanded the three hundred guards until Amintor's arrival, a baby-faced scoundrel named Imamura, was naturally resentful of the Baron, who had appeared as if from nowhere to take over his command. Amintor understood this reaction perfectly, though Imamura did his best to mask it. Accordingly the Baron had done his best to placate his displaced colleague by promising him that he would soon have more people to order about than he had ever dreamt of—and, of course, all the wealth, rank, and privilege that went with such a powerful position as chief of staff of a large army.

But now even that problem was going to have to wait. Somehow, for some reason, they were going to have to move against Tasavalta, leaving at once and doing all their planning en route.

The urgency of Burslem's decision had apparently been increased by an unpleasant discovery he had just made and had related tersely to Amintor: A hostage that the wizard had thought he was holding securely, one of the minor Princes of the Tasavaltan house, had somehow escaped or been set free. That in itself did not seem to the Baron a reasonable cause for panic. Obviously more was going on here than he had been told about, a state of affairs that he intended to rectify as soon as possible.

Amintor had already put forward the suggestion that if for some reason it was really essential to move at once against the Tasavaltans, the wisest idea would be to try to kidnap Prince Mark and his heir, rather than recapturing the hostage who had somehow got away. (And the mere fact of that reported escape preyed upon the Baron's mind as well—had he somehow overestimated the quality of the magical power with which he was making such an effort to ally himself?) It was almost certain that Prince Mark, traveling as he was with an escort including a caravan of baggage, had not yet reached home; though probably the invalid child, having benefited from treatment with the Sword of Mercy, was now riding as robustly as anyone else.

If both Mark and his offspring could be taken and held for ransom, there would probably be little need to do anything else to bring the proud Tasavaltans into the position of a subject state. It was even possible, thought Amintor, that then, with a little face-saving diplomacy, even the Tasavaltan army might become available for certain tasks.

The Baron had already suggested that possibility to Burslem, and it had been moderately well received by the wizard; but in truth Amintor himself had grave doubts about it. He had just received Princess Kristin's answer to his demand for pearls, and that answer had not been at all encouraging. Possibly the lady was even tougher than the Baron had suspected—or maybe she really wanted to get rid of her husband.

He still thought the blackmail scheme had been a worthwhile gamble, but there had been several drawbacks to it from the start, not the least being, as in all extortion, that you had to reveal yourself as an active enemy before you really struck at your victim. And as for the weapon employed, the last line of its verse in the old Song of Swords certainly signaled caution:

> *Farslayer howls across the world*
> *For thy heart, for thy heart*
> *Who hast wronged me!*
> *Vengeance is his who casts the blade*
> *Yet he will in the end no triumph see.*

Other verses of the old song had turned out to have truth in them, all too often for Amintor to feel that the warning in this one could be disregarded. He meant to be very cautious when it came to actually using Farslayer; but he had hoped to profit from the threat.

And then, in these matters there was always the nice question of exactly how much to demand from the victim. Amintor, an experienced hand, was convinced that it was at this stage that many blackmailers went wrong. They asked too much, so that the victim elected a desperate defiance rather than cooperation. And he ought not to have underestimated the Princess Kristin. He had carefully calculated—or miscalculated, as it now appeared—his demand for two pearls. Maybe, he could not help thinking now, if he had asked for only one . . .

Behind the Baron, the flap of his tent was rudely, without warning, jerked open from outside. An image of Burslem's head, swathed in a purple turban, appeared in the magic mirror. "Come!" summoned the wizard's voice imperiously. "We can delay no longer!"

Amintor had thought that he was waiting for Burslem, but he made no argument.

"Very well," he replied, and gave his collar a last tug as if it were indeed his uniform that had been engaging his attention. As he turned away from the mirror he saw from the corner of his eye how it went out, like a blown candle-flame.

Squaring his shoulders, he marched out of the tent after Burslem, to where servants ought to be holding their riding-beasts for them. He—

He stopped and stared.

Forty meters or so ahead of Amintor, the great worm lay quiescent, its mouth closed, eyes half-lidded, enormous chin resting on the ground. A dozen humans, clambering on and around the vast hulk of its body, were attaching what looked like a howdah—a roofed basket big enough to hold five or six people—on the back of what would have been the creature's neck if it had had a real neck. The howdah was ornamented with rich side hangings, now furled out of the way, and it appeared to be stuffed with pillows. Standing on the ground in front of the legless dragon's enormous nose, several minor magicians chanted and spun things before its glassy eyes.

Two more assistants held a ladder and beckoned to the leaders. Burslem was the first to climb into the basket, an honor that the Baron had no intention of disputing.

The worm, carrying the two partners in the howdah on its back, led the procession toward Tasavalta, with the army of three hundred following, and after that a baggage train. As soon as the march got under way, some of Amintor's apprehensions about the worm—though not the worst of them—were confirmed. This despite the fact that, in its regular mode of forward travel, the head and what corresponded to the neck were preserved from the most violent of the side-to-side undulations that propelled the legless body forward.

The howdah, just behind the head, balanced aloof from almost all the lateral vibration. The mass of the body just beneath it poised nearly motionless, armored belly a meter or two off the ground, for a period of several seconds, long enough for a human to draw a breath; then, accelerating fast enough to jerk a rider's head back, it shot straight ahead, more or less, for twenty or thirty meters. After the shudderingly sudden stop, there again ensued a nearly motionless balancing as the twisting body behind caught up. The cycle repeated endlessly.

The motion, and the sense of the earthshaking power latent in the enormous body underneath him, began to make Amintor giddy almost at once. He could easily picture the walls of castles going down before this battering ram beneath him. As always, Shieldbreaker and Farslayer were both riding at his sides. The chance to use both of them, he was sure, would come in time.

Dizziness became transformed into a kind of giddy exaltation. In the silence of his own mind, the Baron cried out: *With wizard, worm, and weapons of the gods, all to do my bidding, who shall stop me?*

Exalting, in a way, the motion of the worm might be, but in practical terms such lurching back and forward made it all but impossible for the passengers to conduct any rational discourse. Accordingly, after a quarter of an hour, the partners called a halt and by mutual consent switched to more conventional transport. Climbing down from the basket, attempting to appear nonchalant, Amintor had the distinct sensation that his guts and possibly his brains as well had been churned into a homogeneous jelly.

Soon the whole column was under way again, the two leaders now mounted on riding-beasts. The monstrous, legless dragon, still of course under Burslem's magical control, propelled itself along in the same direction, on a parallel course some hundred meters distant from the mounted humans. The sound made by the dragon's passage was a continuous, hoarse crashing, a pronounced, slithering roar of displaced rocks and dirt and vegetation.

All human attendants were also keeping themselves at a distance from the leaders. Now at last Burslem could broach the subject he had been unable to discuss coherently in the howdah.

"It comes down to this, Amintor: we are both of us being tested."

"Ah? How so?"

"The failure of your extortionary scheme and the escape of

my hostage render it all the more imperative that we succeed in this, our greater effort. It will not be well for us if we do not succeed.''

''I eagerly await the details.''

''Even as you applied to me for a partnership, so I too applied to one whose power stands above my own.'' Burslem was on the verge of adding something to that, but refrained. His manner was uncharacteristically defensive, even worried; their double failure had affected him even more than Amintor had realized until now. The wizard wiped his forehead nervously. Now it seemed that he had said all that he intended to say.

''What do you mean?'' the Baron asked with what he considered heroic patience. ''You have applied to someone as a partner?''

''I mean just what I say.'' And the magician looked around again, as if he thought they might be followed by someone or something other than his own small army.

This news of another and even more senior partner was startling to the Baron at first. But when he began to think about it, certain matters that previously had puzzled him started to make sense.

''At our first meeting . . .'' he began.

''Yes!'' Burslem examined the sky carefully.

''When I first observed the presence on the high rock, I thought that it was merely one of your—familiars—''

''No!'' Burslem swiveled his head back, glaring. ''That was *he*, sitting on the ledge above our heads.''

''I had thought that—whatever it was up there—was some kind of beast. I thought I saw it fly away.''

''Hush!''

''I only mean—''

''You did see wings, large wings, take to the sky. But let us have no discussion about shapes.''

Amintor remained silent for a few moments, listening to the methodical hoofbeats of the riding-beasts and the serpentine roaring of the dragon's progress at a little distance, scales scouring the land. But it would be too stupid to remain indefinitely in the dark on this subject. There were things he simply had to know.

"I meant no offense," he resumed presently in an apologetic voice, "to whatever—whoever—was up there. But I had the distinct impression that it flew away. I mean, it looked to me just as if—"

"Yes, yes. The—ah—personal configuration of the Master's body has—ah—become unusual. But what you saw—at least *part* of what you saw—was a griffin."

"A griffin."

"Yes. The Master frequently rides on one."

Again the Baron remained silent for a time. The Master, hey? And he had thought that griffins were purely mythological.

Now Burslem peered at him closely, as if aware of his doubts and reading his thoughts. "It would not be wise," the wizard counseled, "for you to inquire too closely into the Master's nature, shape, or other attributes. It is enough for you to know that he exists and that he has triumphed at last over his ancient enemies—even over Ardneh himself. And that we, in partnership with him, may conquer the world."

"Indeed."

"Indeed. And that, if he should decide we are inadequate, he has but to lift his hand to replace us with other partners. In that case, it would be better for us if we had never been born." Burslem choked just a little on that last word, but he got it out with an air of finality. Then he turned his gaze back to the sky.

"I see," said the Baron, and rode through another interval of quiet thought. But when he spoke again it was as firmly as before. "You may believe," he said, "that you have now told me all you want to tell me. But it seems to me that it is not enough.''

''No?'' Burslem, incredulous, frightened, and ready to bluster, glared at him again.

''No.'' Amintor did his best to sound firm and soothing at the same time. ''Look here, if I am to cooperate intelligently, there is more I need to know. Just what is the nature of this person, or power, that we are serving? Just what does he, or it, expect from us? And what can we expect in the way of help in return?'' Amintor's earlier mood of exaltation was rapidly dissolving in the radiance of Burslem's fear. And, even as the Baron spoke, he could feel his resentment continuing to grow, that he had been led into such a relationship with some unknown being, without the consequences of his bargain being explained to him beforehand.

But now Burslem too was growing angry. ''It was you, was it not, who approached me and pressed me for a partnership? You did not demand of me then to know who else might be my ally, nor that all the possible consequences be explained to you ahead of time. Indeed, I would have thought you a madman if you had done so.''

And the Baron, though he scowled darkly as he thought this over, eventually had to admit that it was true enough.

Now again both rode on for a little way in silence. Then Amintor asked: ''But tell me this—is this power you call the Master overseeing us now, this very moment? Is he somehow listening to our every word?''

''To the best of my knowledge, no, there is no such program of surveillance. The Master has many other matters to occupy his time.''

''Such as what? Or is that too impertinent a question?''

Burslem was dourly silent.

''All right, then, I withdraw it. I am a reasonable man and do not pry unnecessarily. But, if I am to cooperate intelligently with the Master's plans, and yours, I must have a better notion than I do now of what is going on. To begin with, where is our Master now, and what is his chief strategic objective?''

The wizard heaved a sigh. ''I believe that he is somewhere far to the southwest of here. Even, perhaps, at the far edge of the continent, ten thousand kilometers away.''

''Ten thousand!''

''But one who rides on a griffin can be here and there in a matter of only hours.''

''Really,'' said Amintor. ''What does he—'' Suddenly he frowned and nodded past his companion. ''And where is the great worm going now?'' The gigantic creature had suddenly taken a diverging course, bearing more to the south.

Burslem looked too, and altered his own course accordingly, waving a signal to his army to do likewise. ''We must keep close to the worm now. It possesses certain senses that will be of great help in locating our objective.''

Then he turned in his saddle to glare at Amintor again. ''As to what the Master requires of us, all I know with any certainty is what you have already heard: we are to proceed against Tasavalta. The method is up to us, so long as our efforts are forceful enough to distract the rulers of that land, keep them from undertaking any adventures elsewhere. Bringing the house of Tasavalta into complete submission would be ideal, but it is not essential. For some reason it is of great importance to the Master that someone or something connected with that land be neutralized, prevented from interfering with his own plans elsewhere. Also, there is one of the Swords that he particularly desires to have.''

''Not one of mine, I take it.'' If that were the case, the Baron assumed that an effort would have been made to get it from him already.

''No, nor one of Prince Mark's either. The Master is

especially interested in the Mindsword, of which both you and I, I think, have had some experience in the past. I take it you have no clue as to its present location?''

"No, none," Amintor murmured abstractedly.

"You and I, to be sure," said Burslem, "play a secondary role in the Master's designs. But if we do well, greater things will be entrusted to us."

"I see," said the Baron again.

"As to what help we can expect from the Master against Tasavalta, I should say that, for the moment at least, the answer is: very little."

"Hah."

The wizard looked at Amintor severely. "I know more than I have told you, but at the moment I am not at liberty to share my knowledge. I would remind you, however, that as between the two of us, I am the senior partner. Let it suffice for you that I am satisfied."

"You are the senior partner," agreed Amintor meekly. "And if you are satisfied with our arrangements with this one who is called the Master, I should be foolish to proclaim myself discontented."

"Exactly." Burslem, grimly satisfied at having made his point, sat back in his saddle. In his mind's eye he could see himself hauling Shieldbreaker out of its scabbard and riding away, letting those who wanted to stop him try it, washing his hands of the whole business. But he wasn't sure what such a move would accomplish for him, except that it would certainly make enemies of two very accomplished wizards.

And, there was the worm. How fast could it move? If Burslem sent it after him, perhaps it would catch him and gobble him up, along with his two Swords and his riding-beast to add a little body to the snack.

Amintor rode on in silence. Since his first meeting with Burslem, he had been confident of his ability to manage the magician. But the mysterious Master added new dimensions. An ancient foe of Ardneh, still alive? Amintor did not believe all that he had just been told.

But the complications were growing. He was getting in deeper, but this wasn't the time to break away. It would have to be sometime when the worm was distant, if he decided to break away at all.

Under the edge of his new turban he could feel his forehead sweating.

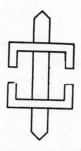

CHAPTER 21

ZOLTAN sat his loadbeast, looking down on something totally unexpected, in the shape of a mighty cruciform scarring of the earth. He had come to a place where the trail of the great worm intersected itself.

There was no other way to read the sign, no doubt that that was what had happened. It was plain also that the new segment of the trail was much fresher than the old one; the loop that the worm had traveled before returning to this spot must have been a lengthy one. Nor was there any difficulty in telling in which direction the new trail led.

He moved first to scout out the area surrounding the intersection. Running parallel with the new trail, at a distance of about a hundred meters from it, was another broad obvious track, this one instantly recognizable if still surprising. It had been left by what Zoltan took to be an entire army—certainly many more riders than were in the Tasavaltan patrols whose signs he had observed much earlier. Nor was the army Tasavaltan. Here and there a clear hoofprint, showing the form of an iron shoe, indicated that very clearly. And a few bits of equipment, worn or broken and cast aside, offered confirmation of this conclusion.

They were headed in the same direction as the great worm in its most recent passage, and certain signs indicated they had passed through here at about the same time. Were they hunting the creature? Or might it have been hunting them? Zoltan's imagination, when he beheld that scoured-out track, could create the image of a monster whose proper prey was armies.

He shuddered a little, despite himself, and regardless of the fact that Dragonslicer hung at his side.

All he could do was continue what he had started, the job of following the monster's trail; if there was an enemy army ahead of him as well, he would just have to do his best to avoid it. He moved now with a new urgency and a new alertness, for neither monstrous creature nor enemy army could now be much more than a day ahead of him, and might be considerably less. The signs in both cases were unmistakable.

And both army and worm were headed east, in the general direction of Tasavalta.

Praying for some kind of guidance, Zoltan forged on.

Ben and the small column of the command that had been entrusted to him were moving in the same direction, toward Sarykam and home. Ben was not praying for guidance, but muttering oaths under his breath as he listened uncomfortably to the blind Princeling's babble from inside the nearby litter. Today the mad crooning and muttering was almost continuous. At least the child did not sound as if he were suffering. Crazy, maybe, but not in pain.

Partly with the goal of avoiding that sound for a time, partly out of general impatience, Ben spoke a word to the cavalry officer, who was now his second in command, and then cantered on ahead of the column, taking a turn at scouting.

A few minutes later, while trying to discover the best way through a large outcropping of rocks, he was distracted by a sudden jumping of the land beneath his feet. It felt to him like an earthquake, or the sudden manifestation of an elemental.

In another moment Ben was confronted by the bizarre figure of a small wizard wearing a strange robe covered with symbols of obscure meaning.

This apparition, crouched among the jumbled rocks, waved to Ben and shouted at him: "Go and find Prince Mark! Hurry! Prince Mark is in trouble and he needs your help."

Ben turned his mount around. The image he was looking at was obviously just that and not an ordinary human being. He judged that the only way to deal intelligently with it was to get magical assistance.

As soon as he had turned his mount, the ground beneath the hooves of the riding-beast shifted back again, so he was left facing the same way as before.

The strange magician-figure, in front of him again, cried out: "Don't run away, Ben! Listen to me!"

"I have my orders," Ben managed to get out, and tried once more to turn his steed.

But he had to listen to more shouted pleadings before he was allowed to leave.

When Zoltan saw that the fresh trail he was now following was bringing him back to the river—or *some* river—once again, his spirits rose as before. He was looking forward to possibly encountering the mermaid again.

The trail was going upstream now, along what looked like the same river he had followed downstream only a few days earlier. He wondered if something out of the ordinary could be happening to the geography of the land through which he traveled.

At least it did make sense that the dragon should need the river, as the maid had told him. Here was another indication, a place where the beast had obviously tried to submerge itself, to wallow in the stream, though the channel here must actually be smaller than the diameter of its own body. Both banks and the vegetation on them were spattered and coated with dried mud for many meters, and a small pool had been scraped and scoured into a pond.

The thrown-out mud looked dry. But when Zoltan probed at a thick clot of it with his fingers, the center was still moist. Certainly not very many hours could have gone by since the creature passed here.

The Sword at Zoltan's side remained quiet as he crumbled the dried mud between his fingers.

He had no more idea now than when he had left the farm, of where his uncle Mark might be. The idea was beginning to grow on Zoltan that he might be the one who had to wield the Sword of Heroes when the time came. He could neither accept the idea nor reject it. It was just there, like a boulder in his mind.

Doggedly he stayed with the trail until nightfall, doing his best to overtake the thing that had made it.

A few hours before sunset he came to a place where at last the parallel trail of the human riders diverged from that of the dragon. And here the mounted force had split into two unequal groups, which had then ridden off in different directions.

Now there were three diverging trails. Zoltan stayed with that of the great worm.

After dark he once more made his fireless camp beside the stream. And once more, to his joy, the maid appeared, popping up briskly out of the water shortly after he had wrapped himself in his blankets and lain down.

"I was afraid to show myself during the day," she began calmly. "The leather-wings might have seen me again."

"I have seen none of them," said Zoltan.

"That is good. You know, don't you, that the dragon is

not far away now? Under water I can hear him burbling and splashing. I think he is resting right in the river somewhere.''

Zoltan swallowed, with difficulty. ''Does it ever move around at night?''

''Oh yes. Sometimes . . . listen! It may be that you will be able to hear it moving now.''

He concentrated, listening intently. There was the sound of the river itself, and he could not be sure of anything else.

The maid asked him: ''Where is your uncle?''

Zoltan shook his head. ''I still don't know. I have no more idea than I did before.''

''What are you going to do, then?''

''I don't know that, either. Except that I must keep on following the dragon. Once I get within sight of it, keep it in sight. And, when Uncle Mark shows up, give him the Sword.''

''You will not try to use the Sword yourself?''

''Not if I can help it,'' said Zoltan after a pause. ''He's— he's much better at it than I am. He's done it before.''

''I will weep for you,'' the maid breathed, ''if you are killed.''

He didn't know what to say to that.

In the morning Zoltan started before dawn; there was no need for a great deal of light to follow a trail like this one. He came in sight of the dragon's tail as it was heading out of a huge thicket.

In the growing daylight he recognized the farm ahead, its distinctive boundary of trees no more than a kilometer away. And he saw that the dragon was now heading directly for it.

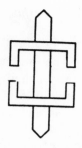

CHAPTER 22

BURSLEM, after much heavy conjuring in the firelight of their nightly camp, announced to Amintor that the time had come for them to split up their forces.

"Is it permitted to ask why?"

"Prince Mark and his child are both within our reach, but they have separated. The Prince himself is now coming toward us again, either alone or with a very small escort; while the child is being taken on toward Tasavalta. If you, with a small squad of cavalry, can intercept and capture Prince Mark, I, with the remainder of my army, will overtake the force escorting Adrian."

"Where is the Sword of Mercy now?"

"Mark does not have it."

"Ah. And why this particular division of labor?"

"Because, my friend, you are the one equipped with Swords and should not need an army to protect you against one man—and I feel more comfortable with most of my army where I can see it. Would you like to exchange assignments?"

Amintor thought it over. "No," he said presently. "No, if matters are as you say, I can take him prisoner. What of the worm?"

Burslem demonstrated anger. "Some kind of magical interference has come up. It's interfered with my control."

"Karel, perhaps, is striking at us?"

"I suppose so. At any rate, we can't count on the worm just now. Neither can the enemy properly control it, of course; and I expect it'll give them something to think about besides us as it goes ravaging their countryside."

"You've lost control of it?"

"I've said that, haven't I?"

The Baron stared at him. "What if the demon-damned beast had got away from you while we were riding it?"

Burslem glared back. "I had it more directly in my grip then—anyway, nothing happened. You have your orders. Carry them out."

Zoltan, meanwhile, was doing the best he could to get himself and Dragonslicer in front of the great worm and to keep the creature from getting at the farm. There was no mistake; it was the same farm; he could recognize the gate and certain trees of the boundary, even at this distance. But even as he tried to get his loadbeast to gallop, he was confused by the fact that the farm did not seem to be at all in the same place, geographically, where he remembered it as being. He had ridden for days away from it, and here he was already back again. He had not, he was sure, been traveling in a great circle ever since he left. That would have been too elementary an error. Yet there they were, the boundary hedge and gate, just as before . . .

But now, they lay directly in the dragon's path.

The monster, fortunately for Zoltan's plans, was in no great hurry. If it was yet aware of him and his loadbeast, it was so far willing to ignore their presence. It let him get himself and his beast in front of it.

Once having reached the position he wanted, he dismounted and paused to let his loadbeast rest and to await the thing's advance. Zoltan could still nurse a hope that the dragon might, after all, decide to go off somewhere else, avoiding the farm altogether.

Meanwhile, the monster was moving only intermittently, and he had a little time available. Enough to open the medical kit that was still tied to his belt and extract from it a certain glass bottle that he had noticed earlier. This one was labeled AGAINST THE HARM OF FIRE AND ACID. Dragons, according to everything that Zoltan had ever been told about them, had plenty of both those powers with which to assail their opponents.

He smeared himself—face, hands, then as much of his skin inside his clothing as he could cover—with the vile-smelling stuff of the bottle, using the entire contents. Only then did he wonder if he ought to have saved some to give to his uncle. Well, it was too late now.

The dragon had been moving again, and now it reared its head over the small rise just in front of Zoltan, not fifty meters from him. There was no doubt that it saw him now.

The immediate effect was that the loadbeast panicked and threw Zoltan off just as he was trying to leap back into the saddle and before he really had time to panic, himself. Furious anger rose up in him and for the moment drove out fear. Dragonslicer was humming in his hands now, the full undeniable power of a Sword at last manifesting itself for him.

The monstrous head confronting him raised itself, eyes staring intently—then lurched away, angling to one side at the speed of a runaway racer. It was as if the demonstration of power in the Sword had been enough to warn the creature off.

The dragon changed its course slightly again. It was still headed for the farm, but it was going to detour around Zoltan to get there.

Zoltan stood frozen for another moment, watching—then

he looked for his mount. But the treacherous loadbeast had run away.

He chased it and was able to catch it—the animal would exert itself fully, it appeared, only when the dragon was coming directly at it.

Back in the saddle, he rode desperately. His mount shied at the last, and he couldn't get close enough to the worm to strike. Quickly he leaped from the saddle and ran forward desperately.

The monster was almost past him now—but he managed to reach one flank of it, back near the tail, and there he hacked into it boldly with his humming Sword.

Amintor had been provided by Burslem with good directions as to exactly where to find Prince Mark. Now the Baron, with Shieldbreaker and Farslayer as usual at his side, and what he trusted were a dozen good cavalrymen at his back, was very near the calculated point of interception. Given the force at Amintor's disposal, it seemed to him very unlikely that he could fail to take the Prince, most probably alive rather than dead; but he was wary of Mark's ability, and of the unfathomed powers of the Sword of Mercy as well, if the Prince should have that weapon with him.

When Zoltan hewed into the dragon's flank, the blade in his hands parting the armored scales like so many tender leaves, the beast's reaction came fiercely, though somewhat delayed. The vast scaly body looped up over his head and came smashing down, making the earth sound like a drum and knocking Zoltan off his feet with the violence of the shock that shook the ground beneath them. The dragon did not turn or pause to see whether he was dead or not. The spur of Dragonslicer had been enough to send it into flight.

Its first flight was not straight toward the farm, which gave Zoltan time to recover and catch his loadbeast again.

Mounted again, he was once more able to get between the indirectly advancing dragon and the farm. The loadbeast was not unwilling to be ridden in the dragon's general direction, or at least no more unwilling to carry him that way than any other. Only when Zoltan tried to get it to go within what it considered actual striking distance did it rebel.

The dragon now had reached yet another of the river's pools, and halted there. Zoltan could hear it drinking and saw it twisting the forward portion of its snakelike body in an apparent effort to splash cooling water on its sun-heated upper scales.

Zoltan urged his mount as best he could to get in front of the dragon. It was here or nowhere that he must stop the beast; he was now almost within a stone's throw of the farm at his back.

He jumped from the saddle, Sword in hand.

Now he saw that, whether by accident or design, a bight of the huge scaly body had been thrown across the stream, making a crude dam. A deeper pool than before was rapidly forming upstream from this obstruction, and now the dragon's head was lowering toward the pool to drink.

I will kill it now, thought Zoltan, or I will never kill it.

Raising the humming Sword above his head, he ran silently toward the drinking beast.

Dragonslicer, Dragonslicer, how d'you slay?
Reaching for the heart in behind the scales.
Dragonslicer, Dragonslicer, where do you stay?
In the belly of the giant that my blade impales.

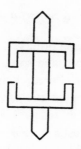

CHAPTER 23

THE Baron was belly-down in the desert, watching from concealment Prince Mark's slow mounted approach. The Prince, as Burslem had predicted, was quite alone. Behind Amintor, the dozen troopers who had been detailed to go with him were presumably making their own preparations to carry out the ambush. The riding-beasts of Amintor and his party were in concealment too, being well-trained cavalry mounts that would lie down and jump up on command.

The Baron turned his head partway in the direction of his men, and whispered softly: "Let him ride right into us, if he will . . . save us the trouble of a chase. That's a powerful mount he rides."

Then Amintor, his attention caught by some sound or perhaps unwonted silence among his men, turned to observe them more carefully. He saw them all in the act of divesting themselves of their weapons.

In the blink of an eye he was on his feet, with a Sword out in each hand. He had thought ahead of time about the possibility of some such move as this. Prince Mark could wait.

Shieldbreaker, because it could be relied upon to manage itself in a fight, was in the Baron's left hand. And Farslayer, in his right fist, was ready to exert its magic too—if any such magic should become necessary beyond that of sharp steel and skill.

The lieutenant gave terse orders, and a few of the troopers, some brandishing weapons and some not, tried to close in on Amintor. The Sword of Force, hammering loudly, picked out their weapons as they came against it, and disposed of them, along with a limb or two. And Farslayer, working superbly if in mundane fashion, took care of those who tried to attack Amintor unarmed.

Half a minute after it had started, the fight had reached a bloody standoff. Three men were down, dead or bleeding to death rapidly. Amintor could not chase down all his enemies, nor did he dare relax his vigilance. But there appeared to be no way for the surviving troopers to overcome him.

The officer changed his tactics and tried negotiation. He called to the Baron: "Our master Burslem says if you give up the Swords, we are to let you go."

"Yes, of course. To be sure. And what has he promised you and your men?"

No one answered.

"Whatever it is, I can give you more. And I will do so if you, or any of you, will switch your allegiance to me."

Refusal was plain in the officer's face. Mixed emotions, with fear and doubt predominating, ruled in the faces of the other men.

The Baron looked them all over as well as he could. Then he picked out one of them and locked his gaze on the man's eyes. "Sergeant? What about you, ready to join me? Or are you determined to collect one of these god-forged blades of mine in your guts?" The Baron paused, then once more addressed them all. "I repeat, those who are loyal to me are well rewarded. Not like these three on the ground. If any of you know anyone who served in my army under Queen Yambu, you know I speak the truth."

He got no immediate response, but now the officer was worried. The situation, balanced.

When the break came, Amintor was almost as much surprised as the lieutenant was. The sergeant approached the officer as if for a private conference—and then struck at him without warning. The officer managed to parry most of the force of the swordcut, sustaining only a light wound, and in the next instant striking back. In the next instant a bloody melee had broken out, the troopers in two opposing factions hacking and slashing at each other energetically.

In a matter of only moments, the lieutenant and a few who remained with him retreated. First one group and then another reached the riding-beasts, and in a few moments more the fight, now a small cavalry skirmish, had swirled over the next dune.

Discipline, thought Amintor, could never have been good in Burslem's little army—and now, doubtless, it was never going to be.

"After them! Finish them!" he shouted orders after his new allies.

Now the thudding noise in Shieldbreaker quieted and Amintor was able to sheathe the Sword again. His whole left arm felt strange from holding it, but he was confident that the sensation would soon pass.

And now, with distractions out of the way momentarily, for the Prince. Quickly Amintor looked back in the other direction. There was Mark, a hundred meters or more away, evidently out of earshot of the noise of fighting. Mark was upwind, which would have muffled the noises somewhat. The Prince had dismounted, as if he meant to camp for the night, though nightfall was still hours away. No, now he was tugging at one of the legs of his mount. It looked like there was some trouble with his riding-beast's hooves or shoes.

Amintor, studying the figure of the Prince as well as he could at the distance, frowned as he observed that Mark was apparently unarmed. Oh, there might be a knife at his belt. Doubtless there would be a weapon or two somewhere, but . . .

Burslem had said that Woundhealer was now with the caravan escorting Adrian, and doubtless that was the case.

Now, the Baron judged, was the time for him to act boldly, before his own treacherous escort, or any part of it, could reappear. He rose partially from concealment and hurried forward, alternately trotting and crawling. For the moment he preferred to leave his own mount behind, so he could get closer without being seen.

When he was about fifteen meters away from the Prince, he stood up straight and called out in a loud voice for Mark to surrender.

Mark jumped to his feet, giving little sign of surprise. Apparently unarmed, he stood silently facing Amintor.

Shieldbreaker was thudding faintly again, and the Sword's hilt stung the Baron's wrist as his arm swung past the scabbard; he feared that the weapon was going to leap out into his hand. Let him once grasp the hilt of the Sword of Force now, and he would be unable to cast it down whatever Mark might do. And Shieldbreaker would never be effective against an unarmed man. To be safe, Amintor unbuckled the belt that held the Sword of Force at his side, and let belt and all fall to the sand.

Next the Baron drew Farslayer—obedient, controllable Farslayer—and smiled. He advanced upon his foe.

Mark waited until Amintor was quite near him. Then the Prince bent swiftly, plunging his arms into the sand at his feet. When his hands emerged, they were holding the hilt of a bright Sword.

Amintor assumed the weapon was Woundhealer, though there was no way he could be absolutely sure. Damn Burslem for an incompetent wizard!

"I suppose there is some logic in your behavior," he remarked, doing his best to conceal his rage.

"As much as in yours, I suppose. The next time you try to set an ambush, you should bring quieter companions."

The Baron glanced back over one shoulder, directing a contemptuous look in the direction of his vanished patrol. "Your advice is good, Highness—had you no trustworthy friends either, that you come seeking me alone? Or is it some other object that brings you here like this? I cannot think why you would want to encounter me again."

"Can you not?"

"No."

"Then tell me, bandit chieftain, how you worked your trick." Mark's own quiet rage could be heard in his voice.

"Bandit chieftain!" The Baron genuinely felt offended. "Come, Prince, you should know by now that I have advanced a step or two beyond that status."

"Really? You have acquired fine new clothing since I saw you last, I see that much."

Amintor frowned. He still did not understand Mark's presence here, and it bothered him that he did not. "Which trick do you mean?" he called to Mark. "It must have been a good one if it has brought you here seeking me with such determination."

The Prince, his face quite unreadable, stared back at him for a long, silent moment. At last Mark said: "The Sword of Healing will not heal my son."

"Ahh." Amintor let out a long, soft breath. Then he added, more to himself than to Mark: "Then it may be, after all, that there are powers in the world that can overmatch the Swords." It was not a reassuring thought for one who was relying upon Shieldbreaker against tremendous wizards.

"I have no explanation," the Baron continued aloud, after a moment's thought. "But then, I gave you no guarantees when I traded you that Sword. No, Prince, I worked no trick upon you in that way. There would have been no point in my doing so. I was content to see you go your way in peace—of course, now that you are here—''

The Baron had weighed the probabilities as best he could. Now he raised Farslayer and rushed in to strike. His object was not to kill but to disable, and he had little fear that Woundhealer would be able to do him any direct harm. Anything was possible, but a man had to be ready to take some risks.

But Mark, younger and more agile, evaded the rush. Then, running to get past his opponent, he dashed toward the spot where Amintor had cast Shieldbreaker down.

The Baron had not been careless, and had not let himself be drawn too far from where he had dropped that most effective Sword. In fact he had even begun to count, in a way, on Mark's trying to get to it. Still, it was a near thing. Amintor, hurrying back to defend his treasure, had to lunge desperately with Farslayer at the last moment to keep Mark from getting his hands on the Sword of Force. Mark nearly lost a hand in reaching to grab it up but managed to pull his arm out of the way of the slash in time, and danced away unhurt.

Still, Amintor did not want to pick up Shieldbreaker and bind himself to it indissolubly for the duration of the combat. Farslayer would do just as well for now. Holding the Sword of Vengeance ready, he slowly advanced once more.

Mark held his ground, waving Woundhealer gently before him in a two-handed grip.

The imponderables brought into the situation by the Sword of Mercy slowed the Baron's feet and stayed his hand. If he were to throw Farslayer against it, what might happen?

Then, behind him, he heard the unmistakable sounds of several riding-beasts approaching, at a slow pace.

He backed away from Mark until he felt he could risk a turn-and-look. Then he allowed himself to relax slightly; it was the sergeant and three of the men who had been with him. One of them at least was wounded, pale and swaying in the saddle.

The sergeant, after pausing to take in the situation, spoke. "The lieutenant"—he paused to spit—"and those who followed him are dead, Sir Baron."

"Good," said Amintor, breathing heavily. "Now we have another problem here."

"Indeed we have, sir. Though perhaps it is not the one you think."

Careful to keep Mark in one corner of his field of vision, the Baron turned again and regarded the sergeant silently.

"Colonel Chou, at your service," said the mounted man with stripes on his sleeve. "I am, I may say, a trusted friend and adviser of the Magister Burslem. At the moment I am charged with collecting all the Swords for him—the late lieutenant was to undertake the same task for our former commander, Imamura, but he, as you can see, has failed. I shall not fail. Both of you, put down your Swords, please. The Sword that would help you now is at the moment out of reach of either of you, I see."

Amintor, with his eye on the speaker's midsection some thirty meters away, began to swing Farslayer in an arc. It was a certain killer, having the serious disadvantage that with one use of its power it was gone. Once the erstwhile sergeant was dead he would have to deal with the other people somehow—

Only too late did the Baron see the practiced motion of the slinger's arm on the mount beside the newly self-proclaimed colonel. With a shock of mind-splitting pain the smooth stone struck the Baron on his left leg, near the knee. He went down before the impact, as if the leg had been taken off completely. The world was a mosaic of red and black before him.

Yet he would not, could not, give up. Farslayer was gone, out of reach somewhere, fallen from his grasp before it could be launched. He crawled forward, dragging himself by his hands toward Shieldbreaker—

But at the same time the former sergeant was galloping forward like a trick rider, reaching down from his saddle to grab up the Sword—

The shaft of a small arrow sprouted from the rider's turban, and he fell from his saddle, rolling inertly toward the prize. His riderless animal swerved away.

Amintor groaned, heaving with his arms to drag himself forward toward the treasure. But now he could not move. His broken leg was caught, snared in some trivial trap of desert vegetation. When he tried to move, he blacked out momentarily with the pain. He drew breath, then let out a piercing whistle, calling his war mount. In the background he could see Mark raising Woundhealer, sparring with one of the mounted troopers. The trooper was hesitating to close against the unknown Sword, but still he managed to block Mark's path toward the greater prize.

And, beyond that, on the crest of a small rise, was a huge mounted figure Amintor could recognize as that of Ben of Purkinje. A figure now cocking a crossbow, with a single simple motion of arms so thick that they made the weapon look like a child's toy.

And Amintor still could not move forward—

He looked back, then centimetered himself backward on hands and belly and the one leg that worked. Farslayer's dark hilt came again within his grip.

He saw Ben shoot a second trooper from the saddle, then duck under the swing of a battle-ax, aimed at him by a third.

Amintor's own specially trained war mount came near enough to brandish its shod hooves defensively above its fallen master— By all the gods, a bit of luck at last! The beast crouched down when Amintor gasped another order at it. It got down low enough for him to hoist himself somehow aboard it, into the saddle.

Mark and Ben between them had now finished off their last opponent. Mark dashed past the Baron and grabbed up Shieldbreaker.

Baron Amintor, sweating and grimacing with the agony of his broken leg, of broken plans and broken life, hauled out Farslayer—he had had to sheathe it to get himself mounted—and began to twirl the Sword over his head.

He had known, for a long time, the proper recitation, and he began it now.

"For thy heart, for thy heart—"

Mark now had Shieldbreaker in hand. Quickly he tossed Woundhealer to Ben, who held it before him like a shield.

"Who hast wronged me—"

The Sword of Vengeance, howling, left Amintor's hands in a streak of rainbow light.

Burslem, consulting certain indications, saw that now, as he had hoped and expected, his magic had completely over-whelmed the small Tasavaltan escort force that had been protecting the Princeling Adrian on his way back to Sarykam.

On separating from Amintor, the wizard had led the bulk of his miniature army to the place where, his magic assured him, Adrian was to be found.

Leaving his troops waiting on a small rise of land nearby, Burslem advanced alone toward the camp of the paralyzed Tasavaltans. His magic was in full control here, and he felt more than adequately protected by it.

Some of the riding-beasts and loadbeasts were on their feet, others lying as if dead or drugged. None of the humans were standing. Some sat on the ground, staring ahead of them with empty eyes as if they were drugged or dead. Others lay at full length, or curled up, eyes closed as if they were only asleep. Some people had been starting to put up a tent when they were overcome, and canvas, attached to a couple of erected poles, flapped idly in a small breeze.

In all that small section of landscape, as Burslem had intended, only one figure moved. He had withheld the full power of his magic from the Princeling himself. Valuable goods should not be damaged unnecessarily.

The child himself, small and golden-haired, had gone a little apart from all the rest to sit right beside the stream. Appearing unperturbed by what had happened to the members of his escort, the boy was dipping a hand into the current and pulling it out, over and over again, letting the water run out of the cup made by his frail fingers. With each trial he watched the result carefully, as if the way in which the drops fell sparkling in the sun might be the most important thing in all creation.

The child turned as Burslem approached, looking up at the wizard with pale blue eyes. At first those eyes stared almost blankly, but then they widened with growing fear.

Burslem, as he took the last few steps, was not even watching the child closely. Instead his thoughts were on Amintor—ought he to have trusted the newly-promoted Colonel Chou to be able to get the Swords from him? Burslem had, or thought he had, a magical hold on Chou that would make rebellion on the colonel's part all but unthinkable—but one could never be perfectly sure of anyone or anything.

But Burslem had been too much afraid of Amintor, and of the Swords, to make the attempt himself. Prince Mark had Woundhealer with him. Let Amintor and him fight it out.

Burslem would be ready to face Swords again when he had his great worm back under control.

And where was the great worm now? Would his inexplicable loss of control over it bring on the Master's serious displeasure? Burslem was in fact looking up and around at the sky again, even as he bent to snatch up the small body of his hostage from the riverbank.

His reaching arms passed through empty air. The ground he walked on had changed beneath him in midstride so that he overbalanced in his movement and nearly fell.

Where was the child?

The sky above Burslem, calm a moment ago, was going mad, as was the land around him. Discolored clouds swirled about the zenith, and the ground heaved underfoot.

Only a moment ago those hills on the horizon had been arranged in a configuration drastically different from the one that they presented now. The land was stretching and recoiling, like fabric stretched upon the earth's tremendous loom, with titans' shuttles plying to and fro beneath.

The boy was gone. The stream at the wizard's feet was boiling coldly, like water in a churn, with clouds like chunks of darkness coming up from it. Chaos, like gas, appeared to be escaping from the tormented surface in great bubbles.

Something stung Burslem in the back; he skipped away from the attack and turned to see how the altered plants of the riverbank were lashing at him with new arms and claws.

Only now, belatedly, did the wizard realize that his own protective powers had been scattered like blown leaves before this change. The soldiers of his army, too, had scattered— he could hear them howling their terror and could see some of them in panic flight, going over the next hill in the altered land, and then the hill after that. This, then, was the vengeance of the Master, Burslem's punishment for some known or unknown sin. It was useless to resist, he knew, but still he had to try, to fight for his survival.

His intended victim had disappeared completely, no doubt preempted in some way by the Ancient One himself. Burslem was standing all alone under a darkling sky, his feet rooted in the middle of an enormous and forbidding plain. The clouds were quiet now, and the river had vanished completely from this odd space that centered itself upon him. Even the distant mountains now seemed to have been ironed away.

The colors and shapes of everything that he could see were changing.

Even if he had somehow displeased his Master, why should punishment be visited upon him only now, when he had at last achieved a measure of success? The wizard could not understand it.

And now, gratefully but incomprehensibly, his scattered powers were coming back to him. Was there hope in resistance, after all? Or had the Master relented?

No. This was not the Master's doing after all. Burslem could achieve no sense that the Ancient One was here at all, or acting here. And the overwhelming magic that had so wrenched out of shape the world around him had no real feeling of art to it at all. It felt like nothing but raw power. Like something born of rage and fear compounded . . .

On only a few occasions in his seven years of life had Prince Adrian sensed the presence of people who truly wished him harm. The presence of other human beings was usually a matter of indifference to him, though there were a few—his parents, a small handful of others—who were almost always welcome.

One instance of terrifying hatred, accompanied by direct violence, stood out sharply in his experience. It had taken place on the day when he and the other children had gone to play in and around the caves. On that day Adrian had been a witness to the slaughter of the soldiers who had been detailed to protect them.

Not that the little Prince had been physically present at that scene of horror, or that he had seen it with his sightless eyes. Rather he had observed and experienced it in the same way that he saw the rest of the world around him: with the inborn vision of a true, natural magician. And even that vision had been blinded for a time by the horror of the killing of the guards. For Adrian that experience had been shattering.

From that moment a profound transformation had begun in Adrian. The first manifestation of it had been his mind's instinctive defense of the cave against the magical, demonic powers assaulting it from outside. After that had come an even deeper withdrawal from the world.

Then the defense of himself and his friends had been resumed in a conscious though indirect way.

Adrian had also been steadily aware that his parents and the other humans with whom he had close contact had also been alarmed and horrified by the ambush, and that they were in some way doing what they could to meet the threat that it represented.

From Adrian's infancy he, like other infants, had been able to sense the feelings of those around him as well as hear their speech. Now, after the shock, he paid more and more attention to their words. Not that they often spoke in his hearing about things of real importance. But more and more the constant threat of physical danger, remote though it was, had turned Adrian away from his lifelong absorption with the magical aspects of the world, had made him reach out beyond the suddenly inadequate perceptions of the world that he could achieve with magic.

The little Prince knew when his father rode off from the train alone, though he did not fully understand the reasons. He missed his father and could follow him, most of the time, with his nonphysical perceptions. In the same way Adrian had a fair grasp of the locations of many other people whom he knew as individuals. And he had already begun to do more than keep track of their whereabouts.

If no one would listen when he tried to tell them things directly, perhaps they would listen to a wizard.

And the elementals, the ones originally aroused by Karel on the day of the children's entrapment in the cave, had not been allowed to meld their energies back into those of the earth itself. Instead, Adrian had discovered how to keep them alive. He had played with them like toys, sending them here and there, augmenting their power and then allowing it to diminish while he tried to decide what else he might be able to do with them. It appeared that they might possibly be a useful means of defense.

And then, at the moment when he belatedly become aware of the presence of Burslem, almost upon him, Adrian had called the elementals back to full life and had concentrated them all close around himself. It was almost a purely instinctive reaction, the only thing that he could think of to do at the moment. Another small child might have hidden his head in his arms, or jumped into the river to get away.

From the day of the alarm at the cave, Adrian had spoken directly to no one else about what he feared, or what he was trying to do. The experience of his life to date was that no one else was really able to communicate with him. His parents tried to do so only through speech, and then almost always spoke only of the simplest things. It was as if they were totally unable to see the world of magic that lay all about them. The physicians who attended Adrian were hopeless, being concerned, as far back as he could remember, with nothing but getting answers to their questions about his body: Had he eaten? Had he slept? Had his bowels moved properly? Did anything hurt him, here, or here, or here? And the magicians, if anything, were even worse. They looked around him, never exactly at him, with their arts; like the physicians, the wizards peered and probed and examined, going about their own preconceived plans as best they could with their limited perceptions.

It was the way the world was.

Adrian had experienced something of a shock when he realized, at a very early age, that the workers in magic, like everyone else he knew, were at least half blind. They seemed almost totally incapable of any real communication with him, even when he sought their aid. And magic, Adrian was beginning to realize now, was not a very good tool of communication anyway. It was much more effective as a means of concealment and manipulation.

The friendly workers in magic who sometimes attended Adrian were often more clever in their manipulations than he had yet learned to be. But in many ways they were also weaker and less able. And Adrian was beginning to realize that often they could not see as well as he could what was happening around them.

The notion of using his physical powers of speech to try to warn them had scarcely crossed Adrian's mind. One difficulty was that few people ever listened to him anyway; another was that most of the people with whom he was suddenly anxious to communicate were now scattered well out of the sound of his voice.

Among the several new needs that he was beginning to feel strongly was a better way to see. He had to establish stronger contact with the perilous world around him in order to find new ways to control it.

Entrancing discoveries rewarded his first real efforts to use his eyes. The new sense could not be quickly perfected, but now, day by day, and even hour by hour, he was making progress in its use.

A time came when Adrian realized that magic from some threatening source had ensorcelled everyone in the caravan around him. The threat was definite, though not yet immediate. He was disturbed enough to get up from his bed and leave his tent. His vision was developing strongly, and for almost the first time in his life he went wandering through the physical world unguided.

He ought to help his friends who had been struck down. But he did not yet see how. Looking, thinking, he allowed himself to be distracted by the glory of the physical, visual world surrounding him. His eyes were focusing properly at last, and his brain had learned to use the signals from them. For almost the first time he was able to see the world in full color and crisp detail. The sound of the stream drew him, and he approached it cautiously. Then the familiar feel of water became attached to the sparkling, never-before-seen dance of droplets in the air.

The magician Burslem had been able to approach very near to Adrian before the young Prince sensed his presence. The perception came in the form of an image of evil magic and threatening physical size, compounded into one.

Shocked into panic, Adrian did what he could to remove himself from the evil presence and to erect barriers between himself and it. He saw with all his senses that the effort had created a perilous turmoil in his immediate surroundings, an upheaval through which he himself was forced to struggle, as through a dream.

And suddenly he was aware of a place, not very far away, where he should go.

Burslem's own powers had recovered in time to protect their master from the shock of this local alteration of the world. The alteration could be undone, and they could undo it for him; only a little time was necessary for the task.

He was just begining to be able to establish some mastery over his environment when a new sound distracted him. His powers were massing on one side of him, laboring there to build the most impenetrable wall of magic that they could create.

The impenetrable wall burst open at its center. Burslem had no time at all in which to hear the howl and only a moment of life remaining in which to see the streak of rainbow color coming straight at him.

CHAPTER 24

A S Zoltan ran toward the great worm and the pool that the creature had created, the head of the monster turned toward him. Then it rose and swung away, avoiding the shrilling Sword that Zoltan held before him as he ran.

Recklessly he ran in under it and hewed again into the gray-green wall of the creature's flank at the first spot he could reach.

Scales the size of flagstones flew left and right. Again the Sword emitted its piercing sound and carved into the worm's integument as if those armored plates were so much butter.

This time Zoltan was closer to the heart and brain, and the reaction of the beast was swifter than before. A vast wounded loop, spraying dark blood, went coiling up, high as a house, to come smashing down again almost on Zoltan's head, with a noise like a falling castle wall. The carvable plates of the scales were suddenly impervious armor once again, so long as they avoided Dragonslicer's gleam. The descending mass crushed into splinters the riverside trees that happened to be beneath it. It shattered sandstone into sand and dust.

Once more, Zoltan narrowly escaped being caught under the falling bulk and flattened.

The upper limbs of one of the flattened trees caught him in

the whiplash of its fall and sent him rolling, bouncing across the ground. He was bruised, scraped, and dazed.

He stumbled to his feet. The Sword had been knocked from his hand. Now it was gone.

There it was, only a few meters away. In a moment he had the hilt of the Sword of Heroes in his grip again.

But by now the dragon was a hundred meters away and receding swiftly to an even greater distance. It was still thrashing like a hooked fishworm and hissing like a windstorm with the pain of what he'd done to it. But it was not about to come back and try to get revenge against the Sword.

Zoltan realized that it was still making headway toward the farm.

He ran to get ahead of the monster again, with Dragonslicer howling in his two-handed grip. The Sword seemed to leap in his fists, as if to urge him on and drag him with it faster.

Momentarily the beast stopped its retreat to turn and raise its wagon-sized head and stare at Zoltan with its enormous eyes. Vague memories of childhood dragon-stories had started to come back to him; now there stirred one of such a story in which these beasts sometimes developed hypnotic powers, feeding themselves by bidding herds march down their throats. The nameless mermaid had mentioned something of the kind.

He felt no compulsion to let the dragon eat him. But now it was moving toward the farm once more, and he wasn't going to be able to catch up with the thing on foot.

Zoltan turned and ran after his loadbeast. It allowed him to catch it once again.

The animal allowed him to mount and ride, and willingly carried him ahead of the monster. He had lost count now of how many times he had overtaken it.

And now, for a second or third time, the dragon got around him. As long as he stayed mounted, his mount panicked at the crucial moment and fled; if he was afoot, he could not go fast enough to keep the thing blocked from its goal. If the dragon had had wit enough to keep moving quickly, it might have easily got around him to the far side of the farm and entered there to begin its devastation before he could catch up with it again. But it had no more wit than an earthworm, as far as Zoltan could tell.

And once it made a short detour, pausing to scoop up the carrion carcass of a feral cow or bull into its mouth.

Taking advantage of the delay, Zoltan was once more able to get directly between the giant creature and the farm. Then he jumped off his mount for the last time, drew Dragonslicer, and quickly cut the loadbeast's throat with the keen blade.

Working feverishly, he opened the loadbeast's belly with the same sharp tool and pulled out the entrails still pulsating and steaming lightly in the chill air.

Then Zoltan worked himself into the dead beast's body cavity, where he lay in gory warmth and darkness, gripping the hilt of Dragonslicer with both hands.

Trying to control his own breathing, he could hear the breathing of the dragon as it approached, perhaps lured on by the odor of fresh blood. Next Zoltan could feel it, feel the earth quivering with the movement of the approaching mass.

His plan had been to jump out at the last instant, when the head was lowering over him, mouth about to open. But it was impossible to time things that exactly. The creature was very near, and for an instant the noises stopped. Zoltan was suddenly afraid that it had sensed the presence of the humming Sword. But his next fear was of something else altogether. In another instant, darkness and swift motion had engulfed the dead loadbeast. It was being swallowed.

The boy could feel the carcass that enclosed him being crunched and ingested by the great worm. The process was tumultuous, almost deafening, the noise a compound of gaspings, crunchings, hissing, and the throbbing of the gigantic internal organs. Accompanying this came a wave of incredible stench, so that Zoltan found it almost impossible to breathe.

The great teeth, actually small for the size of the creature that they fed, hooked the loadbeast's carcass no more than twice as they sent it along into the dragon's gut.

Zoltan struggled to draw breath. Utter darkness had closed around him, and air had been almost entirely cut off. The physical pressure was such that he could hardly straighten his arms or move his elbows. Though Dragonslicer shrilled loudly, he was almost helpless. With wrists and forearms he wielded the blade, and then, with a desperate, surging effort, succeeded in straightening his arms so that the Sword of Heroes thrust out blindly.

The blood of the dragon jetted over him from some deep reservoir. The fumes of blood burned at Zoltan's lungs next time he managed to draw a little breath.

By now he had worked his arms and shoulders free of the loadbeast's carcass and was carving a space clear around his head. There came a whistling roar and a blast of air as he cut into the windpipe. Blood was threatening to drown him anyway. And now Zoltan thought that the blade in his hands was trying to pull him with it in one direction, as if it would lead him toward the heart.

Meanwhile, the titanic body around him was convulsing with redoubled violence. Only the tight, soft cushioning that gripped Zoltan's body on all sides saved him from severe injury.

With his last conscious energy, he strove to hack a way out through his enemy's ribs. In utter darkness he could feel how massive bones were separating before Dragonslicer's magic. He carved and carved again. At last light struck his almost blinded eyes, and again fresh air hit Zoltan, like a rush of icy water. Simultaneously the great worm's body convulsed in a spasm more frenzied than any that had gone before. Still inside the thrashing body, Zoltan could see that the opening he had cut was sometimes toward the sky and sometimes toward the earth.

Mark and Ben found themselves in possession of two Swords, Shieldbreaker and Woundhealer, and of the field of battle.

Amintor, having hurled Farslayer, creating a streak of light that dwindled rapidly toward the horizon to the east, had at once urged his mount to speed and was now rapidly disappearing in the opposite direction.

Neither Mark nor Ben were ready to pursue the Baron at once. Ben had been wounded in the skirmish just concluded, and the use of Woundhealer was the next order of business.

"Why are you here?" Mark demanded. "Where is my son?"

"I'm here to save your neck. Acceptable?"

"Sorry." The Prince drew a deep breath. "But what's happened to Adrian?"

"Happened to him? Nothing. All was well when I left the escort. He's well on his way home, many kilometers from—"

"Then what is *that?*"

Ben turned to look. Then the two men stood together, looking with awe at the bizarre effects that appeared to be transforming a portion of the world before their eyes. It was the same area into which the Sword of Vengeance had vanished when it left the Baron's hands. And on the fringe of it the Tasavaltan camp was visible. At the distance a few people, moving about slowly and lethargically, could be seen within it.

"That cannot be," said Ben. "I left the encampment days ago, to try to follow you."

Mark said, at last: "Reminds me of the time we looted the Blue Temple."

Ben nodded. "We seem to have entered a land of magic again—and this time without a wizard."

"I don't know about that."

"What do you mean?"

The Prince looked up at the sky and at the dead enemies on the earth around them. "I'd say that someone's been trying to take care of us. I was thinking that Karel must be responsible for some of this at least."

Some of the magical distortion of the landscape was clearing away, but something else, also out of the ordinary, had appeared.

"What in all the hells of Orcus can *that* be?"

"It looks like a farm. A well-kept, irrigated farm, here in the midst of nowhere. In the midst of a cauldron of magic."

"I," said Mark presently, "must go to that encampment and see about my son." The Prince turned his head and pointed. "You scout that way. Take a look at that farm, if that's indeed what it is. We can hope it's something Karel's sent us; we could all use fresh food and rest. But good or bad, we must know."

And the two men separated.

Karel was still kilometers to the east of the epicenter of the magical turmoil, though he was riding as fast as he could toward it. Even from a distance, he got the distinct impression that the local geography had been pretty well jumbled, and he was impressed. It was a long time since he had seen anything of the kind. At least there was no doubt of where he ought to go. You didn't need to be a wizard to see the signs.

Elementals had created most of the turmoil before him. As he approached, the wizard watched with awe the elephant dance that they were still performing.

"What have I done?" he asked himself. "How did I ever manage to accomplish it? Ardneh himself could hardly . . . but wait."

Karel assumed the elementals were the same ones he had created many days ago, now revivified and stalking the plain before him and the nearby hills, diverting the little river from its proper channel. But if these were indeed the same elementals, someone had really been working on them, had salvaged and reenergized them from the entities that Karel had left dying, like so many smoldering fires buried in the earth. They were now bigger, more powerful, more sharply defined, and closer to sentience than any that Karel had ever managed to raise before.

He rode a little closer to the turmoil, until his steed began to grow restive at the mumbling and the rumbling in the earth. Then he stopped and looked matters over again. Now he could be certain that this was not the work of the one who called himself the Master. He hadn't really thought it was, but—

But now he could let out a long, faint, quivering breath of relief.

And now someone—the figure of a wizened little old man, clad in a peculiar stage-wizard costume—was standing a few meters to Karel's right and waving at him.

Karel had been looking forward to this encounter. He turned, nodding to himself. Beth and Stephen had done a good job of describing the apparition. The image was really very good, though slightly transparent along the edges.

The lips of the figure moved. "Karel, Karel!" it rasped at him in its old man's voice. "You must help me!"

"Yes, I will help." The magician who was seated on the riding-beast shook his head and pulled at his gray beard. "Do you know, some of this is my fault . . . I know who you are, by the way, though it is not easy to believe."

"I know who you are, too, Karel. Who cares about that?" Now the voice sounded angry, and frightened, too. "Go back home if you can't help me. Can't you help?"

"I will help. I see that things are starting to get away from you here. But be calm, you have done marvelously well, considering everything. These elementals have doubtless saved your life, and others' lives as well. But now they're turning dangerous to you. Dangerous even to your—"

"Help me, then! Help me!"

And Karel did.

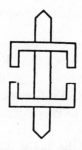

CHAPTER 25

IT took the experienced wizard even a little longer than he had anticipated to soothe and quell the elementals down into quietude, for their rebellious power had grown great. But eventually even their gargantuan energies had been tamped and dampened back within the earth. The local clockwork of the world was ticking on reliably once more. The image of the ancient-looking wizard in the unintentionally comic dress had disappeared, and Karel did not expect ever to encounter it again.

Once the job of settling the elementals was done, Karel remounted his riding-beast—the animal, relatively experienced though it was in these matters, required some soothing first—and proceeded on his way.

The unruly portion of the world had quieted—if it had not exactly gone back to its original conformation—and the local geography was once again almost completely stable. Almost, because Karel could see the farm still there ahead of him, and he knew from past experience that the farm had a way of its own with geography. He was not really surprised to see it right before him now, though the last time he had seen it (under quite different circumstances) it had been many kilometers from here.

When he reached the tall gate, with its green wreaths of

vine and its decorations of horn and ivory, he found it unlocked. That was no more than Karel had expected. He rode on in, remembering to close the high gate carefully behind him lest any of Still's livestock wander out. Here on the farm you always had to keep such practical matters firmly in mind.

As Karel approached the house he saw that he was expected, which by now came to him as no surprise. Outside the front door, two people were standing waiting for him. The first of these, to Karel's great relief, was young Zoltan. The boy looked older than when Karel had seen him last, and a bit banged about and bruised, but essentially unharmed. Zoltan was dressed in clean farmer's garb, and his half-curly hair was damp as if he might just have had a bath. He was holding a piece of pie in his fist, and his mouth was full.

Bulking beside Zoltan was Ben of Purkinje, still grimy and smeared with dried blood as if he had just come from a war. Ben was looking somewhat confused—Karel, remembering his own first visit to the farm, could sympathize. Ben welcomed the appearance of Karel as that of a familiar face in a strange land.

As Karel dismounted he smiled reassuringly at Ben. When the first round of greetings was over, he told the huge man: "There is magic, Ben, and then there is magic. Not all of it is accomplished with a chant and a waving of the arms. Not all of it turns parts of the world upside down."

And then the Stills themselves were coming out of the house, and Karel spent some time in the joyful task of greeting his old friends in the way that they deserved. He showed them great respect, and also some of the envy that he could never help feeling when he visited here.

The Stills were prompt to assure him that Prince Mark himself was safely on his way to join them and would be arriving at the farm presently.

And now one more figure, a small one, had appeared in the open doorway of the house. Prince Adrian stood erect, looking at Karel with clear blue eyes; and then he somewhat shyly held out a hand in greeting. Karel was much moved. He half genuflected as he grasped the child's hand and muttered something.

A minute later the gathering had adjourned to the kitchen— something that always seemed inevitable in this household— and everyone but Mother Still was seated at the table while she bustled around it, dealing out heavy plates and cups. A feast was rapidly taking shape before them.

Ben, who had stopped at the sink first to wash the stains of combat from his arms and face, was marveling at the seeming ease with which these preparations were being accomplished. Karel caught his eye, and said to him in an aside: "Whatever the task on this farm, working or fighting, it will be done well and quickly if someone works at it. That is the secret magic that these people have."

Ben smiled vaguely, wanting to be reassured, not really understanding as yet. It took most people several visits, Karel had observed.

Adrian had been listening. "And it works for reaching the farm, too," the child said. "Don't forget that. My father is going to find it, because I'm here, and he's really working at finding me."

It seemed to Karel that the preparations had hardly started, the last clean plate dealt out on the table, before Mother Still was announcing that the feast was ready and taking her own chair at the table. At that point conversation was abandoned for a time except for the terse courtesies that were required to maintain a flow of serving dishes from hand to hand around the table.

Everyone took part in the cleaning-up that followed, and again it was all done almost before the visitors were sure that it had started. Each of them felt faintly disappointed that there had not been time for him to contribute more.

And then the party were all seating themselves in the parlor, and Farmer Still was lighting the lamps there against the first lowering of the shadows outside.

When Mother Still had established herself comfortably in her rocking chair with her knitting, she turned at once to Karel across the table and asked him: "Tell me, are you blood kin to the Princess Kristin? Or are you this child's relative by marriage only?"

"Indeed I am blood kin. The mother of the Princess was my sister."

"That explains it, then." Nodding with satisfaction, the goodwife rocked her chair and shooed away the calico cat that was menacing her supply of yarn. "I thought as much," she added. "Then the child has a powerful inheritance of magic on both sides of his family."

Adrian, sitting close beside Father Still at the moment, was listening intently.

"How's that, Mother?" The farmer squinted at his wife. Meanwhile his large, gnarled hand had paused over the lamplit table, where he was starting to show Adrian the game of pegs.

"Father, I do wish you would try to keep up with family affairs." The goodwife's needles clicked. Her chair creaked, sawing at the floorboards, back and forth.

"Haven't heard much from that part of the family," he grumbled mildly. "All busy over there wearing crowns and being royalty and such."

"Never mind," his spouse chided him. "It's still family, and they have a lot of things to worry about." The cat (who was really quite ordinary in appearance) now sprang right up into her lap. Rocking industriously, Mother Still added: "His grandfather on his father's side is the Emperor himself, you know.''

"This lad? Oh yes, I know." Not appearing overly impressed, Still was now jiggling the Princeling on his knee.

"When," Adrian asked them all in a clear firm voice, "is Daddy going to get here? I want to see him. I know he's on his way, but when?"

Ben had turned his head and was looking at the child again with profound amazement. The huge man had eaten well at dinner—it was hardly possible to do otherwise in this household—but had had little to say, before the meal or after. Continuing to wear his battle-harness, and still showing some of the marks of war, Ben sat in a chair and marveled silently.

"The Emperor himself," Goodwife Still repeated with quiet emphasis.

"Yes, of course," her husband agreed. Either he had remembered all along about the Emperor, or he was trying to sound as if he had. Now he went back to teaching Adrian the game.

No one had yet answered the Princeling's question. "Your father," Karel said to him, "is really safe, and he is really on his way here. The people who were trying to harm him are either dead now, or far away."

"I know," said Adrian.

"Good. Well, then, about your father. People, or certain people anyway, can find this farm whenever they really start to look for it. At least they can if it's anywhere near them at all when they start. And you're here, and I'm sure your father is really looking for you. So he's going to be here very soon. If you're impatient, you could look for him yourself."

"I've walked so much today that my legs are tired," the small boy said. And in truth he looked and sounded physically exhausted. "And I don't want to do any looking with magic. I don't want to do any magic at all for a while."

"A wise decision," Karel nodded.

"Then play the game with me," Still encouraged the child. "It'll help you keep awake until your daddy gets here." Then, having caught yet another pointed glance from his wife, he protested: "I *did* remember about the Emperor."

"And I, for a time," said Karel, rubbing his eyes, "forgot about him, and that Adrian is his descendant. To my own peril, and that of others, I forgot."

"Will someone tell me one thing, clearly?" Ben of Purkinje boomed out at last, startling everyone else. "Why couldn't Woundhealer help the lad? And what've you done for him now that's worked this cure?"

"The Sword of Healing could not restore his sight," said Karel, "because he was never blind."

Ben only looked at him. Ben's mouth was working as if he were getting ready to shout again.

Karel sighed. "I did not express that well. Let me say it this way: Adrian's eyes, and the nerves and brain behind his eyes, had nothing wrong with them. He simply had not learned to use them yet."

Mother Still, busy with her knitting, smiled and nodded. The farmer frowned at his pegboard game. Adrian was looking from one of the adults to another, and his expression said that he was too tired to talk just now unless it became necessary, and at the moment they were doing well enough without his help.

Ben muttered exotic swearwords under his breath. "Then why, by all the gods and demons—?"

"He began to use his eyes to see with," Karel went on, "as soon as a real need arose for him to do so. He was ready by then to use his eyes. When that time came, he turned away from the world of magic, for almost the first time in his short life, and he entered the world that is shared by all humanity."

Ben was still staring—now, the wizard thought, with the first glimmerings of comprehension.

Karel pressed on. "Take Woundhealer's blade and draw it through the legs of a day-old infant—the babe will not jump up and begin to walk. Its legs have not been healed, because they were not crippled to begin with. The child is simply not ready to walk yet."

"Talk about children!" burst out Mother Still. Her fingers continued their tasks with yarn and needles, but she gave the impression of someone who was unable to keep silent when a favorite subject had come up. "If you've ever had little ones about and watched 'em closely, you'll have noticed that they generally work at learning one thing at a time. The important things, I mean, like walking and talking."

"And seeing?" Ben was trying to grasp it.

"There are different ways of seeing," Karel continued. "To Adrian—who has, I think, the greatest natural gift for magic that I have ever encountered—the most natural way to see is not with the eyes at all."

Mother Still impulsively threw her needlework aside and held out her arms. Adrian, faced with this silent summons, jumped down from her husband's lap and came to her on tired legs.

She lifted the boy into her own lap and passed a hand across his forehead. "These little eyes are learning to see now. But for a long time there was no need—or so it seemed to the little mind behind them. Because there were so many other things for that mind to do. So much to be learned, to deal with the other kind of vision that he has. Things that vision brought him might have hurt him badly if he had not learned how to deal with them."

"To my shame," said Karel, "I never really looked at him until today." Turning to Ben, the wizard added: "Until now, Adrian has seen every person and every object in the world almost exclusively by the auras of magical power and potential that they present. It took me decades to learn such seeing, and I have never learned to do it as well as he can now. It is of course a fascinating way in which to perceive the world—but for a human being it should never be the only way. And for a child of seven there are certainly dangers—you remember the seizures he was subject to.''

Ben said: ''He's not been troubled with those, I think, since the Sword touched him.''

''Nor will they bother him again, I trust. Now he should—I think he must—put away all the things of magic for a time. Let him look at the world by sunlight and moonlight and firelight. Let him see the faces of the people in it. Let the struggle that has separated him from them be at an end.''

''For a time,'' said Adrian suddenly, and they all looked at him.

''For a time only,'' the wizard confirmed, ''let magic be put away.'' He looked around at the other adults. ''It is a shame,'' he said again, ''that I did not understand the problem. None of us understood it—but I might have. Only I did not take the trouble. When I considered the child at all, I wasted my time, looking into the air and space around him for evil influences, spells and demons that were not there.''

''Come along, boy,'' said Father Still, getting up from his chair suddenly and holding out his hand. ''Someone's at our door.''

Adrian stared at him for a moment, then jumped up.

At the front door of the house the two of them, with the others crowding close behind, met Mark just as he was lifting a hand to knock.

Adrian stared for the first time at his father's face. Then with a cry he jumped into his arms.

Dusk had deepened into moonlit night when Zoltan wandered out of the house, closing the door behind him on the firelight and laughter within. He paused, content for the moment to breathe the fresher, colder air outside. Then an impulse led him along the short wagon road, not the one leading to the gate but another track, which terminated at the edge of the cultivated land, just where a ditch fenced with a grillwork barrier let in water from the stream flowing just outside the farm.

Zoltan, standing just inside the fence and clinging to it, looked for a long time at the undiminished stream outside as it rushed down a hillside. At length he turned away, starting back to the house.

There was a splash behind him, and he turned back just in time to see a small log bob to the surface at the foot of the miniature waterfall. Then the piece of wood went dipping over the next brink down, moving along briskly on its journey to the distant sea.